T0128857

PORTRAIT OF A DRUG DEALER

PORTRAIT OF A DRUG DEALER

TOM CELLAR

iUniverse®

PORTRAIT OF A DRUG DEALER

iUniverse books may be ordered through booksellers or by contacting:

iUniverse
1663 Liberty Drive
Bloomington, IN 47403
www.iuniverse.com
1-800-Authors (1-800-288-4677)

ISBN: 978-1-4917-6902-7 (sc)
ISBN: 978-1-4917-6903-4 (e)

Library of Congress Control Number: 2015908357

Print information available on the last page.

iUniverse rev. date: 6/9/2015

A FEW SHOUT OUTS

To my brother, for his tireless work editing this book. Your knowledge and suggestions were invaluable. I consider myself extremely fortunate to have a man with such intellect and integrity as both my brother and friend.

To my mother, for her unconditional support. I could not have made it through those hard times without you. Saints do walk among us. You are proof of that.

To my wife, for her unwavering love. You are a constant source of edifying struggle and amazement for which I am grateful for. Life is far more beautiful with you by my side.

The off ramp came as a surprise. Mechanically, I turned the steering wheel. Windshield wipers were keeping time with the pulsing bass pumping out the amp in the trunk, rain sliced through the night sky pelting a dreary line of soulless metallic shells. My knuckles were white, my palms sweaty. As I tried to light a cigarette, the numbness permeating my whole body intensified in my thumb, thwarting my attempts to spark the lighter. I had lost too much blood. Tears came rushing to my eyes, but I stifled them with a long snort. This was no time for weakness. It did not matter that I was alone in the car.

Weakness is a choice. Certainly there are those who are predisposed to weakness, to cowardice, but it is inevitably a choice for which there is no excuse. One may point to past traumatic experiences, one may use their upbringing to rationalize character defects, but it always comes down to a choice. People choose to be weak, and that for me was not a choice. Well, it was a choice, but one that would ultimately lead to either prison or the grave.

I accidentally blew through a red light as I finally

succeeded to spark my lighter. Transfixed by the flickering flame, I nearly sideswiped a van. Blaring horns jolted me from my reverie. The flame died along with the last bit of my confidence. I could not take it. I pulled into the nearest parking lot which happened to be a 24 hour porn store. After taking a few moments to breathe deeply, I placed the cigarette between my dry lips and lit it up. Smoke poured into my lungs, helping to calm my quivering hands.

Screeching tires caused me to drop my cigarette and go for the pistol under my seat. No sirens, no flashing lights, false alarm. I winced as I bumped my left shoulder on the steering wheel. Pain shot through me, paralyzing the entire arm. I composed myself by staring hatefully at the other car while tears of pain ran down my face.

It was an older style Cadillac Coupe Deville. The paint was peeling, exposing large portions of rust, but the rims sparkled in glow of the parking lot lights. Those four wheels were worth more than the rest of the car. Two Hispanic males with flat-brimmed caps hopped out. I recognized one of them, and even though I knew it was too dark for them to see inside the car, I still lowered my own cap. Not that anyone would be looking for me. It had been nearly two years since I had been back for anything more than a quick stop at a hotel room.

The thought of a hotel room caused me to yawn. It had been almost forty hours since I last slept. My nerves were strained to point that if one more thing went wrong, I would be liable to snap. Like Charles Bukowski once wrote, "It's not the large things which send a man to the mad house... no, it's the continuing series of *small* tragedies that send a man to the mad house... not the death of his love but a shoelace that snaps with no time left." The intensity in which I understood that had left one of my shoes untied for hours.

I had no idea what had brought me back to Eugene, Oregon. I could have gone anywhere. I could have driven a couple hours south and been in Mexico, but I would have been forced to ditch my cargo. And what was in my trunk was worth more than what the average American makes in a year. Perhaps I had come back to Eugene simply because I knew of a reliable hotel. The search for suitable shelter would have been too grueling for my agitated nerves. Plus, I had my arm to clean up. The threat of fainting was the most pressing issue. I contemplated what would happen if the police found me unconscious in a ditch. Violently shaking my head, I pushed that thought out of my mind. After flicking the butt out the window, I slowly pulled out of the parking lot and headed to the outskirts of town.

The hotel I had in mind was near the train tracks tucked behind a small grove of trees. There was a large sign stating that weekly and monthly rates were available. After cleaning my hands up and double checking to see if the plastic bag I had duct taped to my arm was still sealing off the blood, I stepped outside the car, holding myself up for a few seconds to test my legs. The pouring rain was cold and refreshing which helped clear my head. With much effort and concentration, I slowly put one foot in front of the other and walked to the office door.

I was greeted curtly by a balding, middle aged man at the front desk whose corpulent face blubbered out a few noninvasive questions to which I responded with ambiguous answers. We both knew the drill.

"How long you staying?" he asked while licking and smacking his dry lips.

"Not sure. I will pay by the week." I pulled out two hundred dollars, fifty-five more than I needed. "Keep the change. Just keep my room open, and I do not wish to be disturbed. If I need my room cleaned, I will let you know."

The man nodded and handed me my key.

My room was on the far end, an extra kindness from the proprietor for my generosity I assumed. I parked my car in the designated spot and began unloading as my

3

eyes nervously scanned the area. One backpack was in the rear seat filled with clothes, the duffel bag in the trunk contained my life savings. With one last look over my shoulder, I opened the door to my room.

The bed filled most of the room. As with most cheap hotel rooms, the floral wallpaper was yellowed with stale smoke. Cigarette burns covered the comforter. The stains in the shower had an origin which I shuttered to contemplate. Yet this was to be home for now.

I stashed my pistol in the drawer of the night stand, and then I unscrewed the cover to a heating vent. Inside that I deposited the contents of my duffel bag. Granted, this would be one of the first places the police would look, but it was better than leaving it lying on the floor. For good measure, I turned the heat off. If I got cold, I would layer up.

It was late and there was very little to choose from on the television, so I mindlessly flipped channels as I rifled through my pockets. I found the small plastic bag I was looking for. Two different colored pills appeared in my fingers. I laid them on the end table and pulled out my knife.

I chopped up the first one into two lines. The right nostril railed the first line and a half, the left finished the rest. My nostrils squealed in masochistic ecstasy as the powder scorched the mucus membrane. While methadone takes fifteen to twenty minutes to kick in, endorphins started pumping into my blood stream just from the pain. I immediately began feeling euphoric though I knew that was simply my brain happily anticipating its much needed vacation.

I only shaved off a small portion of the second pill. 200 mgs of morphine might have put me in a coma which, honestly, sounded quite nice at that moment. But that was the weakness talking.

I never understood those who pop pills unless, of course, one is actually taking them for chronic pain. Perhaps I have an unhealthy partiality for a quick come up. I prefer opiates to hit me like a brick wall. That being said, I never enjoyed smoking pills unless it was in a blunt. So much of the active chemicals are wasted when the flame hits it.

After railing my fair share of powder, I lit up cigarette and continued surfing channels. For some reason, I gravitated towards the coverage of some South American Polo Championship. I had never watched polo, did not even know it was polo until the first commercial, but it seemed more entertaining than watching infomercials. By the time I finished my cigarette, I could feel the methadone start to kick in. Methadone drips are horrible, but not quite as horrible as morphine drips. I needed something to wash away that horrifying mixture of mucus and chemicals which was working its way down my throat.

Grudgingly, I rose from the bed. After tucking my pistol in my pants, I left the room and headed to the vending machine. On my way, a scrawny, nearly toothless woman who could have been anywhere from twenty-five to forty asked me if I was up for having a little fun. I did not even bother to reply. On my way back, she tried to hit me up for money. Same response.

With a Sprite in hand, I relaxed back onto the bed. The polo match was starting off the last half of the game. The teams were lined up on the opposite sides of the field. A whistle was blown, and they charged to the center of the field.

I had no idea what team was which, more precisely, which was Argentina and which was Peru. All I knew was that one team was red and the other blue. They all looked so similar. However, there was one player on the blue team, the captain or the polo equivalent of a captain, which caught my attention. He always took the lead, storming recklessly towards the white ball brandishing his mallet. More than once, my heart would race as I thought there was going to be a collision. However, the red team always backed off. With a swift blow of the mallet, the captain would send the ball sailing towards the goal. The red team would knock it back to the midfield, and from there it was a game of back and forth.

Polo struck me as a rich man's soccer. The whole affair seemed laughable except for the captain. At one point, his horse swung hard to the left to avoid a collision, and he was thrown from the saddle. Yet he still held on. The network replayed it in slow motion. There he was, hanging from the side of his horse, one leg wrapped around the back of the horse, the other dangling underneath. Still galloping, the horse continued careening towards the ball. With the deftness of an acrobat, he flung himself back onto the saddle. The crowd roared. He raised his mallet high in triumph and charged straightway in the fray.

In a past life, he must have been one of the Light Brigade which Lord Alfred Tennyson glorified in his poetry. Every movement he made was calculated and executed with the precision of a surgeon. Gradually, the blue team widened their lead.

As the match was winding down, the red team hopelessly behind, something terrible happened. It affected me in a strange way. The captain was charging after the ball, his mallet raised high as if he was a flag bearer storming the enemy's front lines with one of his comrades following close behind. Two of the red team's players were also charging for it. Yet this did not quell the captain. He continued to ride furiously as if Hellfire was licking the flanks of his horse. One could almost see him foaming at the mouth. As usual, his opponents gave way, leaving him an open shot. He lobbed the ball towards the goal, another point for blue. However, his teammate was not so fortunate.

When the two red players veered away from the captain, they found themselves directly in the path of the other blue player. With a desperate pulling of the reins, he managed to avoid a collision, but the horse's legs crumpled underneath it throwing the rider from the saddle. He sailed through the air and landed viciously on the ground.

The match came to a halt as medics rushed the blue team player off the field. In a few minutes, it was announced he had a broken leg, a dislocated shoulder, and most likely a few broken ribs. While there was very little time on the clock and the blue team had an insurmountable lead, they played out the last few minutes anyway. Yet the captain did not resume his gallant display. He lingered on the sidelines, his mallet nearly dragging on the ground. In those few minutes, the red team managed to score twice, but that did little bridge the gap. The match ended. The captain held up the trophy listlessly as he tried to force a smile.

Then came the press. They swarmed him, some with congratulatory remarks, others with angry accusations. A heated debate ensued about his forceful way of playing the game. It was how he made his name, yet it seemed that every other reporter had, at one point, prophesized that something disastrous would happen because of his aggressive tactics. Then the somber news was announced that his teammate was being rushed to the hospital. Speculation said that a broken rib had punctured a lung.

And there he was, the victorious captain staring into the camera as reporters lunged at him like a pack of crack-addled hyenas. His nose was held high in defiance as he viciously defended his tactics, yet I could see his eyes filled with terrifying doubt. And at that instant I recognized him. I lost control and wept.

I awoke the next morning with my hair plastered to the pillow by snot and hardened saliva. My moment of weakness the night prior had stained the pillow with a few bodily juices. Also, I would be buying the hotel some new sheets as my plastic bag leaked a rather alarming large pool of blood. After railing a few lines of methadone, I headed to my car to grab a first aid kit from the trunk. I had been too paranoid to use it on the drive up as I did not want to draw any attention to myself, but I should have properly cleaned the wound as soon as I arrived at the hotel.

The gash along my left arm, at its worst, was nearly three quarters of an inch deep. Luckily, the bullet passed through. In my haste, I had torn a piece of cloth from my t-shirt and stuffed it in the wound. Then I had taken a large plastic bag and duct taped it in place.

I hopped in the shower and inspected the wound. There was coagulated blood oozing out from under the cloth. I gently tugged at it, and the pain brought me too my knees. Deciding I was nowhere near intoxicated enough to deal with this level of pain, I snorted a lot of methadone and morphine, popped some Xanax, and then headed back into the shower. I turned the water up as hot as I could stand it. Then I waited for everything to kick-in. Time passed. I dropped to my knees and gripped some of the loose cloth.

A revelation shot through me. I quickly stood up, wobbled a bit from the light-headedness, and then stumbled to the bed to fetch my pants. After grabbing the leather belt from my pants, I headed back into shower, dropped to my knees, breathed deeply watching the drops of water slowly creeping down the translucent shower door, folded the belt in half to make it twice as thick, closed my eyes, thought real hard about praying, bit down into the belt, grabbed the loose cloth with tears in my eyes, decided against praying, inhaled long and deep for one last time, and then everything went black.

I awoke feeling very fatigued and woozy. Hot water was scorching my body. The tub was stained with blood, and I had only succeeded in removing half of the cloth. A bunch of dirty looking curdled blood was oozing out of the wound. Cursing, I viciously grabbed it, and as there was enough for me to get a good grip on it, I successfully tore the rest out.

Triumphantly, I held the bloody rag in front of my face, and then everything went black.

What happened next could barely be considered waking up. It was a haze of splashing rubbing alcohol on the wound, screaming into the belt, more alcohol, more screams, some blackness, more alcohol, more screams, some surgical glue not meant for wounds this serious, alcohol, screams, gauze, and then everything went black.

After crawling out of the shower, I fought to stay conscious long enough to order some pizza. Bitter tears welled in my eyes when I learned that the Pizza Hut down the street did not open for another hour. I tried a Chinese place only a block away. Lunch would be served in one hour. Attempting to retain my composure, I slowly put on some clothes, checked to make sure I was not bleeding through the bandages, and then walked outside.

The morning sun was painful to my eyes. I lit up a cigarette and started walking towards the golden arches in the distance. The cigarette proved to be a bad idea. A head rush nearly brought me to my knees. Plopping my butt on a curb, I flicked the cigarette onto the street. It took a few moments for the world to stop spinning. After my equilibrium balanced, I heaved my way back onto my feet and took an unsteady step forward. My destination was not far. I had to keep telling myself that to keep my wobbling legs upright. Nourishment, man's most basic need, was not far away. I just had to fight the dizziness and the nausea and the pain and the overwhelming urge to throw myself into oncoming traffic. The quicker I walked, the sooner I would be sitting down and consuming some much needed calories. It had been over twenty-four hours since I had last eaten. Every step I took seemed to use up the last of my energy. I thought I would simply wither away. Right then, I knew the agony of Tantalus. How I was still alive was beyond me. Apparently, a body can go without a substantial portion of blood. The thought of blood forced me to sit down again. I was nearly at the entrance, plastered with glorious pictures of food, each more delicious looking than the next.

As I made it to the entrance, I praised whatever god ruled over this domain and pushed open the door to the succulent smell of America's signature cuisine. The blonde haired, teenage angel awaiting my arrival, whose unrivalled youthful beauty could put me away for five years with a simple loosening of a button, asked me in a voice as soothing as a babbling brook playing a harp, "Welcome to McDonalds. Can I take your order?"

"I want three of the McGriddles. Those are the ones with the maple pancake bun things, right?" My ears were starting to ring, so I pretended I understood what she was saying. "Good. Yep. Three of them and three large hash browns."

Her lips moved slowly as she looked up expectantly at me. I was not sure what she asked, so I answered, "And a large coffee."

She began speaking again. I heard something about it being cheaper to order the combo. "Look, I don't care about the combo or anything, just get me what I ordered," I replied as my equilibrium started doing summersaults. I needed to sit down.

I pulled out my wallet and handed her a bill from my violently shaking hand. "Here's twenty. Just keep the change, but if you could do me a big favor and bring everything out to me in a to-go bag. Thanks."

Somehow I made it to the booth. The girl was quick with the coffee. She even offered to put some cream and sugar in it for me. I politely told her I liked it black.

"Must have been some party last night," she said coyly.

I smiled bitterly and nodded. "Yeah. Some party."

Her blatant stare was making me uncomfortable, so I turned and glared bleakly into her eyes. That sent her running back into the kitchen though she was still very nice when she delivered my food. While I had anticipated the McGriddle more passionately, it turned out that all I wanted were the hash browns. I attributed that to the loss of blood. Washing down the hash browns with coffee, I began to feel a bit stronger. The world was coming back into focus. However, before I finished my breakfast sandwich, I felt my stomach churn. Apparently, I should have consumed my food at a slower pace. Grabbing my bag, I dashed out the door making it to the sidewalk before I fell to my knees and vomited.

Back in my hotel room, I finished my meal in the bathroom. I would eat a few bites, drink some coffee, vomit a bit, and then try a few more bites. It was a wearying affair, but I was hungry. However, by the time I finished throwing up the last of the fast food, Pizza Hut had opened. Feeling a little farther from Death's door, I patiently waited for the pizza as I smoked a fat joint. The high soothed my stomach, distracted me from the pain, and when the pizza arrived, I was able to keep half of it down before I vomited again.

With a sigh of relief, I rolled another joint and railed some pills. It was time to recuperate, and I would hardly leave my bed for the next week.

It was late April. A chill still clung to air, yet the breeze was warm and humid. Torrential downpours would give way to sunny skies in less than an hour's time. And just as quickly would the storm clouds roll overhead. The first time I went out for a walk, it was clear outside. I walked maybe two miles. By the time I returned, it had started hailing. The valley only intensifies this season of flux.

As I verged on the two week anniversary of my triumphant return to Eugene, I became alarmed at the state of my finances. Down five hundred in cash, I had to start moving product if I was going to be able to stay much longer. I took a shower, cleaning my wound which was healing very slowly. The pain restricted full movement of my arm.

After smoking a joint laced with Provigil, something to give me a boost, I ventured out of my hotel room. First, I headed for the liquor store. I kept my cap pulled low over my face, but not so low as to look suspicious. Then, I stopped by a convenience store to stock up on microwavable burritos, chips, and a pre-paid phone, or a "burner" as people in my profession call them. Burner phones have a few advantages, the first primarily being that your name is not attached to it, deterring police from tracking your location. As there is no contract, it is easy to ditch one and simply purchase another. This is especially helpful if there are people who you no longer want to deal with.

Lastly, I roamed around Springfield, a smaller town outside of Eugene. While Eugene may be only a shell of its former hippie self, Springfield is nothing but a cesspool of meth. Granted, there are some nicer parts, quiet cookie-cutter suburbs tucked away from the filth and grime, but a good portion of the town tweaks. It is so prevalent that it is not uncommon for tweakers to be holding full-time jobs at a factory or fast food joint. To say meth is socially acceptable in Springfield would be an exaggeration, but since a good majority of the population hits the spoof pipe, it is less objectionable than it would be in most towns.

I drove around the town for a few hours, recognizing more people than I cared to. However, I did not find the one person I was looking for. I knew where I would find her, yet it was too early in the day for her to frequent her favorite hang-outs. Probably was still fast asleep. After reacquainting myself with the layout of the city, I headed back to my hotel.

Breathing a sigh of relief, I closed the door of the hotel room behind me. Then I eased my way onto the bed. It was rewarding to complete my errands so early in the day so I treated myself with a drink and another joint. Then I railed some more crushed up pills, even opened up the heating vent to fetch some klonopin I had stashed away.

PORTRAIT OF A DRUG DEALER

Vermouth is to a martini as klonopin is to a pilltini which is I what I call an assortment of crushed up pills. Like vermouth, klonopin does not have much of a kick, but it helps smooth out the whole experience. Unlike other pills, klonopin does not burn when it is railed; on the contrary, it feels as if one has snorted a breath mint. It's cold which is why it is a great compliment to any pilltini as it offsets the burn. And nothing washes away the drips like a gin and lemonade.

My whole day was spent on the bed unless I was headed to the bathroom to relieve my bladder or my stomach. By the time Cartoon Network started playing adult cartoons, I had finished only half a fifth of gin, yet I was extremely drunk. Then I realized I probably was still in need of more blood. With a shrug, I continued to drinking and railing well into the night until I made one last trip to the bathroom.

As I kneeled before the porcelain god and offered my sacrifices, I could feel my heart rate slowing. Mixing downers with downers is risky business. Normally, I would end a night of drinking with a few lines but rarely mixed them three hours after I woke up. Yet this was not a normal day, and these were far from normal times. As I stared down into a tumultuous sea of burnt yellow with small floating chunks of partially digested processed beef, small black dots began appearing in my vision. First one appeared, then another, until I could see nothing but blackness. It was warm and inviting. I gave into the darkness and sighed happily, completely at ease for the first time in years. If this was dying, I should have done it a long time ago.

When I awoke the next evening, I was overwhelmed with disappointment. It took a few moments for me to regain my composure as I fought back tears. There was blood on the floor next to the toilet which was bewildering at first, yet I flinched as I touched the side of my head. My fingers had come across a deep gash. Apparently, I must have crashed my head into the corner of the sink cabinet as I lost consciousness. Surprisingly, my bandages were holding up, though they were in desperate need of changing.

The pain served to shake the drowsiness from my eyes. With a groan, I rose to my feet. I poured myself a drink, smoked a joint, and railed some morphine. No methadone today. Well, not enough to get high, just enough to get well. I thought about how I had nearly died the night before, the fact that I had emptied by bowels during the night was proof that I had overdosed and was quite close to death. This bothered me a little but not as much as it should have.

I sat for nearly three hours on the bed, wondering what my next move should be. I knew who I had to meet; I simply did not want to make the effort to find her. My last burner phone was lying in a few pieces alongside the freeway, and I did not have her number memorized. So I headed over to Springfield again hoping to run into her. I spent the next few days casing various strip clubs I knew she frequented.

After five days creeping around town, I spotted her exiting a strip club. As usual, she was decked out in red from head to toe. Short cropped blonde hair was covered by a Chicago Bulls flat-brimmed cap. Her baggy shirt covered up the fact that she was built like a starving twelve year old boy. On the shirt was a large picture of nude woman with glittering rhinestones that covered the breasts and crotch. Her blood red shorts hung down to her calves, only inches above a pair of Air Jordans.

She was leading another girl wearing fishnets and a tube top to a beaten down red Chevrolet Berretta. They entered the back seat. Patiently, I chain smoked cigarettes as I waited for the car to stop shaking. The two women exited the car; my contact began walking aimlessly down the street while her companion went back inside the strip club.

I followed her at a distance, always keeping a block or two away from her. While she never looked back, I knew she was aware of my presence. She swaggered down the road, calling out to various people. Sometimes they would stop for a moment as product and money switched hands. For over an hour, I followed her down side streets and waited outside various strip clubs.

Then came that fateful turn into a dark alley, just like I had taught her to do when someone was tailing you. I took a deep breath and rounded the corner. As expected, a pistol flashed in my face which I deftly knocked to the side. A small fist came hurtling towards my face, but that was anticipated. I deflected it with ease and quickly jabbed into the darkness. My aim was true. There was a crunch and an angry curse.

She was backpedaling. With a forceful shove, I knocked her small frame to the ground as I pulled my own pistol from my pants. She looked up at me with bewildered angry eyes. Her nose was a bit crooked and leaking blood.

My words came out slow and quiet. "Should know better than to try that shit with me." I put my pistol back into my pants

It took her a moment to digest my words. "Isaiah?" she asked hesitantly.

I smiled and held out my hand to help her up. She hopped up to her feet and flung herself at me with open arms. "Goddamn it, Isaiah!" Though reeling in pain, I managed to suppress the urge to cry out.

I held one finger to my lips to shush her. "Quiet. Nobody knows I'm here but you, and I would like to keep it that way."

She nodded and stared at me as if I was some exotic animal at the zoo. Then she shook her head. "Fuck, bro. Where you been?" As the blood began to trickle into her mouth, she wiped it away only to wince at the pain. "Damn it! Fuckin' broke my nose, you bitch."

I put a gentle hand on her shoulder. "Sorry about that, but you shouldn't be waving around a pistol like it's a fucking dildo."

Defiantly, she retorted, "You was creeping on me. Fuck, you know how many fools on the lurk for me. This hustla has gotta keep on her toes, you know what I'm saying." Her voice was raspy as if she had never quite recovered from a sore throat.

Same old Tiffany or as most knew her, Tizzy or Tiz for short. A big black thug trapped in a skinny white chick's body. At least that is what she thought.

Delicately, she touched her nose again and immediately recoiled. "Goddamn, that fuckin' hurts. Might have to go the fuckin' hospital, you goddamn prick."

"Whatever it costs you let me know. I'll cover it."

She took a few moments to gently push on her nose. "Fuck it. I'll just tape it up," she muttered angrily.

Pausing to light up a cigarette, she began to smile at me. "But what the fuck you doing here, fool? Been almost a year since anyone's fuckin' heard from your bitch-ass. People beginning to think you was dead or busted."

I sighed. "Look, we should talk about this someplace safe. There a bar or restaurant we could go to without raising a few eyebrows?"

"Shit, everybody knows Tizzy in this hood."

I sighed, knowing she was right. It would be hard to keep a low profile with her in my company. "Then let's get out of town. You free tomorrow?"

"I ain't doing shit but grinding, but my bitches should be able to handle shit for a day."

"Alright. I'll pick you up... say noon?"

She nodded. "Aight, playa. Where at?"

I lit up a cigarette before replying. "How about the gas station on Olive and 18th?"

"You got it."

I stared at her sternly. "And be there on time. I'm not looking to sit around all day."

She punched me playfully on the shoulder. "Shit, bro, I'll be there. Don't be sweatin' me."

I nodded. "Alright then. Keep your head up. I'll see you tomorrow."

"Good to see you, Isaiah. Shit, we got some fuckin' catchin' up to do. Stay up, bro."

And with that, I left her and headed back to the hotel.

Tiffany Hardlock. Tizzy. Thizzin' Tiz. She and I go way back. We first met when I was twelve. My foster parents took her in. She must have been eight or nine. Back then, she was a quiet and timid girl with long curly hair who loved ballet. I remember her teacher said she was a gifted dancer. After our foster father took her to a ballet completion in California when she was thirteen, a drastic change occurred. When she returned, she took a razor to her hair, started wearing baggy clothes, stopped doing ballet, and began break dancing. That was right about the time when I was hitting the streets with a pocket full of dub sacks. While she wanted in on it, I refused to let her take that risk to make me money.

When I was seventeen, there was a physical altercation between the foster parents and me causing me to leave abruptly. Tiz was always running away to come stay with me. Whenever she was taken back to our foster parents, she would turn into a hellion so nobody would want her. That lasted for about a year before she was emancipated and moved in with me.

One day, I was scowling at my jar of weed. It was short by a whole ounce. Tiz never took anything without asking. I could not for the life of me figure out me why I was so short. Suddenly, Tiz popped in the door with one of her girlfriends. They were carrying large bags of groceries.

"What up, Isaiah. Hope you're hungry," Tiz said happily. "Cause we gettin' some muthafuckin' steak up in this bitch!"

Tiz and her friend started unloading the groceries as I stared at her in disbelief wondering how she got that kind of money.

"Did you steal that?" I asked.

"Nah. We'll talk," she replied hastily. She looked at her friend and ordered, "Aight, bitch. I gots to talk to my bro, so how 'bouts you start cookin' and we'll be back." She kissed her, and we headed off to my room.

"What's going on?" I demanded as I realized what happened.

She pulled out two hundred dollars from her pocket. "That's for you."

I shot her a nasty glare. "You took an ounce didn't you?"

She smiled guilty. "Look, Isaiah, you been supporting my bitch ass for a grip. I just wanted to fuckin' help out."

"I don't want you selling for me."

Indignantly, she wrinkled her scrawny nose at me. "I ain't fuckin' sellin' shit for you. I need some fuckin' skrilla in my pocket too. How the fuck am I supposed to get them fine bitches with torn up pants and dirty Jordans." She stared at me sternly. "Look, these muthafuckas at school ate this shit up. I could probably push a fuckin' QP in a couple days."

I shook my head. "I don't like it, Tiz."

"Don't fuckin' worry about it. By the way, can you get some thiz?"

"No," I barked. "I'm not hooking you up with that shit."

She shrugged her shoulders. "Whatev. I'll find it myself. You know, someday, people gonna know me as Thizzin' Tiz. Fuckin' swear it on my life, bro."

"Is that supposed to be your rap name?" I asked snidely.

"You mu-fuckin' know it, bitch!" she roared. Then she waltzed out of the room barking orders to her girlfriend, leaving me alone shaking my head and chuckling.

Besides having a knack for pushing weed, she also proved to have a green thumb. We started growing weed. Our first harvest made us a half-pound of some descent product. The next one yielded two pounds of some pretty good weed. We were making good money. It seemed every night we were going out to eat, sometimes racking up a hundred dollar tab at a nice Italian restaurant downtown.

However, that would soon come to an end. One day she let some of her friends over while I was away which was strictly against the rules. As luck would have it, one of those friends got too high and freaked out. Parents found a bag of weed she had sold him. Police were called, questions were asked, questions were answered, and, suddenly, I was in handcuffs being hauled off to jail. Spent three months there, but that was by far the least of my concerns. Because of those drug charges, my financial aid was revoked, and, consequently, I could no longer afford to go to college. So I dropped out, ten grand in the hole. I forgave her and never held it against her. But she never forgave herself which is why I trusted her more than any living being on this planet.

As she promised, she was there waiting for me at noon. Without making a scene, she casually hopped in the passenger seat. Her nose was taped up and still a bit crooked, but, to my knowledge, she had broken her nose five or six times. Or to put it more accurately, someone had broken her nose five or six times. She talked some shit, and I never knew her to back down from a fight.

"So where we off to, bro?" she asked as she lit up a cigarette.

I shook my head. "Not sure. I was thinking of heading to the coast or maybe up to the butte."

"Damn, I ain't been to the coast in a grip. That clam chowder bread bowl be a calling me hard, but when ain't them clams calling for the Tiz," she said with a devious smile.

I shook my head trying to suppress a chuckle. "The coast it is."

She rolled a blunt as I headed out of town, and just like her big brother, she busted out some pills and crushed them up sprinkling the multi-colored powder on the weed.

"What you putting on there?" I asked.

"Little Oxy, some Concerta, and a bit of morphine."

"Damn. Oxy. You going all out."

She smiled at me. "Well, shit yeah. Fuck, I ain't seen you since you dropped off that flying girl."

"Yeah. You push that alright?"

"Fuck, I still got bitches up on my cooch begging me for more."

"Good. That's what I wanted to talk to you about."

She looked at me wide-eyed. There was a spark of childish excitement in those eyes. "Really, cause if it's like the last stuff, that shit'll fly."

I looked long and hard at her, pausing before I spoke. "It's better."

She shook her head. "Na... na... I got to see that to believe it. That was some prime shit."

I pulled a small bag out of my pocket and handed it to her. Greedily, she snatched it from my hand. "Well, fuck me like the Virgin Mary. Shit's yellow. And, fuck, little sticky. And the taste. Damn, Isaiah this is about a pure as pure gets. Goddamn, I'm getting wet just looking at this muthafucka. Bro, you gonna let me try this, right?"

I waved my hand nonchalantly. She scooped up some with her pinky nail and snorted it. She slammed her hand against the armrest and banged it a few times as her head flailed back. After letting out a gut wrenching shriek, she shook violently and laughed.

"Goddamn! God-fuckin' damn! That's the shit right there! That's the shit! Burns so good! Ain't that right, brother?"

Burns so good. That had been our motto for years, and we both had that phrase tattooed on our right forearm. She scooped another pile and held it under my nose. I myself disdain melodramatics, so I did not sound off like a porn star faking an orgasm. I looked over at her and smiled. It was good to be back. There she was, rapping along to the music, hat cocked, pants sagging, it was all too endearing. The girl was 5' 6" and barely over a hundred pounds.

"Damn, this is some good shit. You looking to push this?"

I nodded solemnly. "Like I said, that's what I wanted to talk to you about. I'm looking to get rid of some shit."

"How much you got?"

I hesitated for a moment. Then I realized who I was talking to. "I got a pound."

Her jaw dropped. "How?"

"Don't ask. I also got two thousand triple stacks. As well as..." I paused. "Look, I don't know if you fuck around with this shit, but I got some crystal as well."

She stared at me for a moment as if she was waiting for the punch line. "Shit, I fuck around with anything that gets me that cash."

"You just let me know what you need, and you'll get it. And I'm not trying to meet up with anyone. I'm lying low for a bit. And if you aren't comfortable pushing the crystal, don't worry about it. I just don't want to draw any attention."

She stared at me with concern in her eyes. "What happened? Where's T?"

I tried not to balk at that question. "I don't know what happened to Tyrone."

"What! You two been butt buddies since I've known you. How you not know where he's at?"

"Because I don't!" I snapped, causing her to recoil a bit. I regained my composure quickly. "Sorry. I don't want to talk about Tyrone, and leave it at that."

"Whatever," she said with a huff.

We smoked blunt after blunt until I was questioning my ability to drive. I listened as she spit some Busta Rhymes. Her flow had improved since I had last seen her.

We finally made it to the coast. I wanted to walk along

the beach before we stopped by for a bite to eat. As usual, she bitched about how she would scuff her Jordans. One thing I never understood was why anyone would buy a pair of shoes that they were worried about trashing. To me, that seems like the whole point of shoes. Instead of scuffing your feet, you have these neat things around your feet to take the punishment.

Yet my insistence won out. We hung out on the beach long enough to burn through two blunt wraps. Then we headed up to the light house and watched the ocean for a few minutes. Seagulls were perched on a large rock jutting from the ocean. We walked out onto a miniature peninsula where each side was a steep drop off. On the very edge, I held my arms out embracing the warm salty breeze. This is what life was supposed to be. Far from Iphones and shopping malls, simply enjoying one's surroundings. I felt my equilibrium begin to balance. Breathing slowly and consciously, I tried to freeze the moment in my mind. I could have stood at that spot for hours, but maybe that was the molly talking.

Tiz huffed impatiently, and I heard a lighter sparking. I snapped out of it and lit up a cigarette. We stared at one another for a moment. Her pupils were enlarging as were mine. A large, devil-may-care smile crept onto her face.

"You feeling it?" I asked.

She nodded. "Shit... yeah. This is some good shit."

I looked around for a moment taking in the view. The wind was picking up causing the waves to swell in size. The repetitive crashing of the waves was lulling me into a trance.

"So how 'bout we get the fuck outta here," she said.

"You hungry?" I asked in disbelief.

"Na... but I could use a drink."

The drips were terrible, so I readily consented. We headed back to the car and found ourselves a quiet bar in town.

Adorned on this small, wooden planked establishment were all sorts of mounted fish and fishing gear. There were a few men at the bar, all grey-haired or balding, talking in hushed tones. From time to time, they would roar with laughter. Obviously, they were fishermen as one could easily tell from their attire. I thought about how peaceful it must be to do an honest day's labor, go have a few drinks with a couple friends, and then return home to your wife and children. I stared wistfully at them. A few months ago, I would have sneered at such simplicity. But now, there was something enchanting about the idea. Maybe it was simply the fact that I knew that sort of life would forever be denied to me. I had made my choice; no one forced me on the path that I was travelling.

But that was the weakness talking. I had to remind myself of that. That was the kind of weakness that got one killed or in handcuffs. After a crazy month, it was only natural to envy the mundane and tedious existence these men lived. But such a life was not meant for me. I wanted the extraordinary.

Years ago, I was approached by two young ladies representing some Christian college club who were taking a "spiritual survey." They asked a few of typical questions dealing with views of the afterlife, the existence of a higher power, and the origins of morality. I was with an old church friend at the time who was familiar with this club. Her answers were met with smiles and affirmation. Then it was my turn. Scowls and perplexed stares was all I got. Especially when it came to the last section of the survey. "In three words, describe what you want your life to be." My companion gave the cliché answers one might expect from a Christian. Happy, fulfilled, and content. The three things that can be easily filled by swallowing religious fiction. Then their eyes turned to me. I lit up a cigarette and smiled mischievously, riding a wave of narcissism to the vast shores of intellectual superiority.

"What I want my life to be?" I repeated as I held in the smoke. I exhaled in their direction. "In three words. That is a tough one. Well, I would have to say that first and foremost, I want my life to be interesting. Gratifying would be number two." As I brandished my cigarette at them, I spat, "And lastly, I want my life to be extraordinary."

They had no response to that. After mumbling a quick thanks for our time, the scurried off leaving me to deal with the exasperated stare of my Christian friend who was none too pleased with my behavior.

Without being aware of it, the bartender was scowling at me waiting for my order. Tiz nudged me, and I noticed that she had already got her gin and juice. I asked the bartender to pour me a pint of something local. He handed me what I believe to be a Coors though he charged me as if it was micro-brewed IPA.

We headed for a table close to the juke box in order to let the music drown out our words in case someone decided to eavesdrop.

I gave a short but sweet toast. "To our first legal drink together."

She smiled. "Right. I forgot about that. Shit, it's been over a year since we really kicked it together."

I grunted, and the conversation went silent.

It took a couple drinks to loosen our tongues. Both of us were still reeling from the come up. I could see her mellowing out. Her face softened from its perpetual scowl, giving her an almost feminine appearance. Eventually, she cleared her throat and said in a whisper. "Missed the shit out of you, bro."

I smiled at her. "Missed you too."

Silence again. She shook her head and laughed. "God, getting all gushy up in this bitch. So tell me, what the fuck you been up too?"

Shaking my head, I replied, "Same shit."

"Well, you seem to be in a good place. I mean, shit, you

got some weight. You could really make something in Eugene with that sort of startup."

I sighed. "Yeah. I don't know, Tiz. I'm tired of the game. I just want that shit gone."

"And then what?"

"Don't know. I haven't thought that far in advance."

"Bullshit. You always got something up your sleeve."

While I would have liked to unburden my secrets on her, I knew to do so would be utter selfishness. I had no desire to have her in cuffs as an accessory. But the truth was I really did not have a plan. Sure, I had options on my mind but none solidified. Placing one foot in front of the other was all I could manage for the time being. Oliver Wendell Holmes once said that "walking is a perpetual falling." I was beginning to understand the ugly truth in that statement.

"Honestly, I don't know what to do, Tiz."

She looked at me sympathetically. "Well, if you want my two cents, you should stay in Eugene. Hell, we could make some serious cash, bro. You could save up and go back to fuckin' college! You're a goddamn genius. Go back to school; we can pay for it by hitting the streets. With the shit you got, it won't be no thing. It wouldn't be shit. You could be a goddamn professor!"

"No, I can't." My icy response cut off her enthusiasm.

She frowned and wrung her hands nervously. "Can't you get that shit expunged?"

I shook my head. "Not Class A felonies."

Her shoulders slumped. "Fuckin' bullshit that growing weed is a Class A felony. Not like you murdered somebody," she mumbled.

A manic burst of laughter took us both by surprise. It was laughter of one possessed. A crazed, bitter laugh of one being strapped to the electric chair. It took me a moment to realize it was my own laughter. She looked at me curiously, but I could not stop laughing. I laughed so hard my stomach started knotting up, and the men at the bar turned around to stare.

She smiled and tried to chuckle but was too bewildered to let out anything but an amused snort. "Fuck's wrong with you, Isaiah? What's so funny?"

I regained my composure and wiped the tears from my eyes. "I don't know. Just fucked up is all."

Looking at me with the skepticism of a high school nurse, she muttered, "I guess so."

I was feeling good. It had been a long time since I had laughed so hard. Irony is my favorite kind of humor. We changed the subject and began discussing what she had been up to. As I guessed, she had been up to the same old routine. Smoke weed, spit rhymes, hustle fools, eat pussy. Then the conversation veered to people we knew.

"So Bucky's doing three years for grand theft auto. Charles is in a bad way. Ran into him a little while back," she said in a low voice.

"Wait, Charles? The same Charles we went to church with back in the day?"

"One and the same. Fool got on the H."

I shook my head. "Damn," I whispered. "He was a good kid."

"It's a fuckin' shame, but he's a goddamn fool for getting himself hooked."

"Wonder what led him to that."

"No fuckin' clue, bro."

I hesitated before I asked the next question. "So you hear from anyone else from church."

"Shit, fool, I ain't been back since I moved out with you. Fuck, I ain't never took to that religious bullshit like you did."

I was a bit hurt by that comment, but I did not let it show. Granted, I had been with our foster parents much longer than she had and had been subjected to their dogmatism to a much greater degree. For a few years, I had found great comfort in the church. It provided me with the emotional support I never had from my foster parents. I had a particular connection with the youth pastor, John Keersgard. My interactions with him did not cease when I stopped going to church. Though I had given up the faith, I still had found him to be an invaluable confidant and a sure friend. I always suffered a pang of guilt every time I thought of him and how I disappeared without saying goodbye. He was a good man, and though I generally have a low opinion of Christians due to the rampant hypocrisy, he was saved in my eyes as being one of the few who truly practiced what he preached.

I ventured another question. "So, you haven't heard from John at all?"

"Well, shit, I see him from time to time. He always says hello and asks about you."

I sighed heavily. "He's a good man."

"Only motherfucker at that goddamn place with some fuckin' cred, you know what I'm saying."

I smiled and nodded. "I know exactly what you're saying."

Tiz lived up to her name, Thizzin' Tiz. At one rave, she managed to push two hundred tabs and an ounce of molly. She invited me to go with her, but I was still a bit hesitant to wander around town much. It had been a couple years since I had attended a rave. Back in the day, I went to one on an almost weekly basis. But I declined out of fear of who I might run into. Regardless of that fact, I was immensely pleased with how much cash she managed to bring in. With two grand tucked away in my pocket, I began to breathe a bit easier. I even ventured out of the hotel room to catch a little fresh air. I felt that the stuffy air in my hotel was hindering my recovery.

There is a butte outside of the city which I am particularly fond of. It is not too grueling of a hike but enough of an incline to get the blood pumping. It starts off easy enough, a simple trail wandering around the butte. When one is high enough and there is a break in the trees, one can see parts of Eugene. Eventually, the incline intensifies and the trail becomes overwhelmed with rocks. After making it past the trees, a strenuous hike jumping to and from large rocks becomes the most efficient way to the top. However, it is well worth it. The view of the city and surrounding areas is quite interesting. The naked eye can see the football stadium and library from miles away. Soon, it became a daily ritual for me to head up to the top and chill for a couple hours.

One day, I brought Tiz with me. She moaned almost the entire way up. I am a person who dresses appropriately for the occasion. To me, hiking shoes seem appropriate, not the brand-new Jordans she had bought two days ago. However, Tiz liked her style so much that she would wear the same clothes to her funeral. When we made it to the rocks, I had to threaten her to make her climb up. However, she was slightly justified in not wanting to make the trek; it did scuff her shoes. Consoling her, I promised to buy her a new pair.

I brought a small lunch for us, subs, chips, and beer. She brought a large sack of weed and blunt wraps. We blew clouds into a cloudless sky, drank beer, joked around about old times, and chowed down when we got the munchies.

After the lunch was finished, we had the customary after-lunch blunt, or "the lunt" as Tiz called it. While there were plenty of other people roaming around, we did not try to hide it. The way I saw it was we had picked a spot far away from the trail. If some prick did call the police, I doubt they would come charging up the butte to catch a couple potheads. They are too busy dealing with tweakers in Springfield. We killed the blunt and stared up at the vacant sky with vacant smiles.

As I lit up a cigarette, Tiz rubbed her hands nervously and stared at me. "So... I got a full album being mixed right now."

As I exhaled a cloud of smoke, I replied, "Shit, that's chill. All your own shit?"

She nodded. "Yep. I got some whiz kid mixing it right now. Sounds sick, bro. Think I might have some shit I could work with. You know, try to get a record deal, start doing shows and shit, man."

"I'd like to hear it."

Her ears noticeably pricked up. "Well, most if it is still being mixed, but I got a few rough tracks. Not polished, you know what I am saying, but you could at least hear where this shit is going."

I smiled and replied with intoxicated passiveness, "That's fucking awesome, Tiz. You got any ideas for the name of the album."

Her shoulders straightened a bit as she proudly declared, "The Alpha Bitch."

I burst out laughing and clapped my hands together. "That's fucking perfect, man. That is fucking perfect."

"I like it too," she said with a relieved tone. "Cause that's what I am, the alpha bitch cause I got the bitches. Fuck, I make bros my bitches."

"I thought you weren't into that."

Her face contorted in disgust. "Oh hell, nah, I don't mean it like that. I mean that I got bitches with dicks making me that cash."

I shrugged indifferently. "Well, we should listen to it."

"Like now?"

"Yeah, like right now. You got it on your IPod."

"No, but it's on my computer at my crib.

"You mean, the Lair of the Alpha Bitch."

She giggled. "Damn straight, fool."

On the way, we stopped by a hotdog stand we used to frequent back in the day. It was there I gave Tiz her first lesson in dealing drugs. She was sixteen at the time. The owner of the stand had given us a free bag of chips that day to thank us for our steady business. As we sat on a bench, munching away on our food, I began discussing why we chose this hotdog stand over others.

Clearing my throat, I said, "So take this guy over there. We've been coming to him for years even though we could go someplace cheaper. Ever wonder why that is?"

She shrugged. "I don't know. Cause he's a chill motherfucker."

I nodded. "That's one reason. He's personable, and today, he gave us a free bag of chips. He takes care of his regulars."

I lit up a cigarette and handed her one. "What this guy does is not very different from what I do, and you can learn as much about dealing drugs from him as you can from me. Rain or shine, he's always out there. We can count on his business no matter the weather. He's consistent. I go to him because I know he's reliable.

"Also, he always had good product. He's got the kettle chips instead of regular potato chips, high-quality soda, and he has ten different condiments to choose from. Variety keeps it interesting."

Nodding her head slowly, she said, "Aight. I can see where you going with this."

I leaned in and looked directly into her eyes. "What we want to do is emulate him. No matter what the time is, no matter what the weather is, we deliver to our customers. People need to know that they can count on us. People will pay more just because we are consistent. Most drug dealers, as well as food stands, are real flaky. I am successful doing what I do because people know that they can hit me up anytime, and I will deliver. Might charge them a couple bucks more a gram, but no one grovels about that because I am the convenient choice. That's what America is all about- convenience.

"As for product, well, you already know my shit's good. I won't take bad product even if it is cheaper. Customers need to know that they can depend on you to always supply top-notch shit. And like him, it's good to have variety. So one week I am selling some Blackberry Kush, Tangerine Dream, Blue City Diesel, and Strawberry Cough, and the next week I add some AK or OG Kush and take out the Blackberry. Keep a mixture of sativa and indica. I always keep track of what I sell the most so I know to keep re-upping on that. Keep a record of what product you have and how much money you have. While you already know this, don't ever use names of customers. I like to assign them numbers.

"Lastly, like the hotdog guy, I take good care of our regulars as will you. Whenever a client wants to smoke you out, you insist on rolling a blunt of your own weed. That will make you more personable. From time to time, give them a little extra to thank them. Even if you charge a few bucks more a gram, it will keep people coming back to you. Do you see what I am getting at?"

With a large smile on her face, she replied, "Ya, I know what you're saying. We going to be mu-fuckin' professional about this shit."

I laughed. "Precisely."

"And you still won't sell me no thiz?"

I shook my head. "Absolutely not."

Snorting, she spat, "Whatever. Already got a hook for that anyway."

"What!" I cried in disbelief.

She pulled out a tab from her pocket. "Problem is, I'm pretty sure this shit is a fuckin' meth bomb. Don't feel right, I just get jacked like a mu-fucka, you know what I'm saying."

With a sigh, I told her to give it to me. I bit into it, and, sure enough, it was nothing more than meth pressed together with filler.

Shaking my head in defeat, I said, "Well if you are already getting this shit, might as well get you something good."

With a satisfied smirk, she said, "That's fuckin' right."

Tiz's apartment complex was a large, u-shaped two-story complex. A group of ten or so people in dirty ragged clothes hovered around the laundry room. When they asked for cigarettes, Tiz just handed them her pack.

"Either you pay the toll, or you can't leave your laundry without it getting jacked," she whispered.

The entire complex was piss yellow with faded green bordering. Apparently, whoever designed this was color-blind. Also, whoever built this complex also had distaste for grass and trees as the whole property was covered in cement and asphalt. Beat-up cars crowded the parking lots. Loud music was thumping from multiple apartments, and two loud domestic altercations were taking place as we climbed the stairs to Tiz's apartment.

She was living with an old friend from high school. I did not know him. His name was Arnold Vandenbuck, a tall, muscular kid who was recently discharged from the Marines for medical reasons. His Humvee had been hit by an IED. He survived but had serious head trauma, leaving him unfit to work. So he lived off disability, and since Tiz took care of him, she lived there virtually rent free.

"It's a pretty sweet set-up, bro," she explained as we came to her door. "I keep him fucked up and occasionally get him laid, and he lets me stay fo' free, fool."

I balked. "Wait... you... put out for him."

She shot me a disgusted look. "Ahh... fuck no. I send one of my bitches to take care of that," she snorted. "Fuckin' gross, bro."

She opened the door. Inside was a complete mess. Empty pizza boxes covered the kitchen counters, clothes were scattered on the floor, and glass pipes were everywhere. In the living room, huge posters of half-naked women decorated the walls. Arnold was posted up on the couch playing video games on a large flat-screen television. It was some war game, not sure which one.

"What's up, man. I'm Isaiah," I said in friendly tone. He did not reply.

Tiz whispered, "He doesn't talk when he's in the zone. Fucker's world ranked on this shit. It's all he does."

I watched him play for a few minutes while he finished his match. She was not kidding. This guy was running train on his opponents. Every once in a while, someone would angrily curse him, and he would laugh into his headset. When the match was over, he won with an extremely large lead. As there was a short intermission between matches, he turned to me with a vacant expression on his face.

"Hey, dude. I'm Arnold," he said in a monotone voice.

I walked to the couch and shook his hand. "I'm Isaiah. How's it going?"

He took off his headset, and a large smile spread across his face. "Real good, dude. My doctor just changed my prescription, and it is really helping my game."

I looked at the coffee table in front of him. There were multiple bottles of pills as well as a packed pipe which he lit up then handed it to me. "Well... you seem to be pretty good at that game," I replied a bit awkwardly.

He turned around to look at Tiz who was pouring a bowl of cereal in the kitchen. "How are you, Tiz?"

"Good. Just chillin' with this muthafucka right here."

"Is this your brother?"

She laughed. "Yep, this is him."

His smile became even wider as he looked back at me. "It's very good to meet you, Isaiah. I've heard a lot about you."

Another match began, so he put his headphones back on. The last thing he said was that I could help myself to the weed. I quietly stole away back to Tiz who was chuckling to herself.

"Fools something else," she whispered.

I nodded, not sure what to say.

"Aight, well let's head into the Lair of the Alpha Bitch."

Her room was even filthier than the living room. Empty liquor bottles were scattered on the floor along with a heaping mound of clothes. A king size bed took up most of the room. There were some women's underwear pinned on her wall which I assumed did not belong to her as they were thongs, and Tiz only wore boxers. Below the underwear, there was a desk with a computer. The desk was the only area in her room that seemed organized. A few gadgets lay on the desk which I did not recognize but assumed they probably had something to do with music production. Tiz rolled another blunt, hollered to Arnold to join us if he wanted, and then we lit it up. Arnold showed up in a few minutes, boasting that his overall kill to death ratio had reached above 3.5.

"Hey, Tiz, what's Veronica doing tonight?"

Tiz chuckled. "I don't know. I'll call her up."

He nodded indifferently. "Cool."

"That ho loves her some soldier boys. Do you like her new tongue ring?"

Smiling bashfully, he replied, "It's very nice."

"Well, I'll get that ass over here tonight."

"Thank you very much," he said politely. Then he excused himself and walked away.

Tiz picked up her phone and called the girl up. "Yo, Veronica, you got plans tonight... Well, that's too fuckin' bad. Soldier boy wants to see you... Bitch, I don't give a fuck what you doing, you get that tight little ass over here... Look, bitch, you wanna do me like this when you owe me some muthafuckin' money. I will slap the shit out of you and fuckin' drag your ass over here... I already told him you ain't into the whole cutting thing. He knows you don't like knives... Well, he does now. Besides, I got some other bitch who's into that freaky shit... This ain't a fuckin discussion, bitch, so get your ass over here around eight, suck him off, and then you can go suck whatever dick you like... That's my girl. You come over, and we'll be square. I'll even front you a little flying girl... Good. Aight, baby girl, stay up."

She hung up the phone with an exasperated sigh. "Hoes, man. Got to keep them in line."

I chuckled. "Since when did you take up pimping?"

"Fuck, I ain't sending bitches on the street, I just hook up some homeboys from time to time, mainly Arnold. Shit, if bitches want to act like hoes, they get treated like hoes. These bitches ain't worth shit besides a few wet holes." She paused for a moment and grabbed a notebook and pencil. "I like that. 'Bitches want to act like hoes, they get treated like hoes. These bitches ain't worth shit except a few wet holes.' Gonna use that in a rap."

"I like that too," I agreed, chuckling to myself.

"Yep. That's all they good for. Most of them are a bunch of fuckin' e-tards, you know what I'm saying." She paused and looked anxiously at me. "So you wanna hear my shit."

"That's why I'm here," I replied with a smile.

To say the least, I was surprised by what I heard. What she had seemed polished enough. The beats were simple yet well done, and the instrumentals were inventive. One track had a gothic cathedral feeling going for it. However, Tiz's flow was by far the most impressive part. She played around with the rhymes, speeding it up then slowing it down with ease. Plus, it was catchy, and not some stupid hook repeated over and over as modern hip-hop is fond of doing. In fact, I was surprised to hear some fairly intelligent observations. For example, the track "Fuck Dem Hoes" was a perceptive critique that while our culture views female sexuality as a tool for female empowerment, it still reduces women to the status of sexual objects. I myself was not in complete agreement with the message, but I was impressed by the level of thought she put into it. While my paraphrasing of the lyrics might be a bit more eloquent than the lyrics themselves, it captures the essence of the song. My favorite track was the title track, "The Alpha Bitch," which used some clever metaphors when asserting her position as top dog.

> "Cause I'm the Alpha Bitch,
> Gonna fuckin' die or make it rich.
> Bury your hoes in a shallow ditch.
> Trigger finger got that murder itch."

Overall, I liked it. While she did use gross exaggerations about certain exploits and predicted she would die of an overdose before turning twenty-five, she at least was not too distasteful in her boasts. Granted, it was hard to be impartial as this was my little sister putting this out.

"So what do you think?" she asked hesitantly as the last track finished.

Raising my eyebrows, I replied, "I'm actually really impressed."

"For real?" She was rubbing her hands together as she looked up with relieved eyes.

"Yeah. You got some talent. I'm excited to hear the rest of it."

She smiled with relief. "Awesome. The whole album should be ready in a month or so. Then I'll be pushing this shit to producers. Try to get a label and shit."

"I think you might got what it takes."

Still smiling, she said, "That's tight. Glad you liked it."

We chatted for another half-hour or so before I took my leave. She had business to attend to, and I was beginning to itch for some opiates. Before I left, she handed me a burned

CD of the few tracks she had finished. I thanked her and headed back to my car.

On my way back to the hotel room, I stopped by a convenience store to buy cigarettes. Next to the counter was a newspaper stand. When the clerk asked me if I needed anything else, I snatched up a paper. The headline was too enticing. With a concentrated effort, I resisted the urge to read it while I was driving. My heart was racing.

I dashed inside my hotel room and plopped onto bed. "MAJOR DRUG BUST NEAR ELEMENTARY SCHOOL," screamed the headline. Some poor bastards who lived two blocks away from an elementary school got raided. Police found marijuana, ecstasy, methamphetamine, and prescription drugs in their possession. The suspects, five men, ages ranging from nineteen to twenty-five, were being held with bail set at $250,000. My eyes widened at that number.

My eyes nearly watered, not really but it sounds nice to say, as I beheld the public floggings these guys were getting at the hands of the media. "Thugs!" cried some. "Monsters!" cried others. "Public menace!" was the unifying chant right along with "Increased public safety budget!" And that was the crux of the story. Behind nearly every news article lies a political agenda. This one just happened to be in favor of the cops getting new toys. Conveniently, there was a bill being discussed at city hall to put in place some tax to raise revenue for the police department. There was actually a short two-paragraph story about that on page seven.

Each one of these men was facing fifteen to twenty-five years. "You poor bastards," I whispered because someone, somewhere should read this article and not be filled with scorn for these guys. What is ironic is that most likely some of these guys attended that same elementary school. I know the school, and I also know it is on the wrong side of the tracks. What most people do not realize is that a good chunk of a school's funding comes from local property taxes. Live in a poor community, well, guess what, your school is using text books from the early nineties, there are not enough desks to go around, and no after school tutoring programs to help struggling students because it simply is not in the budget. And the vicious cycle of poverty keeps turning.

My disgust turned to rage when I reached the end of the article. The first part dealt with the fact, the body of the article pandered to public fear, and the last part dealt with the events leading to the bust. It did not happen because of astute detective work or because the men robbed someone or committed some act of violence to draw attention to themselves. No, "due to information provided by a paid informant, police placed the house under surveillance."

I flung the paper to the ground, stomped back forth in my room, chain-smoked cigarettes, and cursed to myself.

After a sleepless night, I headed over to the butte before the sun rose. Those early morning hours have always been one of my favorite times of the day, when the world peacefully slumbers before it begins another arduous day of existence. Yet there I was, trudging up this hill, climbing up rocks, and stumbling over tree roots in the darkness. I finally made it to the top and looked over the city. The sun was rising, and I could see the city clearly. In the distance, low-hanging clouds could be seen coming in from the east.

The butte was completely vacant of people save for me, a rare and precious treat. As I smoked a joint, I watched the clouds begin to overtake the city. In silent, reverent wonder, I watched as the city slowly disappeared in a veil of gray fog. Soon, the clouds began to surround the butte, and I was left with nothing but clouds below me. The child in me squealed with delight to survey such a scene. I could have been on some high mountain top. All I could see was the small patch of rocks I sat on, the fog below me, and the rising sun.

For an hour, I sat there silently and simply contemplated my situation. It had been almost a month since I had arrived in Eugene, and things were going as smoothly as could be hoped for. There were some big decisions ahead, but none of those were all that pressing. For one, I had to decide how long I planned to stay. If I needed to bounce out in a hurry, I wanted to push what I had as quickly as possible which would be risky. I had managed to stay under the radar, but if we were going to move serious weight, I would have to get involved. Not that I did not trust Tiz. There was simply too much at stake to let her go it alone.

I tried to shake away thoughts of business. It was too beautiful of a morning to be weighed down by materialistic cares. The elevated air was doing me some good. As the sun burnt through the fog, I could see the city again as it began bustling with activity. My eyes began to droop. Sleep had been something I dreaded. Nightmares awoke me every night in a cold sweat no matter how intoxicated I was. Yet as the sun caressed my face and warmed the slab of rock I was sitting on, I felt more secure and at ease. I closed my eyes with the intention of letting them rest for a moment before I headed back to the hotel room. However, I fell fast asleep, and not even the sun could burn away the terrors in my dreams.

A large man was standing in front of me wearing all black, from the Nike shoes on his feet to the do-rag on his shaved head. We were in a white room completely unfurnished. He stared at me with large brown eyes filled with worry as he walked towards me.

"Listen, Isaiah, these ain't some wannabe gangbanger punks we be dealing with."

A pistol materialized in my hand. It began to rise, pointing the barrel at the man.

"These are the Sanderros. These fools be packing heavy, bro."

I desperately tried to lower my hand, yet it would not obey me. It continued to point the pistol at the other man's chest. With my other hand, I tried to force it down but with no success as if my pistol arm was made of solidified concrete.

"I'm just saying that the risk ain't worth the profit. And the fuck we doing fuckin' around with crystal, bro?"

The trigger was pulled putting a bullet right into the man's chest. However, he did not flinch.

"Not trying to be a bitch, but we got to look at our options. LA is a whole other fuckin' beast."

Two more bullets burst from my pistol. Still he kept walking towards me. A warm wet sensation began covering my face. I wiped my face off with my free hand.

"Isaiah, you trippin' if you think we are in league with these fools. Them fuckers got connections, bro. And we ain't got nobody but each other to watch our backs."

Shot after shot erupted from my pistol peppering his torso. Blood began seeping from the wounds, but he did not seem to notice. Yet as he reached me, he slumped to the ground. I tried to catch him, but my arms were paralyzed. I could not even muster the strength to shield off the mysterious onslaught of wetness which was slapping me in the face.

"Jamie!" a female voice called from a distance.

"Isaiah," said the man in a weak voice. "Just cool it for a moment. We been going heavy for a bit. We should cool it for a grip, or we gonna get into some shit we ain't prepared for." A look of horror crossed over his face.

Then came the eerie female voice again. "Jamie! Where are you, girl?"

The man cried out, "Isaiah! I don't want to die. Not like this. Not like this!"

"Jamie! Come here, girl!"

The wetness on my face was overwhelming. I struggled in vain against it.

"Don't let me die, Isaiah. Don't let me go, bro. I ain't

ready to die." Tears were welling up in his eyes. His head seemed to float away from his body and enlarge until I was face to face with this massive head trickling tears from the eyes and gushing blood from the mouth.

Then the disembodied face screamed.

Dazed and confused, I awoke with a start. A large black lab was licking me in the face. Gently, I pushed it away, but it was determined to win my affection. Despite my best efforts to fend it off, I gave in and scratched it behind the ear to which it rewarded me with some more sloppy licks. For some reason, I immediately took a liking to this dog. When I realized there was something strangely familiar about the dog, a knot formed in my stomach. I frantically looked around me. The butte was crawling with people and the sun was already halfway done with its daily journey. Inwardly cursing my carelessness, I checked my pockets as I continued to pet the dog. Everything was in order. At least I had not been jacked.

"Jamie!" The knot in my stomach turned into a boulder. At that moment, I recognized the dog, and with that, the owner of said dog.

I jumped to my feet and saw a small group of people nearing my position. The dog jumped up onto a rock and wagged its tail in clear view of the group.

"Jamie! There you are! You bothering this poor man," called the woman leading the group. She was wearing loose fitting hemp pants and a plain forest green shirt. Her wavy auburn hair framed a face which never quite lost all of its baby fat. Even at this distance, I could make out the large dimples on her freckled cheeks. She walked with ease, and a gentle smile parted her thin lips.

Indecision paralyzed me. I had not been recognized. I still had a chance to retreat, but that would have been terribly conspicuous. So, I bent down to pet the dog some more, my gut somersaulting as the group approached. Maybe I would get lucky, and they would pass without recognizing me. After all, it had been over two years since I had seen any of them. Of all the reasons to stay in my hotel room, this was one of the biggest.

I looked up at the group, five people with only two of them recognizable. They were within twenty feet and closing. As I stood up again, the dog jumped onto me, tongue hanging out, tail wagging, demanding more attention.

"I'm so sorry," said the woman with a laugh. "She's a love though."

My throat was clogged. I tried to say something but instinctively lowered my hat and looked at the ground.

"Come here, Jamie! Come on, girl! Stop slobbering on the poor man."

Finally, the dog ran to her. My heart raced as I had hoped that would be the end of it. But I was not so fortunate. She continued walking towards me.

"I'm so sorry about that. I hoped she didn't bother you too much," she said to me.

I cleared my throat. "Don't worry about it," I said softly.

She halted in her tracks and looked me over. "Isaiah?" she asked hesitantly.

Caught. I looked up and tried to smile. "What up, Michelle."

A squeal erupted from her, and she dashed towards me, throwing her arms around my neck. "Oh my gosh, Isaiah! I can't believe it's you!"

Hesitantly, I gave her a hug and gently tapped her on the back biting my tongue to control the pain shooting down my arm. I had no idea what to say. I looked at the others in the group and locked eyes with the one male I recognized. Justin Cloward, who was looking every bit of the self-righteous prick as when I had last seen him. He was exactly what Nazi eugenics had in mind. Tall and muscular with bleach blonde hair and clear blue eyes with a fanatic dogmatism which would make an Islamic fundamentalist blush. He was a snitch who ratted me out to my foster parents and every person in our church when he found out I was smoking weed.

Michelle let me go and stared at me in disbelief. "My gosh, what an awesome surprise running into you here. I haven't seen you since... well, since I left for Africa."

I nodded slowly. "Sounds about right." It was hard to pay attention to what she was saying as Justin was mugging me the entire time. Deciding to forego prudence, I glared back at him. We locked eyes for a few moments as Michelle continued to prattle on about this or that. The man was the epitome of everything I loathed from his designer polo shirt to his barely broken in hiking boots. Each strand of his hair seemed to have been individually gelled, and his nails were as fake as his personality.

I was caught off guard by Michelle asking me a question. "So what have you been up too?"

I shrugged. "Not too much. Just chilling here and there."

She smiled sweetly at me. "Well, we should trade numbers and hang out sometime. Maybe go grab a drink."

I balked. "You drink?" I asked genuinely surprised.

Laughing, she replied, "I'm not as much of a square as when you last saw me."

Justin decided to speak at that point. Even his voice grated my nerves, like someone rubbing Styrofoam together. "Drinks sound nice."

I glared hatefully at him. "How about tonight?"

With perfectly straight white teeth, he smiled condescendingly at me. "Well, not tonight. It is, after all, Sunday."

I matched his smile. "And what the fuck does that have to do with anything?"

Michelle put a gentle hand on my arm. "Now, boys, play nice." Her voice had a slight quiver to it.

"I don't drink on Sunday," he stated flatly.

Shrugging indifferently, I looked at Michelle. "How about you?"

"I'm down."

Hesitantly, Justin said, "Now, Michelle, is that wise? You do have class tomorrow."

She chuckled. "I'm not going to get wasted. Just have a few drinks."

We traded numbers, and I was introduced to the other three people in their group who seemed none too keen on meeting me. Apparently, they were new members to the church Michelle and Justin attended and were taking a stroll with them after the service. With that, I bid them all farewell and tried to leave though Jamie blocked my path. She jumped on me, demanding some attention. I kneeled down and wrestled with her for a few moments.

Michelle was smiling at us. "Well, someone missed you."

"She's a good girl," I replied as I rose to my feet. I told her good-bye and headed down the trail.

Justin got on his knees and tried to play with her, but she jumped back nervously. She looked at him wide-eyed with her tail sticking straight up in the air. He pursued her, trying to be playful, but she would not come near him. With a sneer, I called back to the group, "She's smart too." Justin glared at me. I gave him the finger to the horrified stares of the rest of the group.

If there was ever an archetype for a hypocrite, Justin Cloward was it. That holier-than-thou attitude plagued his entire family. His father had been on the board of directors for the church, and, according to him, a couple decades ago God told him to invest his life-savings in a small, unheard of company called Microsoft. Since he never had to work a day in his life after that, he devoted his time to poking his nose in everyone else's affairs in the name of religion. He also wrote a book about how to invest money in a Christian manner which his son proclaimed on every street corner and pulpit with zeal more befitting of a suicide bomber. His mother was a spineless, submissive house wife and just so happened to be plagued with horrific clumsiness. She always seemed to be getting black eyes and bruises from falling down the stairs or tripping over coffee tables.

Last I heard, he was using his father's enormous wealth to start up his own Christian fashion line using himself as the male model- hence the disgusting over-zealous use of make-up. After coming up with a few catchy quips to put on shirts, his business boomed. At the age of twenty, he was already netting close to fifty grand a year in net profits. That was four years ago. I could only imagine what he was making now. He had even convinced Hot Topic to sell some of his clothing. Whenever I thought of him and his kind of people, the image of Jesus driving the money changers out of the temple with a switch came to mind. I had always been quite fond of that particular scene.

I tried to clear my head of Justin. Maybe I was sore because he not only snitched on me but also beat me in a fight I started. In my defense, he was an all-state wrestler, and I had not planned on him taking me to the ground. After much effort and concentration, I succeeded in focusing on the magnificent scenery which surrounded me.

Oregon is a very green state, in every connotation of the word. After walking around the butte that becomes readily apparent from the hippies in hemp clothing smoking herb to the vines climbing up every trunk and hanging off every branch. The winter rains had flooded the butte creating ample nutrition for the oak seedlings and flowers to burst into existence. Giant pines covered in moss, thickets of wildflowers, three-foot ferns covering the blanket of dead leaves, everywhere there was evidence of the cyclical nature of life. My nose relished in the stench of decay and renewal.

However, my happy reveries were interrupted as soon as

I reached the parking lot. There was a new white BMW M3 parked next to my car. At first, I was close to feeling honored that such a magnificent piece of German engineering had parked next to my humble Acura. Slowly walking around it, I admired every curve in the body, drooled over impeccably done interior, and fantasized the kind of power which lay under the hood. It was my dream car, and I gladly would have murdered a child to own one. Then I came to the rear of the car and a nearly uncontrollable rage came over me. There was a Jesus fish tactlessly plastered on the bumper. It was Justin's car, and it was so like him to own something as beautiful as that just to spite me. I almost smashed out the windows with the butt of my pistol.

By the time my shaking hands managed to unlock my car, I was nearly hyperventilating. I was panic-stricken about the whole ordeal, not just about the car but my interaction with Michelle too. What a fool I had been giving her my number. The best thing I could do would be to smash my phone, grab everything from the motel, and try my luck in Portland. Everything was falling apart. Every square inch of my body was itching, and sweat gushed from every pore. My psyche seemed to be on the verge of collapse.

Then redemption came with a startling realization. It had been a few hours, probably six or seven considering how long I slept on the butte, since I had a fix. A wave of joy rushed over me as I unlocked my glove compartment and grabbed my bag of pills. Not caring who might be watching, I crushed up some methadone and morphine onto a small tin I kept in the glove compartment. With child-like enthusiasm, I snorted them greedily and felt every cell in my body breathe a sigh of relief.

After rolling a fat joint, I turned on my car and began aimlessly driving around with the windows down. It was a beautiful, warm, spring day, and I had no desire to return to my hotel room. However, I also had no desire to run into anyone else. My thoughts turned to Michelle, and I genuinely looked forward to seeing her. For some strange reason, I was extremely excited to see her again. There was a possibility for something, I was not sure what, but an unknown something which made my heart race with anticipation.

For hours, I rode around without any direction in mind. Nearly made it to Bend. Not that I had any desire to go there, but it was a picturesque drive up the mountain aided not only by its pristine beauty but also by the lack of civilian traffic and police officers. Michelle called, and we decided to meet for drinks at nine right after the evening service ended. She invited me to join, but I politely declined.

I stopped by my hotel room long enough to shower and pop a few pills. Not wanting to overdo it, I refrained from snorting them. Plus, it would last longer making it less likely I would feel an itch while I was with her.

We met at a small bluegrass bar in the Whitaker area, one of my favorite spots in Eugene. No big box stores in this area. It is populated by a couple local breweries, a soul food restaurant, brightly decorated houses, and a few community gardens as well as some nice parks which give junkies a scenic place to shoot up. Any large wall either has a mural or graffiti on it, both of which are usually tastefully done. It's a place one can walk around at night and see prostitutes and drug dealers without feeling as if one is about to be jumped. In other words, my kind of place.

Michelle was already there when I arrived, politely conversing with an old tweaker who was making none too subtle sexual advances. When she saw me, she gave me a relieved smile. I ordered the two of us a drink, squeezing between her and the tweaker. Then I asked if she wanted to go outside to the patio which she readily agreed. When the tweaker protested, I said nothing but glared menacingly into his eyes until he averted his gaze.

As we left, she whispered, "Thanks for that."

I smiled and shrugged.

We sat ourselves near a wooden fence which was decorated in Christmas tree lights and bizarre Day-Glo paintings of human and animal heads. Silence enveloped us for a few moments as we both stared at our drinks. I wanted so badly to light up a cigarette but for some reason was hesitant to do so. However, my craving bested me, and I pulled out a cigarette.

Surprising, she sighed with relief and shot me a guilty smile. Then she pulled out a pack and lit a cigarette up.

"You smoke?" I asked in disbelief.

She nodded. "Don't tell anyone. I'm still in the closet."

I shook my head. "Well, well, well, you are just full of surprises. Drinking, smoking… anything else I should know about?"

Again, the guilty smile. "Maybe after a couple drinks we could go smoke a joint."

I nearly spit up some of my drink. She had been this sweet innocent little girl who used to pray that I would quit doing drugs. Not that she was judgmental in a condescending way as most people were. It was not some superficial bid to attain a narcissistic feeling of moral superiority. She was genuinely concerned albeit misguided and misinformed. It blew my mind to see her puffing on a cigarette and sipping on amber ale. And that was not the only change I noticed. There were others less apparent that most who did not know her as well as me might have missed. Her eyes used to be filled with a childish simplicity, a light-hearted joy I always imagined Jesus himself must have possessed. Yet now, those dark brown eyes betrayed a distant anguish that the dimples on her cheeks tried so hard to hide.

"Why the change?" I asked aggressively.

Shrugging, she replied slowly, "Well, Pastor John needs a troublemaker in his life."

I smiled. John always did tend to gravitate to those morally unconventional types which was why we had been so close.

"And how is John doing these days?"

"He's the head pastor now."

I raised my eyebrows. "No shit. Good for him. And good for the church."

"Agreed," she said softly. She paused for a moment, sipped her drink, took a few drags, and continued. "It was a rough transition. Nearly half the church left when he was appointed."

"Damn," I muttered as I shook my head. John was always a bit too unconventional for some of the older church board members liking as well as a good portion of the congregation. While the church had been trying to revamp its image to something a bit more contemporary, many resisted the change. Even though everyone respected John in how he reached out to the youth, I could only imagine the stir it caused when he was appointed head pastor. Especially after the ruckus he caused when he let the children dance at Vacation Bible School.

Michelle let out a long sigh. "But things have gotten better. We've been seeing more and more college students in attendance."

"That was always who he was passionate about."

She nodded and said nothing. Again, we lapsed into silence. I had hoped this would have felt more natural. She had been my confidant for many years, and there was much I would have liked to confide in her. However, her eyes told me that our roles may have reversed.

We finished our drinks in silence then headed back to the bar. I was about to order us two more beers when she suggested we take a shot. She was full of pleasant surprises especially when she wanted bourbon. After we each put back two shots of Evan Williams, she ordered an whiskey lemonade, and I followed suit.

Then we headed back outside and lit up another cigarette. I was feeling a good buzz and could tell she was as well. Silence lingered, so I shot out a question I hoped she was intoxicated enough to answer honestly.

"So how was Africa?"

She looked into her drink for a long while. Not able to suppress a smirk, I thought of one of our last conversations. Before she left for Africa on her mission trip, we had a heated discussion about the existence of God as was usual for us. I speculated that her trip would open her eyes to a brutal chaotic world where if God existed than he was a sadistic asshole. Her scrunched brow, the nervous flicking of her cigarette, the blank stare, all told me that I was right which is why I smirked.

She cleared her throat. "It was... it was... eye-opening to say the least. I worked in one village with an eighty percent HIV infection rate. I saw nine-year old boys carrying fully automatic rifles. I saw a refugee camp that had been raided. There were bodies dismembered, people... women and children hacked to death by machetes." Her voice trailed off into a bitter laughter and coldness crept into her voice. "But it's all part of God's plan, right?" I did not respond.

She lit up another cigarette and painfully smiled. "So how about you? Where have you been?"

"All over. LA, San Diego, Portland, San Francisco. Just been going from place to place."

"Staying out of trouble I bet," she said with an ironic smile.

"Of course," I said as innocently as possible.

"What brings you back to Eugene?"

I shrugged. "Honestly, I don't know. I guess I'm just tired. Real fucking tired and needed a break from it all."

Then she asked the question that I should have expected, but it, nevertheless, caught me off guard. Even worse was she was one of the few people who could tell when I was lying.

"So where's Tyrone?"

I did everything the average person does when they lie. I scratched the back of my head, averted my gaze, shifted uncomfortably, and hesitated before I answered. "Don't know. He just sort of disappeared."

Looking up for a moment, I saw her staring intently at me. My stare turned to my drink.

"That's too bad," she replied. "You two were really tight." Her voice was distant and ambivalent.

Neither of us spoke until we finished our drinks. Without a word, we both came to the conclusion we should leave. We walked along the street for about a half-hour saying nothing. As we passed a small park, she suggested we sit down and burn a joint. I heartily consented.

A few hobos were shooting up and listening to music on one side of the park so we headed to the opposite end. It was a beautiful park. Various members of the community had planted rose bushes, some honey-suckle, and patches of foxglove which are my favorite flower mainly because they are so odd looking and poisonous. The honeysuckle's fragrance wafted towards us thanks to a slow warm breeze. As we sat down at a bench covered in graffiti, she pulled out a joint from her purse which was not expertly rolled but not as sloppy as I had expected.

"You plan on sticking around?" she asked hesitantly.

"I don't know. I really have nothing planned."

She inhaled deeply and blew out a cloud of smoke. "It's... it's really good to see you again, Isaiah."

"It's good to see you too."

She looked at the ground. "I missed you."

I looked at the ground. "Yeah... Missed you too."

She cleared her throat. "Everyone was worried about you. It's like you dropped off the face of the planet."

"Yeah. Shit got hectic for a minute."

She looked at me long and hard. Her gaze was penetrating

which caused me to shift uncomfortably. For a moment, all I could do was stare at the ground. When I looked over at her, the moonlight was glimmering on her cheeks. She smiled sweetly at me, and I returned the smile. We held eye contact for a few long seconds. Then we heard a hobo puking not far away from us which caused us both to look away.

"Things are still pretty hectic for you," she said flatly.

I sighed heavily. "Yep. Honestly, Michelle, I'm real tired of running around all the time."

"Then you should stay here." There was a strange sense of urgency in her voice.

"If it's possible, I'd like too."

"Why wouldn't it be possible?" she asked a bit warily.

I laughed and shook my head. "Just bullshit, a particularly unpredictable kind of bullshit."

She shot me an accusing glare, and I was not sure if it was playful or not. "You need to stay out of trouble."

Holding my hands up defensively, I said, "Look, I'm trying to stay out of trouble, but trouble has a strange way of finding me."

Her eyebrows raised in mock incredulousness. "Really. Trouble just pops out of thin air."

I nodded severely. "Just like that," I replied in a solemn tone.

She laughed and gently punched me on my bad shoulder which caused me to wince. "Isaiah Edward Dummas, you are such a liar."

"One of my favorite deadly sins."

"What's another?" she asked coyly.

That was a question I did not need to think twice about. "Greed."

She seemed a bit put off by my seriousness. "And that is what gets you in trouble."

"I know." Smiling and pausing for dramatic effect, I added, "At least I'm not as bad as Justin."

Her small hands flung into the air in exaggerated annoyance. "My gosh, I was wondering when you were going to remember to slam him."

"What! He is greedy."

Squinting at me, she replied condescendingly, "He's not that greedy."

I let out a mock indignant huff. "You see what he drives and what I drive."

"He makes more money than you." That statement grated my nerves more than it should have. "Plus, he donates a lot of his money to charity."

I snorted derisively. "I'm sure it really breaks the bank too."

She snorted back. "And what charities do you donate to?"

"I don't. I'm not a Christian," I stated simply.

One of the most revolting aspects about rich people is they go around giving to charity, all the while beating their chest on the street corner so everyone will know what a generous person they are. And their charity, oftentimes, comes at a price whether it be a plaque with their name on it or a little league softball field named after them. People praise these philanthropists as if they were some sort of saint like Andrew Carnegie. During the late nineteenth century, some of the bloodiest strikes were fought in his steel factories. Dozens died to secure a decent wage and safe working conditions. Yet history remembers him as some great philanthropist because after he died, he gave a large portion of his wealth to charity. Actually, the library in Eugene was built primarily thanks to Carnegie. While I agree that such charitable actions are beneficial to society, my problem lies in the fact that we esteem these greedy, corrupt, tyrannical men because they gave something they had no use for because they were dead. So instead of going down in the history books as one of the most evil men to ever grace American business, his name is gratefully engraved on libraries across the country. Nothing more than clever public relations.

Without being aware of it, Michelle had been puffing on the joint that had gone out. As she lit it up again, I could tell she was thinking of a response. Immediately, I began running through the possibilities and coming up with adequate retorts. To my delight, she went right where I thought she would.

"Still... shouldn't you judge yourself by the same standard?"

"I do use the same standard just a higher one. I judge us by the standard we impose upon ourselves. He uses Christianity as his moral standard and he fails miserably. I use my own standard, and I pass. Not with flying colors but I pass nonetheless."

"Of course you pass! You make your own rules!"

"Which is more difficult than one might think," I added sneeringly. "Besides, it's not like I pull them out of my ass. I use a variety of credible sources for the foundation of my moral code. There is something admirable about following one's own system."

"And I'm sure every rapist and thief feels the same way," she shot back accusingly.

"Very true, but then it becomes a matter of whose system is more logical. I am a rational being with what I feel is a rational code of morality."

"You... a rational person? That's a laugh."

I was a bit taken aback by that statement. "How so?" I asked slowly.

"With all the trouble you've gotten yourself into, you can still call yourself a rational person. You're something else."

With my pride a bit wounded, I retorted, "I feel that anyone in my place who had experienced what I have experienced and possessed the same sort of self-awareness I possess would proceed in a similar manner as me."

"Same could be said for Justin."

"Then it is a matter of the level of self-awareness an individual possesses."

She looked condescendingly at me. "And how do you judge that?"

I smiled wickedly. "The more self-awareness one possesses, the more one will think like me."

She chuckled. "Gosh, I should have never suggested you joined the debate team in high school. You are positively the most frustrating person to have a conversation with."

"I can't help it if I'm always right." I pointed my index finger at her. "And I know I am fucking right about Justin being a self-righteous, hypocritical, greedy piece of shit."

She let out an exasperated huff and exclaimed, "My gosh, back to him again! You know he isn't half bad. He's got his faults but so does everyone."

"Most people aren't glaring hypocrites."

Wrinkling her small button nose, she huffed, "Ugh. I don't know why you hate him so much."

"Really?" I said sarcastically. "You really don't have a clue?"

She smiled mischievously. "I think you are just butt hurt that he beat you in a fight."

"Oh come on!" I yelled raising my hands in the air. "If he hadn't been a little bitch and tackled me to the ground, it would have been a different story. I can't wrestle for shit, but I sure as hell can box."

She giggled. I knew what was coming. "Then I guess he's just better at wrestling than you are at boxing."

I leaned in and glared at her. "If there was a round two, I guaran-fucking-tee things would turn out differently."

"Well, I hope there is not a round two. It would be nice if you two could kiss and make-up."

I shook my head vigorously. There was no chance that the two of us would ever be on friendly terms with one another.

"He might be down for the kissing part, but neither of us wants to make-up. He's gay, I hope you know."

Giggling, she punched me in the arm. "You are horrible."

Pretending not to hear her, I continued, "I mean, what kind of straight man wears that much make-up?"

Still giggling, she replied, "My gosh, I know! He's actually bought me make-up saying I should take better care of myself."

"What a dick." Suddenly, a question popped into my head. "Why the hell would he buy you make-up?"

"Probably because he doesn't want to be the only one of us wearing blush."

I raised my eyebrows skeptically. She sighed and continued. "And if truth be told, the man is in love with me."

"Really? I had no idea." I tried to sound as sarcastic as possible.

"Yep. He told me that when I decided to stop being such a wild child, he'd marry me."

"Wow. Remember that dating conference we went to with the youth group. They said it was easier to pull someone down than bring someone up?"

Shaking her head, she replied, "That was so stupid, but, yes, I remember that. Trust me, I have no plans on changing what I do for some dude. Besides, I know he wants a submissive little house wife just like his mother, and I have no plan on doing that. Too stubborn."

"And not as clumsy," I pointed out. "You don't seem like the type to fall down stairs much or run into tables."

She glared at me. "That's not funny," she said seriously.

"It's kind of funny," I jeered. "What's even funnier was the time Justin's dad was away on business for two weeks and his mother still came to church with a black-eye saying she slipped while mopping the floor. That happened right after you left for Africa."

There was a horrified expression on her face. She was

at a loss for words, and I was at a loss for an explanation as to why I had lied. Granted, it was a good lie as there was no way she could verify the truth of my accusation, and it was completely believable. What made the lie even more perfect was it had come so naturally to me as it had nothing to do with my own behavior. While I have a natural distaste for lying, this one gave me a warm and fuzzy feeling inside that I get whenever a police officer, who has pulled me over, hands me back my license and tells me to have a nice day.

However, the one drawback to the lie was that it halted the conversation. It had been flowing quite naturally which was surprising considering the time we had been apart. Probably had something to do with the liquor and the weed. While on that train of thought, I pulled out a bag of weed from my pocket and began rolling another joint. She assured me she was stoned enough which I shrugged off saying that only left more for me. Yet when I lit it up, she immediately asked me to pass it.

I was struggling with how to reroute the conversation so I decided to run with what I was thinking at the moment. "I have to say, Michelle, I'm surprised at how easy this was."

"How easy what was?"

"Talking to you. I thought it would be more awkward considering how much time has passed."

"And how much we've changed."

I jolted in my chair. "I've changed?"

She laughed. "For one, you are going grey."

Proudly smiling, I replied, "Makes me look dignified."

With a derisive sneer, she retorted, "If that's what you want to call it. You look like you haven't had a decent night's sleep in a month."

"It's been longer," I assured her.

"And there's something else different. I can't put my finger on it, but something is different about you." She looked directly into my eyes. If it had not been for my habit of staring people down, I would have averted my gaze. "I don't what it is, Isaiah, but you seem… older."

I chuckled. "Well, it's been a couple years."

"I know," she huffed. "But a lot older. But that's not it either. You don't look like you're forty, you just seem… I don't know." She held her hands up in defeat.

Deciding I did not like the direction this conversation was headed, I steered it back to her. "Yet the changes you've undergone have made this reunion much more natural."

"What? Because I drink and smoke now?"

"Precisely."

She chuckled. "I was very anxious about seeing you tonight, and I agree with you. Getting drunk and stoned did help the conversation flow more naturally."

"And if you don't mind me saying, I could not be more pleased with this development."

She sneered, "Well, if you approve, I'm going cold turkey on everything starting tomorrow."

"Oh, come on. I'm not-" My phone ringing cut off my sentence. I cursed it silently. Things were going so smoothly, and there was only one other person who had my phone number. But business is business. Begging her pardon, I answered it.

"What up, Tiz."

"Isaiah! You need to get your fuckin' ass down here and bring your girls! Dustin's having a fuckin' rager tonight and we needed you fuckin' here like- two fuckin' days ago, mu-fucka!" She was slurring badly.

"Alright. How many girls?" Michelle shot me a surprised look.

"A bunch of Tabbys, say two or three hundred and maybe a zip of Molly. Can you do that?"

"Shit, I can do that."

"You should fuckin' party with us tonight, bro! I got's too many bitches to fuckin' handle myself," she screamed into the phone. Michelle's awkward glance told me that she could hear everything Tiz was saying.

"No, I'm good."

"Come the fuck on, you fuckin' faggot!" she screamed.

"I'll think about it."

"Pop a couple, and then let's fuckin' talk."

I laughed softly. "So where you at?"

"At Dustin's. Off of Main by that one fuckin' strip club."

"There are three of them on Main."

"Ahh... 67th. Yeah, turn down 67th. Can't miss it."

"Be there in forty-five to an hour," I replied tersely.

"Bitch! You get here now! Muthafuckas be fiending up in this muthafucka!"

"Aight, baby girl, don't you worry. Daddy will be there soon," I said condescendingly. I hung up to a stream of curses.

Michelle sighed. "Well, I should be getting to bed."

"You alright to drive?"

She laughed. "I should be asking you that."

"Seriously, I'll drive you home in your car and take a cab back to mine."

She shook her head. "Sounds like you got some urgent business needing your attention." I did not know exactly what it was about her tone I did not like, but my stomach churned a bit.

"It's not a problem. I insist. Let me drive you home."

She finally consented to my prodding. Last thing I needed on my conscience was her catching a DUI thanks to me. For me, driving intoxicated was second nature. In fact, it had been quite some time since I had driven completely sober, yet, in all fairness, it had been a long, long time since I had been completely sober period.

The ride back was pleasant enough. We reminisced about old times. We shared some laughs, a couple cigarettes, and one last joint. By the time we arrived at her apartment, she had nearly passed out. I all but carried her up the two flights of stairs to her door. When we arrived, she gave me a very long hug and told me to be careful.

With a yawn, she said, "And I had finally stopped worrying about you, and now you're back, and now I have to worry about you again."

"You don't need to worry about me."

"Someone does."

"Goodnight, Michelle."

"Night, Isaiah. Say, 'what up, homie g' to Tiffany for me," she mumbled her eyes half-closed.

I laughed. "Will do." I dialed for a taxi as I headed for the street.

Back in my hotel room, I crushed some opiates and amphetamine pills up, snorting them to give me a much needed boost. At first, I had not even considered staying at the party. Too many people, too much risk, but after my conversation with Michelle, I thirsted for more social interaction. After all, I had spent nearly a month in the hotel room with nothing but a small TV for company.

I loaded up what Tiz needed as well as a hefty personal stash. Before I turned the key in the ignition, I took a bump of molly. By the time I arrived at the party, I was feeling it.

It was a large two-story house located in a cul-de-sac where a group of people wearing hoodies loitered around the entrance. Plywood covered most of the windows. The ones intact had metal caging around it. Two dozen or so people were outside on the front porch which was an assortment of warped boards and shoddy patchwork. Most of them crowded around some makeshift beer pong tables which were nothing more than doors laid out on sawhorses. Others were lighting up pipes. Loud bass thumped from the house causing the ground to rumble.

As I tried to enter the house, I was stopped by the doorman, a big, beefy thug covered in tattoos wearing a black shirt that simply said, "FUCK OFF!" in large white letters.

"Fuck off, faggot," he snarled dumbly. His head was shaved, and his ears were gauged large enough to fit a quarter through.

"I'm here to see Tiz."

"For what?" he demanded as he let a few other people in.

I understood his hesitancy to let me in as I did not look like I belonged. All my tattoos were covered by a long-sleeved button-up dark gray shirt. While my jeans were not from a fancy designer, they did not have large holes in them either. My shoes were basic off-brand running shoes; no stupid check mark ever graced my apparel. I looked like an average guy with an average build who looked like he did fairly average things which is why I was so successful at doing what I did. I liked to call it the chameleon that lay within me. Police hardly ever looked my way. Whenever I am in an area I obviously should not be, police assume I am lost, and I politely thank them for their assistance.

"None of your business, but please let me through. I need to talk to Tiz."

"You talk to Willy before you talk to Tiz."

I chuckled softly. Classic tough guy bullshit. "I assume you must be Willy."

"Yeah, I'm Willy. Who the fuck you be?"

I smiled painfully. "I am a friend of Tiz. She's expecting me."

"She didn't say nothing to Willy about you."

His referring to himself in third person was starting to seriously irritate me. "Then how about you get her for me."

"Fuck off, faggot. Eat a dick."

"Look, Willy, I don't want any problems," I said as pleasantly as possible though my fists were involuntarily clenching. "But I need to see Tiz."

"Fuck off."

Turning my back to him, I pulled out my phone and called her. No answer, so I turned back to Willy as I fished a tab out of my pocket. "Here, Willy. This is some first-rate triple stack, on me, but I need to get through."

He snatched it from my hand and popped it in his mouth. Assuming our differences had been resolved, I began to walk forward. However, he stuck out his hand and shoved me back.

"Fuck off."

Adrenaline-fueled rage began to coarse through my veins. It was everything I could do not to take a swing at him. I held his gaze for a moment before speaking very slowly. "Look, Willy, that's no way to show your appreciation to someone who just gave you a tab. So let me through, or there is going to a big problem between us."

Then he shoved me with both hands. "And what the fuck you gonna do about it, faggot?"

I answered his question with a quick jab to his fatty throat. He staggered back as he wheezed for air. With both hands clutching his throat, I was afforded a clean shot wherever I pleased. So I threw a low left hook which made contact with his lower side around where his failing kidney should be. He leaned hard from the blow, and I finished the job with a vicious right hook to the chin. Without so much as a whine, he crumpled to the ground. I gracefully stepped over his unconscious body and headed straight into the fray.

It was packed from wall to wall in every room. The kitchen was filled with people, two kegs, and a table full of liquor. The unfurnished living room served as the dance floor where a herd of sweating bodies bumped and grinded into one another. Very few people gave me a second look though I obviously did not fit in. There were ravers and tweakers, junkies and gangbangers, ranging in age from fourteen to forty though the young greatly outnumbered the old.

Not spotting Tiz on the first floor, I headed upstairs.

Along the way, I passed a lanky black kid dressed in all black with a red bandana. He looked at me, and I thought he recognized me. Yet he pushed past me.

"Yo, Kev!" I called to him.

He did not turn around, but I was sure it was him. Kevin was Tyrone's cousin. We had always been chill so I wondered why the cold shoulder. Shit, I sold him his first QP.

Shaking off the offense, I continued up the stairs. There were three rooms and a bathroom. Half-naked people frolicked on couches and beds, performing all sorts of sexual acts in an orgiastic fashion. Not my cup of tea. A few people called mockingly to me as I popped my head in, looked around, and then left, but I paid them no mind. I already had enough trouble for one night. As I cooled off, I regretted attacking Willy. Not that the attack had been unwarranted. I simply worried about him coming after me with some friends.

After I had searched each of the rooms with no success, I tried calling her again. No luck. I headed back downstairs and into the fray of the dance floor. We humans like to think we are so civilized, but the spectacle of people thrashing and grinding on one another with intoxicated abandon reminded me of a Dionysian ritual. Instead of laurel branches, they waved glow sticks. Instead of wine, they ingested ecstasy. The only problem was that it was not my ecstasy. Every time I saw someone pop a tab, irritation overwhelmed me. All I could see was another lost dollar. If only I could find Tiz.

The longer I roamed the house, the more disgusted I became. There was a man with grey hair and tattoos on his face grinding up against a girl wearing little more than lingerie who looked like she was still in junior high. But their pupils told me everything I needed to know. The drugs made the man not care about a statutory charge. The drugs made the girl not care his dick was a buffet table of STDs.

There is nothing inherently problematic about drugs. The problem lies within people. Most people cannot handle them. I have known recreational heroin users, such as myself, though that is, admittedly, not the norm. Most people do not comprehend the concept of moderation which is why people accidentally overdose, especially the younger users. At the first music festival I attended, a fifteen year old overdosed on ecstasy. His friends tossed his body underneath a random car. The body was not discovered until the owner of said car drove over a large bump.

Another thing that disgusts me is that intoxication is used as an excuse to act the fool. If someone performs some offensive or outrageous act under the influence, they laugh it off and blame it on the drug which is a pathetic way to escape personal accountability. If you cannot control your actions then you should not be indulging in intoxicants at such an extreme degree.

I saw Kevin again. This time we made eye contact. I waved; he scowled. My gut was telling me to leave, but my wallet told me I needed to find Tiz. As usual, my wallet won the debate.

I had been at the party for nearly twenty minutes. After trying to call her again, I was on the verge of leaving. People were starting to give me strange looks. Heading to the kitchen, I poured myself a tall glass of whiskey. I thought about trying to sell my supplies myself, but it had been a long time since I tried hustling small quantities. Besides, I was not dressed for the part. Most of the people present probably thought I was a narc.

With my drink in hand, I headed outside. Willy was nowhere to be found. Another nearly identical thug was posted up by the back door. I asked him where Tiz was. He was a bit more polite, but just as helpful as Willy. I took a seat on the porch and lit up a cigarette. My plan was to call her every fifteen minutes. If after forty-five minutes I still did not see her, I was leaving which gave me plenty of time to sip down my whiskey.

After a half-hour passed, I saw Tiz's car roll up into the parking lot. She stumbled out of the driver's seat, vomited on the ground, and then began wobbling her way to the porch laughing recklessly. Four other girls exited who looked like they had forgotten to completely dress. All of them were giggling with large smiles plastered on their faces. I guessed that two were at least eighteen though the other two were questionable.

Tiz nearly stumbled past me until I grabbed her shoulder. She spun around and looked at me with surprise. "Isaiah! Oh shit, I forgot you were coming."

"Really? I had no idea," I shot back angrily. "What the fuck happened to your phone?"

Frantically, she patted herself down. "Shit! Don't know. Probably in the car. You bring the shit?"

The other four girls were now crowding around us, eyeing me in the way that fat people stare down a bakery storefront window.

Grabbing Tiz's arm and leading her away from the porch, I said, "Let's take a ride."

"Can we come?" asked one of the girls shyly.

"No," I replied flatly.

Tiz protested, "Come on, Isaiah. They my bitches. Don't be trippin'. I keep my 'em in line."

With an exasperated huff, I said, "I'm sure you do, but we need to talk one-on-one."

"But they been so excited to meet you," she whined.

"Some other time."

"But-"

I turned around and glared at her. "I've been here for a fucking hour. I already got into a fight. Kevin's been mean mugging me all night, so if I deal with anymore bullshit than I'm hopping in my car and driving away. So if you want what I got, be a good girl and get in the fucking car without another word!" I barked.

I thought she was going to take a swing at me. Undoubtedly, she was thinking about it. However, she muttered something about me being a fag under her breath and walked to my car. We did not say anything until we were on the freeway.

"Fuck, Isaiah, you can be a prick."

"Well, I was sitting around with my thumb up my ass for an hour. You know how much I hate waiting around for some bullshit."

"My bad. I left to pick some of my bitches up, and we got caught up pre-funking."

I shrugged and chuckled. "Figures." And that was the end of our fight. We never really argued much. From time to time, we would irritate one another enough that blows would be exchanged, but it would pass as quickly as it came.

I handed the key to the glove box to her, and she unlocked it. Quickly, she put the two baggies in her pocket. She popped one tab and bumped a little molly.

"So how much you want for this?"

"Same as always. Fifty a gram for the molly. Four bucks a tab."

She nodded and smiled. "Fuck, bro, we gonna make some money tonight."

"That's what I'm hoping for."

"So who'd you get into a fight with?"

"Willy."

She laughed. "He's a fuckin' fool. Let me guess. He wouldn't let you in."

I nodded. "Wasn't much of a fight. He shoved me a few times, and I knocked his fat ass on the ground."

"Whatev. Mu-fucka had it comin' as always. And you said that Kev was muggin' you?"

"He was, which is strange. I thought we were cool."

"Me too," replied Tiz. "I wonder what beef he's got."

Shrugging, I said slowly. "Maybe it has something to do

with Tyrone." I was hoping she may have heard something that I was unaware of.

"Maybe. Was you two cool last time you seen him?"

"Yeah. We were cool," I stated coldly.

"Then I don't know." The conversation trailed off until we reached the party again. The girls she came with were still waiting on the porch. When they saw us, they started waving and walking towards us.

"Ain't they fine?" asked Tiz proudly. I nodded. We had yet to open the door, leaving them out of earshot. "So which one or two you want, bro?"

Laughing and shaking my head, I replied, "I think I'm set for tonight."

"What?!"

"I'm going back to the hotel."

She reached over and put me in a headlock. "No's you ain't, mu-fucka! You partying with me tonight."

I struggled to get away but to no avail. She had shoved me into my car door, and as her feet were pushed up against the passenger side door, there was no way for me to get the leverage I needed to push her off. I heaved and cursed as she talked condescendingly towards me. "Listen, bitch, I been talking you up all night. All you gotta do is say the word and that bitch is yours. So don't you go getting on the rag on me tonight. At least chill for a half a fucking hour, that's all I'm asking. If you want to leave after that, I won't say shit."

"Alright, fine!" I screamed. As she released me, I shoved her back over to her side of the car. "Fucking cunt!"

Giggling outside the car caught my attention. The girls were dancing around provocatively. Sighing melodramatically, I turned to Tiz and asked in a forlorn tone, "Any of them over eighteen?"

She scrunched her brow. "I think that bitch with the orange top is ninteen. And... maybe... the bitch in the green fishnets is eighteen."

I shook my head. "Fuckin' with dem young bitches gonna get you locked up," I said mocking her tone.

"Shit, who ever heard of a dike getting sent up-state for munching some hairless coochy. I know the red head is only sixteen, but she's mine anyway. I don't go any younger than sixteen. So what do you say? You gonna chill for a bit."

I smiled devilishly. "Yeah... but I'm gonna need some more cigarettes."

"What? You got like a full fucking pack."

"I know."

As we exited the car, the girls squealed and rushed us asking for a little something. Tiz began handing out the tabs which they greedily gulped down. One of them asked me coyly if I was staying. I nodded and offered a bump of molly to whoever would buy me a pack of cigarettes. Three mumbled something about forgetting their ID. However, the first girl Tiz pointed out, the one with the orange top, piped up that she would buy me a pack. I told her to get in, and we tore off.

Since I had no intention of conversing with her, I turned up the music and let the bass bump. She looked expectantly at me, and I handed her a small baggie full of yellowish powder. After looking skeptically at it for a moment, she dipped her fingernail in and did a bump.

"That's some good shit!" she yelled happily. I waved my hand signally she could have some more. She did not need to be told twice.

When we reached a discount cigarette store, I gave her a ten and told her to pick me up a pack of American Spirit blacks. I carefully watched her walk in and grinned. As with most of the girls in attendance at the party, her apparel could hardly even be classified as undergarments. As to her figure, I had to give it up to Tiz, she knew how to pick them. Strangely enough, Tiz and I seemed to share a similar taste in women. Not too skinny as there needs to be some curve but not chunky enough for there to be rolls. I nearly licked my lips watching her walk back to the car. The molly was really kicking in.

After tossing me the pack, she asked if she could bum one from me. I handed her my other pack.

"It's pretty much full," she said surprised. "Why'd you need another pack?"

"I wanted to see which one of you were over eighteen."

She giggled. "Oh... I see. Do you want to see my ID just to make sure?"

"Why not," I replied with a shrug.

"Seriously?" she asked in disbelief.

"Seriously. Let me see it," I demanded with my hand out.

She handed it to me, and I made a point of going over it very slowly. Staring at me curiously with a doped-up smile, she asked if she passed.

"Alright, Samantha Teresa Desher. Did you graduate from Thurston?"

"Nope. I dropped out my sophomore year."

"Why?" I asked bluntly.

Noticeably taken aback, she tried to shake it off with a nervous laugh. "Got in the way of fucking partying. Yolo, right." She said that as if it was common knowledge.

Deciding that conversation would only defuse my desire for her, I turned up the music and drove back to the party. She did a few more bumps, and I chain smoked cigarettes. As we left the car, I put my arm around her shoulder which she responded favorably to, leaning her warm body into mine. This time, the doorman caused me no problems. In the kitchen, we took some shots together, grabbed a couple beers, and then went searching through the house for Tiz and the rest of the group.

Girls like Samantha do not have to be wooed or won; they simply need to be claimed. Everywhere I looked was evidence of this. A girl standing alone may turn down a few men who come her way, but, eventually, when either the right one approaches or the night is winding down, she'll go to bed with whoever is convenient. To be fair, boys, especially those of introverted inclinations, are the same way. All a girl has to do is look at him a certain way and he is ripe for the taking. I know this thanks to my own awkward adolescence.

As I looked at the girl wrapped in my arms, I could not suppress a smirk as I thought about Michelle. That was a woman for you. Not one to be wooed, won, claimed, or conquered; she was in independent individual capable of existing on her own terms. Girls like Samantha use their sex appeal merely as a form of validation.

Yes, validation is the new cocaine. People everywhere are looking for it, willing to empty their wallets for it, and can never get enough of it. Due to either a weak mind or a weak will, people are unable to independently create an identity for themselves so they look to companies to dictate what sort of existence they will live. This is the apparel for the outdoorsman, this for the businessman, this for those want to look like they live the bohemian lifestyle, everything is neatly labelled and numbered. We define our existence by what we wear, by what we like on Facebook, by the music we listen to, by our political affiliation or organizations we belong too, and all these things are nothing but fads. In the end, our existence is constantly at the mercy of basic consumerism.

As a case study, Samantha is a girl that possesses neither intellect nor personality, and when staring at herself in the mirror after taking a shower, I can only imagine she must stand naked in a state of revulsion and self-loathing. To hide these defects from the world, she slathers some make-up on, buys some raver gear (light gloves, glow sticks, day-glo lingerie), and whores herself out to whoever has the drugs because the music she listens too, the clothes she buys, the books she reads (or in her case, blogs), and the television she watches all dictate to her, perhaps subconsciously, that this is how her existence should be. Granted, it was an existence she purchased for herself, but it is existence chosen only because it is fashionable these days as the hoard of youths thrashing together in this very room attest to, and, laughably, nearly half of them are only a few bumps away for an overdose. But at least, for a few hours, they can feel validated in their existence, that for an evening they are not alone. While everyone claims they want to be unique, the ugly truth is that we all need like-minded people. A like-minded person, whether it is their taste in music or clothing or television or hobby, makes us feel validated.

That is why advertising is so successful. They sell the one product that will never go out of style, validation. Even if it is simply a dumb rounded checkmark on our shoes, we can all get behind that rounded checkmark as if it is one big circle jerk because we are the "in" crowd that has the inside scoop and the cash to pay for a rounded checkmark on our shoes. And because I can easily see one or two people who spent $300 on a pair of shoes that validates my own purchase and, in some degree, my existence. Not only does it give one a sense of comradery, but it also bestows on the wearer of the shoe a sense of superiority over those who do not because either they "don't know" or "can't have" due to either ignorance or inferior financial capability.

If I was ever going to land an honest job which would make me rich, I would go into marketing. However, being the open-minded person that I am, I do not completely discount the notion of an afterlife. It is a possibility, granted a terribly minute possibility, that there is a heaven and a hell, but if there is, I am certain there is a special place in hell reserved for those in the marketing business. Probably in the same section for child molesters and those affiliated with the 700 Club.

Samantha squirmed in my arms demanding attention

distracting me from a wave of disgust I was being assaulted by. However, Samantha simply was not all that entertaining or interesting so I scanned the room for Tiz. I spotted her leaning against the wall, her eyes squinted, her brow scrunched, as if she was working out some complex physics problem. And then she leapt into action. Of all the lessons I gave her, she possessed one thing I never had. Showmanship. After dropping off product to some of her crew, she began maneuvering through the crowd. She grabbed a girl dancing with a guy and began to make-out for a moment. The guy just laughed as he pulled them apart. Then some tabs flashed in her hand and two twenties appeared in his.

For a moment she disappeared from view, so I gave Samantha the attention she was craving for. Yet even as our lips locked, my eyes restlessly scanned the room. Some of Tiz's boys were posted up in a corner with a small crowd of people around them. My product was flying. Every once in a while someone would approach me asking for drugs, and I would politely shake my head. Those were the ones smart enough to figure out I was the guy Tiz bought from. I rarely partied with Tiz for that very reason, yet I never tired watching the show she put on.

A circle began forming so I pulled away from Samantha to see what was happening. I saw Tiz in the middle of the floor break dancing. She was on her head twirling around as the crowd cheered her on. Deftly handspringing back to her feet, she began doing an odd sort of Robot dance with more fluid motions. I believe kids these days would call it a "pop and lock." Her hands would reach into her pockets, and bills popped into the onlookers hands. Still dancing, she exchanged product for money, not once missing a beat. This continued for three whole songs, and a rough estimation of mine said those ten minutes got us close to three hundred dollars. When Tiz left the dance floor, a small portion of the crowd left with her.

There was a warm wet sensation on my neck which jolted me from my contemplation. Intoxicated as I was, I did not notice Samantha's lips suctioned to my neck. I pulled away a bit as I did not want her to leave any noticeable marks. While I did try to lead her away to look for Tiz, she was resolved to dance with me. So we did for a short time, if what we did could be considered dancing. Essentially, I more or less performed the same function as a stripper pole.

Eventually, I grew tired of simply standing there and was hungry for a little more gratification. First, I needed to even myself out and find Tiz to see how business was going. We headed outside for a cigarette for which I was not offered a single moment without her touching me. I could tell she was rolling pretty hard so when she asked for more, I warned her to slow down. Last thing I needed was for someone to OD on me. However, she insisted and promised all sorts of fun things for another bump, so I unwillingly obliged.

There was a loud shriek which came from inside. I shot up and darted towards the commotion. On the dance floor, Tiz was screaming at some skinny thug-looking kid as people began to form a circle around them. Before I could even figure out what was going on, a pair of brass knuckles flashed on Tiz's right hand. It came crashing against the kid's face. He hit the floor with Tiz right on top of him brutally bludgeoning him. Afraid she might kill him, I jumped in to stop her. She cursed loudly and pushed me away. Yet I did manage to stop her from punching him anymore. Instead, she dragged him to his feet and shoved him against a wall. A knife appeared in her hand and was shoved against his neck.

She snarled, "Look, muthafucka, if I catch you around here again, I'll slit your goddamn throat, cut out your fuckin' intestines, shove 'em up your ass, and pull 'em right out the fuckin' slit, bitch!" Then she hit him in the temple with the butt of the knife sending him sliding to the floor unconscious. "This is my hood, muthafucka!"

She walked away as some other people grabbed his body and tossed him outside.

"What was that all about?" I asked. I had seen her fuming with anger over a deal gone bad; hell, I was there when she went through those first horrendous, hormone-fueled teenage temper tantrums. But I had never seen her red-faced and shaking with rage.

Her chest was heaving as she seethed through gritted teeth, "That piece of mutha-fuckin' shit roofied some thirteen year old at a party! Fuckin' raped her! Fuckin' piece of shit! She's just a little girl! So fucked up! Fucked up!"

She was nearly wheezing she was so upset. "That shit's traumatic for a little girl, you know what I am saying. Fucks 'em up in the head, you know like psychologically and shit. Just fucked up!" she bellowed, her voice quivering with anger.

Then she cooled off a bit. Staring off into nowhere, she whispered, "She was just a little girl." I could have sworn I saw her eyes begin to water.

After that little commotion, a group of us headed upstairs which was a tiring affair considering I had to support Samantha's wobbling legs. Despite my warning, she was over doing it. Not in any serious danger, but I was slightly worried she might not be able to perform some functions which I felt I had paid for with the amount of my drugs she had ingested.

We all posted up on a couple couches. While Tiz's hands were still trembling with anger, she still managed to roll a fantastic blunt. No one talked as we passed it around. I could see Tiz start to mellow a bit. After the blunt was smoked, Tiz and I talked business. She had managed to put another eight hundred in my pocket. The molly was completely gone as well as most of the tabs, and it had been little over an hour since I had given her the drugs.

Samantha was becoming more and more touchy-feely, and I was repeatedly pulling her hand away from my crotch. It was about time to head back to the hotel room. While most of the party-goers had no problem exposing themselves to complete strangers, I possessed a more dignified restraint in that regards. I told Tiz to roll another blunt and then I was taking off with Samantha. One of the other girls asked to come too, but I politely turned her down unless she could show me a state-issued identification card. This prompted a not so polite response.

The night was going better than I could have expected. I was getting paid and getting laid, both of which were long overdue. However, I never shook that pit in my stomach which only grew the more smoothly the night progressed. My mind would constantly replay how Kevin snubbed me. Then the music died abruptly.

As I heard my name angrily screamed out, I uncovered the source of my anxiety. Tyrone was dead. For some reason I had completely forgotten about that small detail. Tyrone was dead, and the only person who knew was me. Well, plus some Hispanic gangbangers in Los Angeles. Again, my name reverberated from the molding plaster on the walls. I knew who was screaming my name. I knew why Kevin snubbed me. Tyrone was dead, and his family was coming to me for answers. Kevin must have called Tyrone's half-brother, Devante, who was the source of those angry cries. Tyrone was dead, and his family would be looking to repay blood with blood. His body must have been discovered. I had thought the Sanderros would have disposed of the body properly, yet it must have been found. Tyrone was dead, and Samantha tried to squirm her way out of my arms. I told her everything was going to be fine and ordered her to stay put. Then I forced myself to remain passively nonchalant about the whole situation. Tyrone was dead, and I could hear loud footsteps charging up the stairs. Cursing my intoxicated state, my mind raced for solutions, yet Tyrone was dead, and it was my fault, and there was no way of shooting my way out of this situation, and if I was caught slipping I was dead, and Samantha was squirming nervously in my arms, and Tyrone, a man who had been like a brother to me since I was seven, was dead, and it was all my fault, and his family was looking for revenge.

With a carefree smile plastered on my face, I stared at the four men barging in the door. Of the four, only two I recognized. There was Kevin again as well as Devante, Tyrone's half-brother. His pupils were pulsing with cocaine. There was a pistol indiscreetly tucked into his waist band. I stared into those big brown eyes, looked over the pitch-black scars which crisscrossed his face, and met his snarl with a shrug. He was a giant of a man, 6'9" carrying around at least three twenty. He could have gone pro in any sport he chose if it had not been for his legendary temper as well as his insatiable taste for narcotics. If this was to be the end for me, at least I was not being taken out by some skinny punk.

"What up, Devante," I said slowly as he eyed me. I leaned back on the couch with my arm around Samantha. My goal was to appear relaxed.

"What the fuck you think, bitch?" he shouted aggressively.

I shrugged. "I don't know. What's the problem? Sit down, take a hit of this, and tell me what's on your mind," I cooed as I tried handing him a blunt which he waved away.

"Where's T at?"

Shaking my head, I lied, "I don't know."

His hands shot into the air. "Bullshit! Fuckin' bullshit! You punk-ass little bitch! You know where he's at!"

"Last I saw him was when we were in LA. Did he get busted or something?" I asked innocently.

The whole room was quiet. Tiz looked at me nervously. Smiling, I gave her a reassuring nod.

"He's fuckin' dead, fool." I let my smile disappear. "The LA police called me a couple days ago. So tell me, muthafucka, what the fuck happened in LA?" asked Devante his voice dripping with hostility.

I looked at the ground and shook my head slowly. "Fuck, dude. That's some shit."

"What the fuck happened?" demanded Devante, seething with rage. It looked like his eyes were going to bulge out of his head.

That was my cue. I stood up very slowly making sure my hands were visible at all times. "Maybe this is a conversation we should have outside."

"And why the fuck is that?" barked Devante, viciously shoving me back on the couch.

With the utmost care, I rose to my feet again. "Because it's just one of those conversations, Devante," I replied coolly.

It looked like he was going to take a swing at me, but his fists unclenched and he exhaled deeply. "Aight, Isaiah, but you got some fuckin' explaining to do," he snarled.

Tiz shot me a nervous glance. I smiled and shook my head. I left with Devante and his crew. Many curious stares followed us out of the house. When we made it outside and were far enough away from prying ears, I lit up a cigarette and waited for the interrogation. Luckily, our walk afforded me enough time to come up with some solid answers.

However, all my answers disappeared when Kevin and another of Devante's crew grabbed my arms and pinned them behind my back. My cigarette flew from my mouth. I was standing face to face with Devante who was puffing on a plastic-tipped cigar and slowly pulling a knife out from his pocket.

"So what the fuck happened?" Devante asked with a malicious grin. I tried to answer but he cut me off by grabbing my throat. Then he put the knife to my right eye and said slowly, "And if I hear one muthafuckin' lie out your bitch-ass, you lose an eye, muthafucka."

Inwardly, I was panicking, but I was able to keep my outward demeanor cool and nonchalant. "Crystal," I stated flatly.

"What you mean?" he snarled.

"Tyrone started fucking around with crystal," I said hastily.

Devante snorted. "How the fuck he get caught up in that shit?" I could tell he was not buying it. Tyrone had always harped on Devante for using meth. To convince Devante that Tyrone had started using would be a tough sell indeed.

I forced my words to come out slowly and deliberately, always holding eye contact with Devante. "We were moving shit from San Diego to LA, mainly thiz and some blow from time to time. Our hook in San Diego had some cheap crystal. Apparently, some real pure shit too straight from Mexico. Our boys in LA were interested in crystal so Tyrone wanted to start pushing it." I paused to shake my head and sigh melodramatically. "I told him that shit was too heavy for us, but he had them dollar signs in his eyes."

"And then what?" he asked angrily, the point of the knife mere millimeters from my eye.

"Well, long story short, we had some weight. He went to go meet with his people."

"What people?"

"The Sanderros," I breathed quietly. That caused Devante to step back and remove the knife from underneath my eye.

"Fuck…"

"Yeah. Heavy shit." I could tell I was reeling him in. The key to any good lie is to insert half-truths throughout. While it pained me to slander my dead friend's name, I would be doing him no service by joining him in the ground. "He started using it too. First, he said it was just to test it, but then he took it to some next level shit."

"Never thought he'd get hooked on that shit," sighed Devante.

I nodded severely. "Neither did I, but that's crystal for you. Anyway, he took off to go meet the Sanderros with a zip so they could test it out. He left one night and never came back. I waited a few days, but when he didn't show, I bounced."

Suddenly, anger flared up in his eyes again. "You didn't ask around?" he asked accusingly. "What! You just left him there, you fuckin' punk!"

Deciding it was safe now to show a little righteous indignation, I snarled, "And who the fuck was I gonna ask? Should I have gone down South Central asking if anyone saw some black kid with an ounce of meth? Maybe knock on some Sanderros' door and politely inquire as to what happened to Tyrone? Tell me, Devante, what the fuck was I supposed to do, all alone there?"

He grabbed me by the throat and shoved the knife against my eye again. "But he always had your fuckin' back! That how you repay him!"

Using all the anger my panic-stricken mind could muster, I managed to choke out as much as I could with Devante's hand around my throat, "What the fuck you trying to say, Devante! What the fuck are you accusing me of! When T was in jail, who visited him every other fucking day?" His grip loosened as he tried to say something, but I cut him off. "That's right. It was me. Your bitch-ass was too busy with a fuckin' spoof pipe to stop by to see your own brother! When T got his ass kicked by those rednecks in Grants Pass, who fuckin' drove out there to pick him up at the hospital? Who found those pieces of shit!"

He stopped me there. "Hey, man, I came out and helped you deal with those fuckin' hillbillies." He was on the defensive, so I kept up the assault.

"After I spent a fuckin' week tracking them down! And, shit, when T was going to court, who paid for his lawyer, huh? Who took out every goddamn loan he could to keep him out of prison? Because you fuckin' know that if he had some fuckin' Public Pretender, he'd of done three to five. Both you and I knew that, but only one of us threw down any cash to pay for a lawyer? Now tell me, Devante, was that you... or was that me?" I knew that last line was either the knock-out punch or my last words.

He paused for a long time before he nodded his head. His crew let me go.

"Listen, Isaiah, I know what you done for him. I'm just hurting-"

I was about to light a cigarette, but I decided to lash out one last time. "You think I'm not! You know me, Devante! You know how tight I was with Tyrone!" The pain in my voice was as genuine as the tear running down my left cheek. "We were like brothers, man... no, we were brothers. If there was anything I could have done, I would have done it! So don't come on like I got him fuckin' killed! Like I just left him on the fuckin' ground bleeding to death! He played a risky hand, and he got burned! Nothing I could have done!"

As much as I wanted for him to believe my lie, I wished even more to believe my own.

He sighed. "Look, I know you two was tight, Isaiah. Don't mean no disrespect, man. Just trying to figure shit out is all."

I paused for a moment. Things were becoming a bit friendlier, so I suggested we grab a drink in memory of our dearly departed brother. No one protested so we walked a couple blocks to run-down bar which was packed with video lottery machines. I never understood the appeal of those machines. It was an arcade for adults that cost more money. I have seen people sit for hours pressing a button, dumping hundreds of dollars into those machines.

I ordered a round of Patron Silver shots for all of us. Patron Silver was Tyrone's favorite. We toasted to his memory and downed our shots. Then I ordered another round. Within a half-hour, I had spent nearly quarter of my profit I had made that night, but I was happy to be alive. Devante was known for viciously beating people who looked at him the wrong way. I could imagine what he would have done to someone he thought was responsible for his brother's death.

By the time we left the bar, I was at my limit for intoxicants. Lights were blinking, the world was shaking, and my stomach was at the brink of expelling all the alcohol I had consumed. By that point, everything had cooled down, so I ventured to restart the conversation about Tyrone.

"So what did the police say happened to Tyrone?"

"Not much. He'd been shot a couple times. They found his body at the dump. Took 'em a grip to identify it. They think it happened a month ago."

"Shit. Anything else."

"Na... They sending his body up here. I'm trying to come up with the cash to give him a decent funeral."

I hesitated for a moment. "Look, Devante, you know how I said that Tyrone left with a zip of crystal right?"

"Yeah."

"Well, we had three pounds of that shit which he was going to deliver."

His eyes nearly bulged out of their sockets. "You still got it?"

"Well, yeah. Not going to throw it all away. My money was in that too. Now I don't know how to get rid of it, but if you can get rid of it, I'll give you a half pound to help pay for the funeral expenses." A half-pound of crystal would pay for the entire funeral and then some. My intentions to help bury my friend were sincere, but I was also hoping he could get rid of some for me.

Devante thought for a moment before responding. "I'd take it. I know some people who would pay whole sale prices for that shit."

"Just let me know when and where you want to meet. I don't like having that shit on me."

"What you gonna do with the rest?"

I shook my head. "I don't know. Tiz is working on it right now, but she only really fucks around with thiz."

"How much you selling it for?"

"I'm just trying to cover my losses. If you'll take it off my hands, a grand a zip or I'll front it to you for twelve hundred."

"And it's good?"

"That's what Tyrone said."

"Let me see where that half gets me, and I'll let you know."

A despondent frown was plastered on my face, but, inwardly, I was smiling. I could not have been more pleased with how the night was progressing. Once we made it back to the party, Devante and his crew took their leave. Tiz was waiting on the porch. After a short conversation about Tyrone where I reiterated the same story to Tiz as I had Devante, we headed back upstairs where her girls were waiting. All in all, it had been a very productive evening.

I awoke to my phone ringing. Scowling at the clock which read 9:13, I inwardly cursed whoever was rousing me after only three hours of sleep. Grudgingly, I answered the phone.

"Hello," I said groggily.

"Hi, Isaiah, it's Michelle." Immediately, I was wide awake. "Sorry to bother you, but my car broke down, and I don't have a way to get to school. Do you think you could come pick me up? Real sorry to bug you, but no one else can drive me. I'm right by the grocery store on 35th."

"Yeah, sure thing. Be there in like thirty or less."

"Oh my gosh, thank you! You're a life saver."

"Don't mention it."

I hung up and hopped out of bed, looking around for my clothes. Something was wrong in the room. There were more clothes scattered on the floor than there should have been. As I glanced back at the bed, I noticed there were two lumps under the covers. Cursing myself and God, I flung the covers off. Sure enough, two girls were under there. One of them was Samantha, the other I had not the slightest clue as to who she may have been. However, I had a sneaking suspicion she was one of the girls who did not have an ID. They mumbled a protest and groped blindly for the blankets.

"Get up!" I barked. "Time to go!"

"What the fuck," muttered the strange girl sleepily.

"I got to go."

"What... why?" asked Samantha.

"I got to pick a friend up. You got five minutes to get dressed, and then I'm kicking you out as you are."

"Can't we stay here?"

"Nope."

As they fumbled to get dress, I rolled two joints quickly and snorted some methadone. I am not a morning person to begin with, and the morning withdrawals from opiates did not help in the least. While seeing an obviously underage girl dress was disconcerting, even more so was the fact I could find no evidence of a condom. Hopefully, I had been too far gone to do any serious damage.

As I lit up a joint, I mellowed out a bit. I gave them each a twenty so they could catch the bus and grab a bite to eat. When they asked me for my number, I kindly turned them down.

Michelle was smoking a cigarette as a tow truck was loading up her car. After a quick farewell to the driver, she hopped in the passenger seat.

"Thank you so much for this," she said earnestly.

"Not a problem. Didn't have shit going on today."

She looked me over. "Looks like you had quite a night with Tiz."

I smiled and nodded. "Yeah... it was something else."

"Have fun?"

"Kind of."

"Stay out of trouble?"

I smirked. "Kind of." I lit up the second joint and offered it to her.

She shook her head and smiled. "Oh no, I got class, but thanks anyway."

I asked her what she was going to school for, and she told me she was in the nursing program. I myself could think of no better occupation for someone as kind-hearted as she was. Then she told me she planned on going back to Africa after she became a certified nurse to do some volunteer work. I balked at the idea. Considering how small she was, I told her that Africa was no place for a woman her size.

She sighed. "Well, I feel like it is God's plan for me."

I shot her a side-ways glance. "Last night you sounded a bit bitter about the whole god thing."

Scowling at me, she replied, "I know, but I was a bit drunk. Whiskey makes me a bit bitter."

"So you're still on that whole god trip?" I asked condescendingly.

She punched me playfully on the arm. "Don't be an asshole."

Shaking my head, I said slowly, "I just don't see how after all that shit you saw you could still keep your faith. I mean, what kind of god let's that shit happen? What kind of god creates such a fucked-up world?"

She sighed. "Look, I'm not saying I don't have my doubts. But I feel like doubt is an important part of a strong faith."

"Then I guess I got one of the strongest faiths around," I said snidely.

Instead of a curt rebuttal, she surprised me with what she said next. "In a way, you are absolutely right."

"What?"

"Pastor John and I have had some long talks about you. He said that in all his years of being a youth pastor, you showed the most potential of going into the ministry."

I nearly dropped my joint. "Seriously?"

"Yep."

I was genuinely confused. Granted, in the few years I had attended the church, I had been actively involved in the youth group, but I had veered hard down another path when I was seventeen. Out of everyone, I was the most outspoken about my disbelief and abruptly left the church after a long rant about the illogical nature of faith. In fact, I had said some fairly nasty things about the ignorance of religion. Why Michelle continued to talk to me after that was baffling as no one else besides John would. Not that I blamed them. What I said had been very cruel.

On the flip side, why I continued to talk to any of them was baffling as well. Sure there was that whole emotional investment side of things, but I was not a sentimentalist. It was as if I still wanted one foot in the door in case I decided to change my mind. Or maybe it was something else. With John, I definitely had self-serving motives for continuing my relationship with him, mainly a pastor for character witness at my inevitable trial.

"Why did he say that?"

"There are things about John you don't know. You two are quite alike in many ways. Did you know he followed the Grateful Dead back in the day?"

"No, but I can't stand the Dead. Probably the most boring band that ever plagued this god forsaken planet."

"Whatever. I like them, but that's not important. He was and still is confident that you will come back someday. Not as you were but stronger. He said you needed to go find yourself."

I snorted. "I did find myself, and I'm no fucking pastor, that's for damn sure."

Her smile irked me. "At least you think you found yourself. To me, you'll always be that shy little boy sitting in the corner all alone reading a book at the Youth Retreat."

She was referring to the first time we talked at this camp for Christian youths which was sponsored by multiple churches. It was free time, but it was pouring rain outside so everyone was in the gym. Most of the people were playing dodge ball while I read a Star Wars book in the corner. Michelle had a bloody nose from taking a hit to the face. Seeing me sitting in the corner reading, she walked over to me and started talking. I remember how I stuttered my responses, the way she kindly smiled at me, and her insistence that I join the next game. After that, she always made sure I was included in whatever activity we were undertaking. I look back at that moment as a critical point in my conversion to the Christianity. Michelle was my main motivation to pursue the faith as deeply as I had.

And perhaps right there is why I enjoyed her company. I was absolutely in love with the image she had of me. No matter how far off the straight and narrow I went, there was good old Michelle thinking I was something akin to the prodigal son, just awaiting my return. If anything ever bad did happen to me, she would weep and think to herself how utterly cruel this world is. It would serve as a stumbling block in her faith, another point for me, some petty revenge for helping me drink the Jesus Juice.

And that, ladies and gentlemen, was the reason why our reunion excited me so much. It was not some sort of emotional attachment, some pathetic yearning for the "good old days;" no, it was far more sinister than that. She presented me with an opportunity to get back at a religion which had caused me so much pain and grief during my adolescence. From my foster parent's constant spouting of "spare the rod, spoil the child" to the scorn and judgment of hypocrites when I stumbled in my faith. I would rob them of one of their most steadfast and influential members.

And then again, maybe it was something else, something I myself was not willing to admit to right then and there.

Honestly, it is hard to look back at that time with a clear head. Memories have a way of warping themselves into something that corresponds to the image one has of oneself.

As of then, I was reveling in ecstasy from this new found understanding of myself and how I perceived the word around me. I decided it was time to change the subject to her. Try to find some weak spot, some area which to exploit.

Innocently, I asked, "So how long have you been in the nursing program?"

There was a long pause as she continued smiling at me. I could tell there was something else she wanted to say on the subject, but she allowed me to veer it off course. "Been in it for almost six months. Could have easily been done by now, but after I got back from Africa, I decided to take some time off to figure out what I wanted to do. Worked at New Frontiers serving coffee for a while."

"I've always thought that would be a relaxing job."

"I could get you job there if you wanted," she replied quickly.

Laughing and shaking my head, I replied, "Thanks, but no thanks. I'm quite content with my job right now."

"Being a drug dealer? Seriously? I'm sure it's fun now, but if you get busted then…" Her voice trailed off.

"I know. But how the fuck else am I going to make it. There's no jobs for a felon that pay decently."

"Have you ever looked?"

"No."

"Then how can you say that?"

The university was coming up which derailed her interrogation for a moment as she gave me directions. I parked and waited for her to get out. However, she paused for a long moment and simply stared at me. There was a strange look in her eyes which caused me to look away.

She cleared her throat. "Just because you are a felon doesn't mean you can't do something meaningful with your life. There are other things you could do," she said with the seriousness of a high school guidance counselor.

"I know. Just prevents me from doing anything that I want to do."

She huffed in exasperation. "Well, if you ever want a job at New Frontiers, let me know."

"I will. Do you need me to pick you up?"

"No, I can take the bus back."

"What time do you want me to pick you up?"

She laughed and waved her hand dismissively. "It's fine. Don't worry about it."

"What time?" I insisted.

She smiled at me. "How about four o'clock right here."

"I'll be here."

She opened the door to leave but paused for a long moment. Then she reached over and gave me a hug. "Thanks for picking me up."

I hesitantly patted her on the back a couple times. "Not a problem. Any time."

She did not let me go. "It's good to have you back, Isaiah. I hope you stick around."

Fumbling for words, I muttered, "Yeah... me too."

Without another word, she hopped out of the car. I rolled another joint in the parking lot then headed back to the hotel stopping by a fast food joint to pick up some food. When I entered my room, I was asleep before my head hit the pillow.

I was in a white room. In front of me was Tyrone. I was saying something, but I could not hear what I was saying. He stared at me with glazed over eyes. I was not sure if he could hear me as I could not hear myself. As I stared into those dead eyes, a peculiar sensation filled my mouth. Large chunks of something started to fill it. Spitting the chunks out, I was horrified to see what they were. Tooth after tooth shot out of my mouth. It seemed like I was losing more teeth than what I had. Whatever I was trying to say was important, but the falling teeth made it harder and harder to speak. I started choking on them as I could not spit them out fast enough.

Then Tyrone screamed, and I woke up.

My head was pounding with a migraine, and my stomach was churning. I stumbled my way to the bathroom and threw up. My sense of time was distorted, so I had no clue how long I was there. The only thing that got me to my feet again was hearing the alarm on my phone go off which meant it was time to pick up Michelle. After railing a few lines of methadone and morphine, I felt much better. I rolled a few joints and was on my way.

I arrived ten minutes early, so I had time to lean my seat back and smoke a cigarette. Of all the places in Eugene, the university is perhaps my least favorite spot second only to the jail. A High Times magazine maybe ten or so years back placed this university on their list of top ten counter cultural colleges in the country. Now I am not sure as to what Nike's involvement with the college was at the time that article was published, but it seems laughable now, considering how much funding Nike pumps into the university's athletic program.

Why sports hold such importance at academic institutions has been something that never ceases to baffle me. When schools today are facing massive budget cuts it seems that the athletic programs would be the first to go, not cutting teachers or skimping on books as seems to be the case. Luckily for colleges, there will always be companies like Nike to funnel millions of dollars into their athletic programs, so they can brand their logo on every nook and cranny. Nike actually gives athletes gift certificates to their own store, allowing athletes to advertise for them on and off the field. Leaving my moral qualms aside, I had to respect their game. They know how to run a racket.

A sharp knock on the window saved me from a wave of

disgust assaulting me right then. I unlocked the door, and Michelle popped in.

"Thanks for picking me up."

"No problem. How was class?"

"Oh, it was interesting. Well, as interesting as math can be."

I laughed. "I always hated math."

"Why's that?"

Shrugging, I replied, "For one, it's repetitive. Secondly, I never cared for subjects that had a right answer. I like room for discussion."

"Fair enough."

"So am I dropping you off at your place?"

She shook her head. "Actually, I was hoping you could drop me off at the church. I have praise team practice tonight."

"I didn't realize you played an instrument."

"I don't. I sing."

I wanted to slap myself in the face. Of course she sang. How could I have forgotten? I always enjoyed her singing. There was something carefree about her style as if she was playing with the notes like a gifted jazz soloist.

There was this one time, years ago, when our youth group went out camping for the weekend at one of our favorite spots by Blue River. We went there at least once a year. For some reason, I had trouble sleeping one night and wandered into the woods. I sat next to the river to clear my head. It must have been towards the end of my stint with the church because I remember being racked with doubt. I remember the desperation I felt as if I was claustrophobic in my own skin. Then I heard footsteps coming nearby. I thought someone was looking for me. Actually, I remember hoping someone was looking for me because all I wanted to do was pour my heart out to anyone. However, it was another person suffering from insomnia, Michelle. To this day, I can replay the exact sounds of her voice as she sang "Michelle" by the Beatles. Her voice sadly melded with the quiet trickle of the water. She sang the song over and over again. I sat very still, not wanting my presence to be discovered. Perhaps she was there for only a few minutes, but it felt like hours. When she finally left, I waited for a long time before moving. Then I slipped back into the campground and fell fast asleep. I never told her what I had heard. It is the small secrets we keep within ourselves which gives life its bittersweet taste.

"What time is practice?"

"Not until six, but you can drop me off now, and I'll hang out for a bit."

"Are you hungry? We could grab something to eat? I'm starving."

Giggling nervously, she replied, "That sounds nice, but I'm afraid I'm flat broke right now. I have no idea how I'm going to pay for the car."

I shot her a friendly sneer. "I didn't ask if you wanted to buy food, I asked if you were hungry. So are you hungry?"

"Sort of."

"Well, alright then. How does the Herb Garden sound?"

"Sounds good to me. I'll pay you back."

I chuckled. "No, you won't. It's my pleasure."

The Herb Garden was a little hippie joint downtown run by only two people. Not sure if they were married or brother and sister, but they were some of the friendliest people around. While there was not much of a selection, what they did have was fantastic. Plus, they had a bunch of pro-legalization literature and posters which was always a good sign. I prefer stoners to make my food because they know how to make a meal both delicious and filling. Plus, being hippies, they were health conscious but not health nuts. They made all their own sauces, and most of their produce came from local farms. Unlike many other restaurants like this one, the food was reasonably priced.

Whenever you walk into a restaurant and are called

"bro" as you enter, you know you have come to the right place. Michelle and I both ordered rice bowls. I cringed when she started interrogating the proprietors about their loyalties to certain dietary fads. What do they serve that is organic? Is it GMO-free? What contains soy? Is their coffee Fair Trade? Is it cage-free, cruelty free, hormone-free, pesticide-free? The list went on. Sure, I too aspire to be an ethical consumer. Actually, I pay lip service to that fact, but rarely will I sacrifice my hard-earned money to back up those convictions. In other words, I am a typical American. After a melodramatic, disappointed huff from Michelle and an apologetic smile from the man taking our order, Michelle and I finally made our way to a table.

Silence lingered as we scanned the walls reading the posters. One of my favorites was one of Einstein sticking his tongue out. I could tell Michelle was reading over one which dealt with the various religious passages about marijuana. Apparently, a poetic sect of Islam spoke fondly of hashish as well as some esoteric sects of Christianity. Deciding the route was a good conversation starter, I asked her about how she justified her life style.

"What? Like drinking?" she replied a bit put off by my accusatory tone.

"I'm just curious. Last I saw you, you were preaching about the evils of drugs every time we ran into each other. Now, you drink and you smoke herb."

She huffed indignantly. "So?"

"So... how does that line up with your religious views?"

Staring at me with a bemused look on her face, she said asked slowly, "Do you see a contradiction?"

I leaned back in my chair and put my hands behind my head as I eased myself into the attack. "Well, sort of. Not many Christians smoke herb."

She scrunched her nose at me. "The Bible doesn't say anything about smoking pot."

"It also doesn't say anything about shooting meth," I retorted.

"True, but how I look at it is weed is a plant. It's natural. The effects are not that harmful, and it has been proven to be medically beneficial. I think it is here for a reason."

"Maybe it is nothing more than a temptation," I offered. "Like dinosaur fossils are nothing more than a temptation to believe in science."

She chuckled. "You are horrible," she replied emphasizing "horrible."

"That being said, do you believe in evolution?"

"Yes," she stated flatly.

That answer caught me off guard. "But if evolution is true, than that sort of debunks the whole Creation story."

"You are absolutely right, but that does not mean there is not an intelligent designer."

I could not contain a burst of contemptuous laughter. "So you still believe in a bearded man floating in the sky speaking worlds into existence."

She scowled at me. "Look, Isaiah, I've changed since you've last talked to me. I'm not some religious hard-liner anymore. I don't take everything the Bible says literally. There is room for interpretation."

"Fair enough. So back to drugs."

"Of course," she snorted, waving her hands despondently in the air. "That's the only thing you ever want to talk about."

"Excuse my curiosity, but this whole hippie Michelle thing clashes with my image of the innocent Christian Michelle I used to know. It seems a bit contradictory to me."

My onslaught was interrupted by the arrival of food. A short pudgy man wearing a tie-dye bandana which matched his shirt and pants put our bowls down, hesitated for a moment, and then said meekly, "Not to be nosy, but why is there a contradiction, dude? Jesus was like the original hippie, man." His eyes were completely bloodshot.

"Thank you," said Michelle with an exasperated sigh.

The man continued with a smile. "Jesus was all like 'don't worry about tomorrow' and 'love everybody' and like 'help your bros out.' That all sounds like hippie talk to me, dude. Just cause the church is all full of ignorant drones doesn't mean that you can't be a hippie and a Christian."

As I stared him down, I asked slowly, "Are you a Christian?"

He puffed up a bit. "Actually, I am. Can't say I go to church very often, but I think Jesus was a pretty rad dude and had some pretty rad things to say, so... yeah... I'm a Christian.

Michelle piped up. "Again, thank you. Not just for the back-up, but the food too. Delicious, as always."

He smiled shyly. "Thank you. I'm sorry I butt in. You two enjoy."

Michelle smiled. "No need to apologize. If you agree with anything else I say, please speak up."

His beer belly jiggled as he laughed. "You two need anything else?"

I shook my head. "This is perfect. I've been out of town for a few years, and I'm glad to see you guys are still open. Always been my favorite place to eat."

His smile grew even wider as he excitedly nodded his head. "Glad to hear it, dude. I thought I recognized you."

Looking down, I replied, "Probably from the time I had to drag my drunk sister out of here when she tried to steal your jug of sweet and sour sauce."

He scrunched his brow. "I think I remember that."

"She was dressed in all red, skinny, butch-looking, wannabe gangster type. Managed to knock over the rice cooker."

A large smile crept on his face. "Oh yeah, I remember, dude. You gave us like, two hundred bucks or something for that."

"Yes, I did, and let me apologize one more time for that. She was very drunk."

Laughing, he waved his hands dismissively. "Don't sweat it, bro. We actually are using the same one. It didn't even break, dude! Can't give you the money back I'm afraid. We donated it to a food bank."

I smiled. "That's fine by me. Glad it went to good use."

"Well, I'll stop jabbering so you can get to eating. Got to get back to work anyway. Enjoy." And with that, he waddled back to the kitchen.

I was starving, and apparently, so was Michelle. We wolfed down our food in a matter of minutes. After bidding the proprietors a fond farewell, we headed outside and walked around downtown for a while.

On more than one occasion, we would pass a bum asking for change or holding a sign, and I would, without hesitation, give them a cigarette or a couple bucks. At one point, I became a bit irritable when Michelle scoffed at my generosity by saying that I would probably being seeing that money again. Sure, a few of the people I gave money too were saving up to buy a bag crystal or some weed, but what is so wrong with that? Many of those on the street are drug addicts or alcoholics, what of it? That sort of living is not easy, and there are very few options available to those on the street to get out of the cycle of poverty. If they decide to snort some meth or drink themselves to death that is their business not mine. Obviously, seeing the condition they are in, life has not been easy on them, and sure, some of them might have made a few wrong choices for which they were punished too severely for, and others are simply victims of circumstance. So when people, especially Christians, criticize others for giving money to the homeless, I am simply beside myself with irritation. Good for you for having easy lives surrounded by safety nets.

After nearly an hour of aimless wandering, we returned to my car and drove to the church. Again, she declined my offer to get stoned. She chided me a little for smoking too much. I did not take too kindly to her preaching about moderation.

As luck would have it, Justin was waiting outside the church when we pulled in. Immediately, he waved at us and started to approach. I parked, and Michelle got out. I stayed in the car.

"How are you today, Michelle?" he asked with obvious faked enthusiasm.

She huffed. "Oh, fine. My car broke down."

His face contorted with feigned concern. "That's too bad. Is that why Isaiah drove you here?"

"Yep, he was nice enough to pick me up."

He shot me a dirty look. "You could have called me. All I had today was an online conference call."

"Well, I thought you might be busy, and I knew he didn't have anything going on," she said with a laugh.

After walking up to my window and putting a hand on my car, he stuck his other hand through the window offering a handshake which I refused. "And how are you today, Isaiah?"

I lit up a cigarette and blew it in his face, hoping it would make him move away from me. "Just fine."

He looked over at Michelle. "You should go inside and tell the others I'll be there in a minute. I want to talk to Isaiah."

"I didn't realize you played an instrument, Justin," I said snidely. "I thought you only concerned yourself with things that made you money or made you look pretty like those fake-ass nails of yours." Apparently, I was spoiling for a fight. The hairs on my neck were starting to rise.

Michelle looked hesitantly at us as Justin glowered at me. She said, "I don't know if I should leave you two alone. I think you need to be supervised."

"We'll be fine," assured Justin.

"Okay... play nice." With that she went inside.

"So what did you want to talk about?" I asked innocently. Readjusting my initial demeanor was crucial to off-balance him. I wanted to keep him guessing, so I decided unpredictability was my best option.

Slowly, he replied, "I wanted to talk about Michelle."

Smiling wide enough to show my teeth, I replied, "Is this a conversation I should step out of the car for?"

His hand was still on my door preventing me from opening it which bothered me. "No. I am hoping to have a civilized conversation with you. Look, I know we have had our differences-"

"To put it mildly," I said abruptly with a forced smile.

With a huff, he continued, "Yes, but I am hoping we can put that all behind us, at least for right now. I know we both care about Michelle, and I am hoping we can both proceed with her best interest in mind."

"Fair enough," I said pleasantly, blowing more smoke into his face.

He wrinkled his nose in disgust. "The last time you left, it crushed Michelle. I don't want to see her hurt like that. I'm sure you have noticed she's changed since you've last seen her."

"I have, and I must say, I could not be more pleased." He uncontrollably frowned at that statement.

"Leaving aside any moral judgments of her lifestyle choices-"

"Which neither of us have any right to judge," I interrupted.

"Of course," he said through gritted teeth. "But I'm worried about her, and, more specifically, I'm worried that if she becomes more involved with you, she may make some poor decisions."

"Like what?"

"Like continuing down the destructive path she is already heading down," he snapped. His cologne was suffocating. I could taste it through my cigarette.

Clicking my tongue against the back of my teeth, I retorted snidely, "I thought we were leaving moral judgments aside."

Exasperated, he exclaimed, "Whether you like it or not, she has been acting more wild lately, and I don't think you are going to help things!"

"No need to raise your voice. It's not like I'm going to try to get her hooked on heroin."

"But you are a bad influence," he insisted

"Says who?" I asked with mock indignation.

"Says everyone!"

"Says you," I said coolly. "And the truth is, you aren't worried about Michelle. You're worried about your prospects with her. I'm an unexpected kink in your plan to woo her which is completely baffling considering you are quite obviously a homosexual."

"What!"

I smiled pleasantly at him. "No need to get offended. I have absolutely nothing against gays. For years, I thought you needed something pulled out of your ass; now, I realize you just needed something inserted in it."

His face contorted violently. "I'm trying to have a serious conversation here, Isaiah."

I continued in the same pleasantly passive tone. "So am I, Justin. Have you looked at yourself lately? Of course you have. You must spend hours in front of the mirror putting your make-up on in the morning."

"There's nothing wrong with a man trying to look nice," he said defensively. "And in my line of work, one has to look their best."

"I'm not judging. I just want to help you realize who you truly are."

"This is not about me!" he snapped. "I'm trying to talk about Michelle."

"What about her?" I asked innocently.

His hands were noticeably shaking. "I just don't want you hurting her again. She's a sweet girl, and you don't need to go corrupting her more than you already have."

"I've corrupted her?" I asked incredulously. "I was long gone before she veered from the straight and narrow."

"Just don't do any more damage than what you've already done." He leaned in with menace in his eyes. "You hurt her again, and I will beat the crap out of you," he snarled. Then with a hateful smile, he added, "Just like last time."

I stared long and hard at him before replying. "Look, faggot, just because I didn't enjoy rolling around half-naked with sweaty boys in high school doesn't mean I can't fight. We go toe-to-toe again, and I guaran-fucking-tee it won't end like last time."

"Well, hopefully, we won't have to test that theory. Just don't go wrecking everything I've done for her."

Laughing derisively, I shot back, "If you think you got a chance with a girl like that than you are out of your goddamn mind. Don't you know, Justin, that women don't like men who spend twice as long getting ready than they do."

He huffed indignantly and scrunched his square face. "Whatever, Isaiah. I was hoping to have a serious conversation with you, but apparently you aren't mature enough for that. I need to get to praise team practice."

"So what instrument do you play? The rusty trombone." I thought that was hilarious which I displayed by my maniacal, overzealous laughter.

He turned and walked away, but before I could throw my car in reverse, he turned around with one last comment. "It's sad when children follow in their parents' footsteps."

Immediately, rage started flowing into my veins. I charged out of the car and stormed up to him. "And what the fuck is that supposed to mean?"

Smiling indolently, he replied, "Just like your parents, you're nothing more than a pathetic drug-addict who abandons people without even saying good-bye. Sad but unfortunately that seems to be the cycle."

Furious, I spat, "Then I feel bad for whoever has the misfortune of marrying you."

I could see anger flare up in his eyes. "And what do you mean by that?"

"He will- I'm sorry, she will be just as clumsy as your mother. Always getting black eyes from falling down the stairs or tripping over the table which is weird since I've fallen down plenty of stairs and tripped over multiple tables, and not once did I ever get a black eye."

"What exactly are you trying to say?" he asked menacingly.

I already had my response. "That your father is an abusive piece of shit, and you probably are as well. Tell me, did you ever once think to stand up for her as he was slapping her around, or did you always think she deserved it for over-cooking the roast?"

"My father never laid a hand on her!" he screamed as he took a few steps towards me.

I advanced a few steps as I sneered, "Right... I'm sure she's just that clumsy."

"He never laid a hand on her I tell you!"

Victory is one of the few tastes which I never tire of. I nearly licked my lips as I was nearing the knock-out punch. I had worked the body, placed a few stinging jabs to his nose, and now all I had to do was come in with a closer. "You're full of shit, Justin, and you know it. At least my parents had heroin as an excuse for their actions. What's your father's excuse for being such a piece of shit?"

Without warning, he viciously shoved me. As I was not expecting that, I stumbled to regain my balance. Violence was the only logical progression of our confrontation, one I was confident I could win without throwing a punch. Smiling condescendingly at him, I came in for the closer. "Just like your daddy taught you."

I saw him swing. I could have blocked it or dodged it as it was a wild hook, but I took it, his fist smashing into the left side of my face. Proving my point was more valuable than avoiding pain. Plus, I was hopped up on enough pain pills that I hardly even felt it. Falling to the ground, the whole world became a bit hazy. Slowly, I rose to my feet again and turned the untouched side of my face towards him. I was willing to take another blow to claim the moral high ground.

"There you go, Justin. Here's my other cheek," I said as I gently patted it.

Then everything went black.

I awoke to the frantic cries of Michelle who was bent over me. A bit groggy, I tried to remember what happened. Then I realized that Justin had punched me in the face, and his second punch must have knocked me out. I pushed myself up so I could sit up. However, my head was still reeling, so I laid back down.

"Are you okay?" asked Michelle nervously.

"Just fine," I said with a smile.

"What happened?"

"Just practicing what Justin preaches," I said snidely. "He punched me once, and then I turned the other cheek. Then I woke up with you hovering over me."

I could hear him angrily explaining to some other people what had happened. A vaguely familiar voice was harshly scolding him.

"Do you need to go to the hospital?"

"No, no. I'm fine." I tried sitting up again. This time I succeeded. Something was moving in my mouth, so I spit it out. I saw the blood but was too dizzy to look at what flew out my mouth.

"Oh my gosh!" she exclaimed. "He knocked a tooth out."

I laughed weakly. "And here I thought he didn't know how to punch."

"I knew I should not have left you two alone."

With more pain in my voice than was necessary, I asked, "Could you do me a favor and go into my car to get a cigarette?"

"Of course."

While she was away, I spit up some more blood. Perhaps I would need to see a dentist. I tried to see who Justin was talking to, but my vision was still too blurry to make out anything besides hazy figures. Michelle returned with my pack. I spit out some more blood and lit up a cigarette. Smoking was a bit difficult as I had to continually spit out blood or be forced to swallow it.

A figure was approaching me. As it neared, I could make out who it was and was simply overjoyed it was him who was scolding Justin.

"Good to see you again, Isaiah," said the blurry figure standing before me.

Weakly, I tried to stand but failed. So I stuck my hand out which he shook. "How are you, John?"

"Doing fine, but I guess I should be asking you that same question."

"A bit dizzy and missing a tooth, but other than that, just fine."

"You must have really said something to set him off."

My vision was clearing, and I could see Justin pacing about twenty feet away. "Well, he started talking shit about my parents, so I said something about his daddy being an abusive piece of shit," I said loud enough for him to easily hear. "But I should have known better. Homosexuals typically have a reverse Oedipus complex, so I should have seen it coming."

"Cool it, Isaiah," John said sternly.

"Tell me, John, now that I've turned the other cheek, is it kosher to whip his ass?"

John let out an exasperated huff. "Violence never solves anything."

"Tell that to fancy pants over there."

"Isaiah!" he snapped. "That smart mouth of yours has always gotten you into trouble. So just shut your mouth and cool it."

Chuckling, I shook my head. "Alright, John."

He stuck out his hand to help me up. "As I've always said, if you ever need someone to help you get back up on your feet, you know where to find me."

As he helped me stand, my legs wobbled a bit. With a chuckle, I said, "I always took that more metaphorically than literally."

"I meant it either way."

Though I have had my fair share of fathers, from the biological one I have no memory of to the multiple foster fathers I have had throughout the years, John was the only man I would have ever called "dad." When I first came to the church, which would have been when I was seven or eight, he took a special interest in me, and I learned later on that he had known my biological mother. When I started getting into trouble, he went out of his way to meet with me every week to grab some lunch or tea. He even took me camping a couple times.

He was a short, sickly thin man who looked like he had his bones wrapped tightly in a well-worn burlap sack. He was in his mid-fifties with thin, grey, curly hair which touched his shoulders. His beard was short and trimmed. As was usual, he wore a pair of loose fitting corduroys, a light-material plaid shirt, and some comfy sandals. There were only rare times when a gentle smile was not plastered on his face.

To my knowledge, no one knew very much about his past, but there were clues. For one, he wore a wedding ring though his wife had been dead for over twenty years, long before he entered the ministry. Another peculiar aspect of him that I was privy to thanks to my connections in the drug scene was that he attended Narcotics Anonymous meetings.

An old friend a few years back who was trying to get well told me that he had celebrated twenty-five years clean. That explained why he reached out to me when he heard I was using. However, he never tried to push me into treatment. In fact, he told me it was quite natural to experiment but hoped I would not become too invested in drugs as it could seriously hamper my future- which it did. The one drug he sternly warned me about was heroin. As he had known my mother, he was worried I might follow in her footsteps though he never told me where those footsteps might lead.

"It's good to see you again, John." As I was regaining my bearing, I began to feel embarrassed not because of the spectacle I had been a part of, but due to the fact that I had been in town and not looked him up.

"Good to see you too. I'd love to stay and chat, but praise team practice is already late because of you. However, we should grab some lunch soon."

"Sounds good to me. My schedule is open, and you can get my number from Michelle."

"I will. Stay out of trouble."

I said good-bye to Michelle who was worried if I was well enough to drive. I probably should have waited a few more minutes, but I told her I was fine. After giving Justin the finger, I hopped in my car and drove away quite pleased with myself.

Devante called me that night. He was ready to meet up with me whenever I was ready. He also told me to bring along a sample of some molly, and, in return, he would throw a sample of something my way. He did not elaborate as to what that something might be. Considering I was watching some dumb reality television show in my hotel, I left immediately to meet up with him.

Normally, I would be a bit anxious about carrying so much weight unaccompanied. However, as I was simply giving the meth to him, I figured there was very little chance of there being a problem. Unless, of course, he discovered some new information relating to his brother's death.

We met in the parking lot of a seedy bar in Springfield. While it was obvious what we were up to, it was also obvious that every other person was doing the same thing. Devante was alone which made me feel slightly more at ease as well as a bit nervous. I hoped no one was lurking around waiting to jump me. Yet it all went smoothly. I handed him the bag telling him to hit me up if he wanted more. For the sake of appearances, we went into the bar and ordered a couple drinks.

As always, he was high on some sort of upper. He was constantly moving his jaw around and scanning the room in a sporadic, paranoid fashion. He order Grey Goose, I contented myself with a local porter. After he had taken two shots, he broke the silence.

I was actually touched by what he told me, not that it was a compliment or a heart-warming story, but he relayed information to me that had the possibility of affecting me. A high schooler had OD'd at a rave, the type Tiz liked to attend. While normally this was not a huge deal, shit like this happens all of over the county, but this particular high schooler was the son of a city councilmember. This councilmember was calling for a crackdown on these illicit raves. However, that was easier said than done because the locations of these raves normally are not released until the night of the party. To even have access to that information, one had to be part of the "in crowd." There would be a pamphlet with the number to some burner phone you would call to find out where the rave was located.

There used to be something to these raves. Something that seemed significant. Like you were part of something magnificent, something which transcended normal human interaction. Something genuine. Sure, we were all high on ecstasy and psychedelics, but there was a real sense of comradery which permeated the scene. We would recognize each other on the street or in the grocery store or in school and we would smile as if we held some beautiful secret between the two of us. I would be hanging out with the church youth group and some kid wearing Day-Glo would come up and give me a hug. We would share a laugh and exchange numbers. No one understood why someone who by all rights was a complete stranger would come up to me and embrace me as a brother. The answer was that I danced next to him at a rave and we recognized one another.

To most, this must seem laughably ridiculous. But to those who have been there; who danced until the sun rose; who sweated and bumped against a mass of smiling faces; who have jumped to the drop; who shared what they had and were given what they wanted without a second thought; who moaned in sorrow and pleasure while their feet still moved to the beat; who have had cold revelations shoot through them like a shot of Dimethytriptamine; who swayed to the cacophony too exhausted to even shuffle their feet; who read the minds of those around them while knowing full well others were reading their mind as well; who saw the writing on the wall though the wall was nothing but flashing lights and smoke; who danced, cried, laughed, loved and learned a little something about themselves and the world around them and laid their head on the pillow as the sun shone brightly through the shades caressing the drug-fueled mind into a comatose slumber only to awake fourteen hours later wondering if it was all a dream; who looked at their wrist and saw a bracelet that was not that there the day before and smiled because it was real, everything was real, the spiritual revelations, the hopes, the sorrows, the moments of self-realization, and the love. It was all real. Especially the love. And to that, I cling too. At least I try too.

Devante's words rang cold in my ears. "I got money

there's going to be a raid, big one too. Streets are quiet. I got a few boys I think are snitches, and they being real quiet. All they need is one fool to put it all on. Just one. Keep your head up. Don't be that fool."

I nodded my head trying to take it all in. I definitely could be that fool whose name is blasted on tomorrow's front page news. Devante's words were almost like a death knell to me. This was it. After one big bust, the rave scene would collapse. It would be restricted to only licensed venues that paid their taxes. There would be bouncers and security patting people down at the door. The lawful supervision would completely stifle everything beautiful about the scene. The chaos, the lawlessness of raves are what created such a unique environment.

Devante chuckled low and deep. "If any of us fools had any sense, we'd all go apply at McDonald's, but fuck it. Every dog has it's day, you know what I'm saying."

He smiled wide. "Shit, been too wrapped up in the crystal." He reached into his pocket and lowered his hand next to mine. Right then I remembered the molly. Discreetly, we touched hands and exchanged small bags.

"Why I asked for this molly was because some fool I know is looking for a new supplier. His dude got popped or something. Disappeared. I told him I knew a guy on the level. We talking weight, fool, if you think you can handle it."

I nodded my head, grinning ear to ear, flattered that he would recommend me. "I can handle up to a couple pounds. I can do that tomorrow. Any more than that and I will need some time to work on it. How would it go down?"

Shaking his heads, he sighed. "Like some fuckin' idiots, that how this dude handles it. He does his dirt at them raves. Thinks they's his fortress. Dude helps put them on, you know what I'm saying."

"And this guy is straight? I don't want to have to worry about getting robbed."

"He always been on the level with me. He's too wrapped up, got too much going on for drama. He's a real businessman. E-tarded as a muthafucka, but he's straight business."

We lapsed into silence. I knew that this was big time. I nearly forgot about the small bag Devante had given me until he cleared his throat and said, "That's some good shit you got in your pocket. I know you don't fuck around with it often, but I thought I'd give you a taste as a token of my appreciation for the crystal. You need more, let me know. I can get that shit all day long."

Inwardly, I squealed. I was about to get real high. My favorite kind of high.

"Well, I ain't looking to become a junkie, but I appreciate the offer." After knowing what was in my pocket, I was itching to get out of there. "Save that for a special occasion."

"Alright, Isaiah. I'll hit you up when I need some more crystal. And I'll see if the E-tard likes your shit. If he does, I'll let you know the time and place. No need for numbers and names, you know what I'm saying."

"If you vouch for him, he can call me."

He smiled wickedly as he rose from his barstool. "Then how the fuck am I gonna collect me a finder's fee."

I chuckled. No such thing as a favor in this business.

I thought my night was done, but Tiz called right as I was lovingly caressing the small bag of heroin Devante had given me. She needed two ounces of molly and needed it tonight. While pleased with the amount of money that would bring me, I was nervous about her handling so much weight. She insisted it was a kid she knew well, and if I came along it would only make him nervous. I trusted her judgment enough to let her go alone, but my gut told me something was wrong. As always, I should have listened to my gut.

After dropping off the molly to her, I was unlocking the door when she called again. She was frantic, and it was hard to understand everything she said. But I got the gist of it. She had been jacked at gun point. I told her I would be there in twenty minutes. In my hotel room, I quickly railed a fat line of methadone and morphine as well as more klonopin than usual. I needed something to take the edge of the murderous rage that overtook me, and I certainly was not wasting my heroin on self-medicating. I really, really hated it when people took my shit, and I was even more pissed at myself that I let her go it alone. While the amount of opiates and barbiturates I ingested should have put me to sleep or a comatose stupor, the adrenaline pumping in my veins staved off any effects. Not even chain-smoking cigarettes and joints did anything to calm me.

Tiz was waiting for me at a park pacing around anxiously. When she saw me, she immediately tried to explain what happened, but I was too busy screaming at her to hear anything she said. After calling her every vulgarity I could think of that meant incompetent or stupid, I finally let her speak.

This is what happened. Some little high school punk named Jude who had bought a gram of my molly at a party said he knew a guy who wanted two ounces and was willing to pay top dollar. Apparently, she had known this kid for a few years, and he had always been on the level. However, the past few months, she had heard rumors he had been using meth and had been changing for the worse. Yet he still was chill with her, so she thought everything was fine. While she did bring two of her people with her to be safe, before she could even say hello, the kid and some of his crew pulled guns on them.

After listening to her story, my rage turned cold. For some reason I laughed. Maybe I laughed because I had every intention of straight murdering the little fuck.

"So what are we going to do about it?" asked Tiz.

I told her to roll a blunt and waited for it to be half-smoked before I spoke. Tiz knew me well enough not to talk when I was thinking.

"This is why you don't deal with high schoolers. They listen to too much rap and think they are bonafide gangsters," I said flatly.

"Look, Isaiah, I know this kid. I've-"

I held my hand up to silence her. "What we are going to do is get our money, and we are going to do this by convincing him to sell for us. Most likely, that little fuck is going to cut it and is probably snorting it up like candy, so we can't just ask for it back. So we are going to get him to pay us for it."

"How we going to do that?"

I smiled mischievously. "Is that run-down cabin out in Venetta still there?"

"Last I checked. I was out there a few months ago partying."

"Go make sure it is still abandoned."

"Why?"

I chuckled and mimicked her tone as I said, "Well, if this muthafucka wants to be gangsta than we going to get muthafuckin' gangsta on his bitch ass."

She smiled. "Aight. I'll go check out the cabin. Then what?"

"We grab him when he's alone."

She shook her head. "He's always with his crew."

"Well, he's got to get his dick sucked sometime, right?"

She shrugged. "I guess so."

"Then we get him when he's with his bitch."

The next few days were spent stalking Jude. Tiz was always a couple blocks away from me, far enough not to be seen but close enough to meet me at a moment's notice. After four days, I knew every house he went too, every chick he fucked, and every place he dined at. Finally, on a cloudy, moonless night he attended a party in Thurston. I watched across the street for hours until he walked out with his arm around a girl who looked like she was in college. They entered his car and drove off. I called Tiz and told her to follow at a distance.

They turned off into a dirt road which led into a state forest. There was not an inhabited building in a five mile radius. I knew this because I used to do a lot of business in those woods. Following with my headlights off, I saw him turn off onto another road which I knew led to a dead end. I parked my car at the entrance. He would have to ram his way out.

An odd calmness enveloped me as I carefully went over the supplies. Gun? Check. Ski mask? Check. Zip-ties? Check. Black bags? Check. Ball gags? Check. Twine? Check. Heavy-duty latex gloves? Check. I slowly put on the ski mask, put the gloves on, and triple checked my newly purchased pistol to make sure it was loaded. The pistol I was carrying was what some would call a Saturday Night Special, meaning it was cheap, unregistered and/or stolen, making it an inconsequential loss if one was forced to toss it after having too much fun on a Saturday night.

I stepped out of the car making sure the interior lights did not come on. Five minutes passed before Tiz showed up who was already wearing her ski mask and gloves. After divvying up half the supplies, I whispered the plan.

"We wait outside the car until they get out of the back seat. That's when we hit them. You take the girl, I got the guy."

"Ahh... fuck no. I got Jude. He's my problem."

"No. You take the girl. Slapping bitches around is more of your thing anyway."

She grumbled a few curses but consented to my plan. We waited for an excruciatingly long half hour. As I listened to them fool around, no doubt snorting up my drugs, a peculiar sensation came over me. It was a strange mixture of the giddiness I imagine a prepubescent girl would have at a boy band concert and the rage of a jealous husband who discovers his wife in his bed with another man. At least, that is the best I can describe it. All I know is that I was nearly licking my lips in anticipation.

Finally, the fateful moment came. The two exited the back seat. Tiz and I were only ten or so feet away from the vehicle. Noiselessly, I sprang to my feet with my gun in hand.

As I smashed the butt of my pistol on the back of his unsuspecting head, I screamed, "Get the fuck on the ground! Get the fuck on the ground!" I am not sure whether it was the blow to the head or my irate tone of voice which sent him tumbling to the ground.

The girl screamed for a moment but was silenced swiftly by Tiz placing a ball gag in her mouth. Jude was sprawled out on the ground, screaming obscenities, but was obedient to every command. After I had zip-tied his hands behind his back, I told him to get on his knees. As he struggled to squirm his way up, I viciously kicked him in the gut. He keeled back over on the ground.

"Get the fuck up!" I ordered. Again, he tried to position himself on his knees, and, again, I kicked him in the stomach. We repeated this for another four times until he was in terrified tears asking what I wanted.

"Get on your knees right fucking now!" I ordered sticking my gun in his face. After letting him rise to his knees, I placed a ball gag in his mouth to silence his inquiries. Then I patted him down, removing the switchblade in his pocket and the pistol tucked in his waistband. He tried to squeal when I brought the black bag out. Shoving the bag over his head, I tied it loosely with twine as I had no intention of suffocating him to death. As he began to frantically squirm, I began to frantically kick him the stomach. After a vicious stomping, he relented in his quest to squirm free.

Tiz had successfully bound the girl which meant it was time for stage two. I drove my car up, and we loaded them up in my trunk after I stomped him again to insure the car ride would not be pleasant one. Before tossing them in my trunk, we tightly bound their legs, first separately, and then when they were in the trunk, we bound their legs together to make it difficult to kick anything. The whole time, the girl was sobbing which prompted many backhands from Tiz.

After our cargo had been secured safely in my trunk, Tiz looked at me with a pleased expression that I could see through her ski mask. "Time to go?"

I shrugged. "I don't know about you, but I could use a celebratory blunt with as many pills you can stuff in there."

I ground up the pills while she ground up the weed. We were silent as we inhaled the smoke which tasted like cleaning supplies and did not say a word when we parted. We left his car there, and Tiz and I left in our respective vehicles.

The ride proved to be a very frustrating one. It seemed that every stop light I came to turned yellow twenty feet before I reached the intersection. Normally, I would try to beat the light but not that night. Also, there was a major accident on the main highway out to Venetta, forcing me to head down a very long, troublesome detour. This only increased my irritation. To make things worse, when we were less than twenty miles away, I noticed my car was on empty, something I bitterly cursed myself for. Tiz had to go grab a gas can and fill it while I waited in a mall parking lot. While I could have taken this time to step back from my emotions and think about the actions I was about to undertake, I was only focused on the murderous rage I was suppressing as well as contemplating this strange excited anticipation which was making my knees weak. What should have been a forty minute drive took nearly two hours.

I drove over the two-track faster than I should have, but I wanted to violently bounce around my cargo in the back. After I parked, I took the time to rail some more methadone and klonopin, hoping it would calm me down enough to the point where I would not lose control and beat Jude to death with my bare hands.

As I popped open the trunk, my cargo squirmed and tried to squeal, but their gags muffled the noise to a strange gargling noise. I cut the twine around their legs and pulled them out of the car. The girl dropped to her knees, Jude was forcefully thrown face first on the ground. Then I proceeded to viciously kick him while I waited for Tiz. When she arrived, I hoisted Jude to his feet by the twine around his neck and drug him to the cabin. Tiz escorted the girl.

The interior of the cabin was as rundown as the outside. At one point, this was probably some sort of vacation getaway, but it had obviously been uninhabited for years besides groups of hobos or teenagers using it as a party spot. Beer cans, used condoms, and broken glass covered the floor. Part of the roof had collapsed letting in sunlight which stimulated the growth of weeds popping through the floor boards. After ordering them onto their knees, I finally removed the bags over their heads. The girl's make-up was smeared with tears; Jude was breathing heavily, staring up at me with terrified eyes.

First I emptied their pockets with my gloves still on. I pulled out cigarettes, phones, keys, and a small baggie full of my drugs from Jude's pocket. As they stared at me, I aimlessly perused through their phones. I looked at pictures, text messages, anything which might give a clue as to where my drugs were. Apparently, they were scattered throughout Jude's high school and the college the girl attended.

After five minutes of this, I walked up to Jude with my pistol in hand. "So... Jude.... any idea why you are here?"

He shook his head violently and tried to talk through his ball gag.

"Really? Because I believe I found something that belongs to me in your pockets. Any idea what that might be?"

He hesitated for a moment then shook his head again which prompted a swift blow to the head from my pistol.

As he crumpled to the ground, he tried rolling away, but the debris and especially the broken glass stopped him from going too far. To punish him for this, I began stomping him in the ribs until he no longer moved. Then I yanked him back on his knees.

With the utmost calm in my voice, I said slowly, "No reason to lie, Jude. I know everything I need to know. So what's going to happen now is I am going to release your ball gag and you are going to tell me what is mine."

As soon he was free to talk, it was an effort to shut him up again. "Look, man, I got no fuckin' clue what's yours. I don't even know who the fuck you are! You got the wrong guy! I didn't take shit from you! Man, please, just let me go. I won't say shit! I won't say shit! Just let me go!"

I held up my hand to silence him. "Hush, now, Jude. While you may have not taken anything from me personally, you do have something of mine. Can you think of what that might be?"

He looked up at me. "Ahh... the molly?"

Smiling passively, I said nonchalantly, "Wow, you aren't as stupid as you fucking look, Jude. There may still be a chance that you get out of here alive. So tell me, Jude, how did you get my molly?"

"Look, man, there's gotta be some big misunderstanding. I paid for that shit fair and square."

Another lie unleashed another blow to the head as well as another vicious stomping. This time, however, he could howl out for mercy.

"Get the fuck back on your knees!" I commanded, and he obeyed. "I know you are full of shit, so stop lying." After pausing for a moment, I continued in a more pleasant tone. "You're just making it harder for yourself."

"Look, man, I don't know what the fuck you are talking about."

Swiftly, I took out my knife with one hand and grabbed

the back of his head with the other. I stuck the point right underneath his eye just like Devante had done to me.

"If you lie to me one more time, you are losing an eye, and just so I am not forced to do this, let me tell you the truth first so you can verify it. Alright? Good. Now let me start by saying that I don't think you are completely in the blame for what happened. An ignorant, uneducated mind, such as yourself, is susceptible to outside influences. As you are undoubtedly a sackless piece of shit, you turn to rap music for validation. It makes you feel 'gangsta.' Problem is, one day you actually started believing you were a gangsta instead of the pasty-faced white-skinned little shit stain that you are. So, as you erroneously assume that listening to a little Tupac makes you an OG, you also assume that you are capable of doing some 'gangsta shit' which, in your case, was pulling a gun on someone and stealing their shit. Just so happens that their shit is also my shit."

I lit a cigarette up, and as he tried to speak, I backhanded him across the face. "I'm not done talking, so shut your fucking mouth!" Calmly, I inhaled some smoke and blew it in his face. "Now I just got back from LA, and let me tell you, LA has got some gangstas. I'm not one, but I worked for some. Now, two ounces isn't all that much, but if you let some little scum sucking faggot, such as yourself, punk you in the small things, you'll get a reputation for being soft. And that kind of reputation will get you killed in my line of business."

I paused to take a few drags, and my menacing glare told him I was not finished. "So, Jude, we have come to an impasse. I don't want my molly back, considering you've already snorted a bunch of it and probably cut it. I can't do anything with that. Now what I am going to do is an unparalleled act of forgiveness that Jesus Fucking Christ might not approve of. Taking into account your youth and obvious stupidity, I'm willing to give you another chance. I got hooks in LA who can get this shit all day long, and you, being a small-minded, short-sighted piece of trailer trash, just fucked what could have been a hook that could have put you into the big time. I'm talking serious weight, Jude. But you had to go waving that little gun of yours like it was another boy's dick. So tell me, Jude, was everything I said the truth or was it the fucking truth."

Dolefully, he nodded his head. "Yeah. That's the fucking truth." He began to snivel. "I fucked up, man. I seriously fucked up. I just thought-"

"You were a gangsta, and you're not. So stop fronting."

"Whatever you say, man." He paused for a moment. There was fear in his voice when he spoke again. "So what happens now?"

I crouched down to be on eye-level with him. "What happens now is you pay me my fucking money."

His eyes widened. "I would, but I don't got it."

"I figured as much, so what you are going to do is pay Tiz five hundred every week. Oh, and the price just raised to twenty-five hundred a zip."

"But-"

Smiling wide, I gently tapped his right check a few times in quick succession. "No buts, Jude, no buts. You do as I say, or I'll fucking kill you. Now you might think this whole scenario is a bit gangsta, but let me tell you something else. If you pulled that kind of shit in LA, they'd fuck that little whore next to you, slit her throat, fuck the slit, light your little bitch ass on fire, and then fuck you in the ass with flame retardant condom. That's gangsta. What we got right now is some small-time drama. That's all it is. Drama. And I fucking hate drama. Now if you go play the fool, if you want to be a gangsta, then shit will get gangsta real fast. I'll find you. I'll fuck your mom, both your sisters, each and every inbred cousin of yours, and then I'll burn down your grandparent's trailer with them inside. Might seem a little extreme, but I'm looking to make a name for myself and am looking for any excuse to fuck someone real hard as an example. Don't give me that excuse. You got it?"

He hung his head. "Yeah, man. I got it."

"Good. Five hundred every week. No excuses. I don't care if you have to sell this little slut next to you to a gang of rapists with HIV, I want my fucking money."

"Whatever you say, man."

I turned to the girl who whimpered through her ball gag. "As for you, I'm not quite sure what to do with you. You can't get me money. All you are is a possible snitch." She began shaking her head frantically.

Jude piped up, "She won't say shit."

I laughed. "As you have proven to be trustworthy so far, I'll take your word for it," I said sarcastically. I pulled out three hundred dollars from my wallet. "My sincerest apologies for the inconvenience tonight, doll. I do hope this will help sooth any bad blood between us." I stuffed the money in her bra.

I undid the gag. She breathed heavily and stared up gratefully at me. "I promise I won't say anything. I ain't no snitch." She sobbed a little.

Smiling, I said in a warm paternal tone. "That's good to hear. Real good to hear because if anything did get out to the police, my boys in LA would come up here, and, well… you already heard what they do in LA. So be a good girl and everything will be just fine."

She nodded her head vigorously. "I won't say anything. Promise."

"Good. So if you'll be a good girl and promise not to do anything stupid, I'll undo your zip-ties, and you can ride in the passenger seat this time and not the trunk. We could even smoke a blunt if you would like that."

She smiled shyly. "I think I could use some weed."

"What about me?" asked Jude nervously.

I laughed derisively. "You? You're in the fucking trunk no questions asked. One word out of you and I swear to god I'll stomp your fucking head in." That shut him up.

With everything squared away, we headed to the cars. Tiz rolled two blunts, one for me and one for her. We decided it was best not to meet up for a couple days to see how things played out. The girl, whose name I cannot remember, smoked the blunt with me, and by the time we returned to Jude's car, we were having a cordial conversation. The molly I had taken back from Jude helped. While none too pleased about his girl accepting my offer to drive her home, he did not grumble too much. However, he would have been even less pleased if he knew that we would not make it to her dorm room until late afternoon the next day. Which was a mistake. I knew that at the time, I could see where that would lead the whole car ride, but I did it. Like Cassandra, it seemed I had the gift of prophecy, except I would never believe my own foresight.

Everything seemed to be falling into place for me. Devante pushed the half pound of crystal within a matter of days. He bought a pound up front the next time I saw him. Also, his boy who wanted a new supplier of molly was pleased with my sample. Devante told me to have a half pound at the ready. So it was time to head back to California.

Apparently, Tyrone's funeral had gone smoothly. Not a huge turn-out but that was to be expected as he had been gone for a couple of years with me. Devante told me where he was buried if I wanted to pay my respects. I thanked him for the information but was too busy plotting my trip to San Francisco to pay much attention.

With pride, I dwelled on the twenty thousand dollars I had to my name, and I had only been in Eugene a little over a month. Jude had made his first payment, and Tiz continued to push my goods. I was actually running low which pleased me to no end. In fact, I would probably need to get another few thousand tabs as well.

Deciding that I deserved something nice, I went out and bought another car. I gave my Acura to Tiz. While I could not afford a brand new car, I could afford a nicer, older model. I found a 1998 BMW M3 hardtop convertible. The original owner had purchased it the day he retired, so there were hardly any miles on it. Even better, he had died two weeks ago meaning the family who inherited it was looking for some quick money. They were asking for seven grand, I talked them down to five.

It was a beautiful car, dark blue like the eastern horizon during sunset. I immediately dropped two grand on some nice black rims. After stopping by an auto parts store to pick up some wax, I headed to a self-serve car wash to polish it. I spent the next four hours there.

While it was nowhere near as nice as Justin's M3, I was still proud of it. Though over a decade old, it was still a sleek looking piece of engineering. While it may not have had the power of the newer models, a 3.2 liter V6 engine gave it plenty of kick. Besides, I did not have any plans on trying to outrun the police anytime soon.

Michelle and I had been hanging out on the regular, at least every other day. Without her knowing it, I went to the repair shop where her car had been taken and paid her bill though I told the mechanic not to breathe a word about it. However, the mechanic did describe what I looked like so she guessed it was me. I did not lie.

One aspect of our friendship which irked me was she continually suggested I find stable employment. She always had some business which she thought would hire me. I spent my life being poor, I was not about to take some working-stiff job. I wanted that new M3; I wanted a nice house; I wanted Armani suits. Being a day laborer at a warehouse or a barista would achieve none of these things for me. At least that is what I liked to tell myself as well as others.

Truth be told, I want my existence to be a middle finger to the powers that be. To me, the best way to do that was to pursue the American Dream in my own way. Stacking cash with nothing but wits and determination and courage. I was blazing trails through the wasteland of the drug world. Sure, I was smart enough to go back to college, land a cushy job being a salesman, get married, and live comfortably. I am self-aware enough to realize that there is nothing inherent in a BMW that I desire. Granted, there are features and aspects I find pleasurable, but what I crave the most is the symbol. Class and luxury which always infer wealth. And with wealth comes envy. And I wanted to display these symbols with the pride knowing I was a self-made man, a term which, tragically, my generation has completely forgotten.

I see a grotesque scale upon which humans are weighed. It is the scale of consumption. That is what name brands are all about. The reason why a logo is plastered on shoes or purses is so society can immediately know how much you have been sacrificing to that gilded idol called "The Economy." And for some strange, completely fucked reason, America has bought that lie hook, line, and sinker. I knew a girl who bought a stolen Louis Vuitton purse for $100. She thought it was hideous, but she took it everywhere she went because it was covered in those two letters. She looked like a tweaker, scabs covered her arms, her cheeks were sucked up, missing teeth and ratty hair all gave that away. But she thought she was pretty ritzy caring around that purse. She talked about it to whoever would listen and a few who weren't. And why did she think that this purse made her transcend her white trash rung on the social ladder? Because her purse told everyone that she was a loyal subject to the Almighty Economy.

And I want to consume more than anyone while creating the nightmares you see on the television. Junkies roaming the streets harassing polo-shirted families on a Sunday for money, tweakers robbing convenience stores, rich spoiled teenagers overdosing at concerts... yeah... you can thank me for that. The guy bumping rap in the brand-new BMW wearing a Rolex. That is what I want, that is my place in society. And you may think I am just a poser, some wanna-be thug. Please do. Irony is my favorite kind of humor.

When one truly sees the absurdity which fuels the operations of this planet, what can one do but laugh? Well... you can laugh, cry, or medicate. I do all three.

I guess we all do. Most laugh at comedies, I laugh at them. Most cry for personal woes or the suffering present in the world, I cry hoping to quell the nausea. People medicate on television or shopping or political parties or religion, I medicate with drugs. Perhaps we are not so different. And maybe, just maybe, that is the key which could unify us. Maybe. Probably not. No, humanity will continue this cycle of self-destruction, this path of sadomasochism which will end sooner than most will think. Humanity will hit the reset button on the evolutionary process so to speak. Who knows, maybe we have done it before. So while the world prattles on about health care and homelessness, about capitalism and socialism, about Christianity and Islam, about the end of the world and the next technological revolution, I am living the good life doing the wrong thing. Who said crime doesn't pay?

To make the façade more perfect, I live a double life. I could go to court tomorrow, and a pastor would be a character witness for me. And not one victim would be in the court room. I would do time. No doubt about it. But my middle finger would still be politely pointing towards the heavens. The judge might even feel a pang of guilt when he bangs the gavel. Might even pop an extra Ativan before he went to bed because I seemed like a nice kid.

And for the most part, I am. I look the part of a young man who is well put together. I fix an old friend's car, I give money to the homeless, and I go out of my way to help out those in need all while dealing drugs. While sometimes I can delude myself that I do these things out of the goodness of my heart, I know that I act the way I do out of sheer narcissism. I know my generosity is noticed, whether that act is immediately acknowledged or not is of no consequence. Because I do not "beat my chest on the street corner" every time it catches my fancy to do something charitable, when my altruistic acts are observed, it is automatically assumed that since I do not brag about those which are acknowledged, it stands to reason that I perform other benevolent acts. So in a way, I am rewarded for those acts which go unobserved. I am rewarded for those and others which I never performed. This all helps to form an identity that I display to the world.

Does this make me an evil person? I do not know. I have analyzed and dissected myself for years with the only result being more paralytic confusion and ecstatic mirth. I pace hotel rooms getting high and drunk simply reveling in my being. Is that normal? Do others do this? I do not know. All I know is that I live my life as if the last chapter will contain some dramatic revelation. Something resembling truth that transcends the realm of communication. I live because I feel as if my story is one that should be told. Perhaps an unnecessary story, I am no Karamazov, but one that needs to be played out. Perhaps the curtain will fall pre-emptively. I feel as if that is inevitable.

As I flick a still smoldering roach out of my car, I wonder how my name influenced my Being. I am the apocalyptic prophet, yet I have no Messiah that I speak of. I see an angel falling from heaven and I see a god forsaking his people. I see the iniquities of humanity pouring out from televisions and smart phones. I see churches flying filthy rags from flag poles. Maybe I'm high, maybe I'm crazy, maybe I'm evil, who knows. But this is my story, and it is a story I feel inclined to tell.

A week passed since I had seen John when he called me. I had actually planned to leave for San Francisco that day, but I figured it would be nice to spend some time with an old friend before I headed out. John and I decided to meet up at a park. He would bring the sandwiches while I brought the iced tea. I knew exactly how he liked it. Green tea with one part lemonade to two parts tea. I also brought some strawberries to put in it.

Summer was beginning to flex. The oppressive heat and smothering humidity was proof of that. I saw John patiently waiting at a picnic table with his eyes closed and hands folded. When I was about ten feet away, a smile broke out on his face and he opened his eyes.

"Hello, Isaiah."

"Hello, John."

He stood up, and I went to shake his hand. However, he pulled me in with a hug.

"Good to see you, kid."

I glared at him. "Not much of a kid anymore, old man."

He laughed. "You're still a kid."

As usual, John's edible creations were delicious. Being a vegetarian, there was no meat on the sandwiches but they were still incredibly tasty despite my fondness for flesh. He had made his own avocado spread, used the top notch bread, and filled it with artichoke hearts, tomatoes, spinach, and other vegetables whose identities were unknown to me.

John always ate in silence, and I respected that odd trait of his. He had picked up that tradition from some Buddhists in India while he was on a mission trip. Perhaps it helped us reacquaint ourselves with one another because when we did begin talking, the conversation flowed quite smoothly and naturally. However, that could have been simply the presence John radiates.

I lit up a cigarette as he cleared his throat. "So, tell me, Isaiah, what kind of trouble have you been getting into."

Shrugging my shoulders, I replied, "Not much. Same shit, different day."

He smiled. "Still slinging dime bags to high schoolers?"

Shaking my head, I replied with a chuckle, "Hell no. Way past that small-time stuff."

"Isaiah," he said with a sigh. "You are going to get yourself into some serious trouble one of these days."

"I keep my head up."

"That's the problem," he retorted. I was not sure how to respond to that statement, so I said nothing.

"You're a good kid, Isaiah, with a lot more potential than what you are doing right now."

Choking out smoke as I laughed, I replied, "Come on, John. Lighten up. We've said like three words to one another, and you are already putting on the screws. Let's talk about something else. Like you. I heard you were the big bad pastor these days."

A wistful smile crossed his face. "I guess I am."

Something was wrong in his voice. The way he said that had a bitter tone to it. "What's up?"

Twiddling with his beard, he shrugged and shook his head. "Well... it's nothing. I really shouldn't say."

I leaned in as I was hungry for details. "Now you have to say it. I'm curious."

He stared at the table for a moment. "Life is very strange. It is a mysterious, fascinating journey which never ceases to baffle me." He paused for a long moment. "I hope you won't be alarmed by what I am about to say, and I trust what I am about to tell you does not leave this table. I have always kept your secrets, so I hope you will keep mine."

"What is it?" I asked, quite literally on the edge of my seat.

"I'm being forced to resign," he said morosely.

"What!" I was in shocked disbelief. "Why?"

With a bitter chuckle, he replied, "Because the church today has become more of a financial institution than a spiritual one. When I took over the senior pastor position, half the church left. More specifically, the wealthy half. While a number of college students have joined, they are not the best at tithing. Which is fine by me but not the board."

"So they are asking you to resign?"

"Yep. I have one month to wrap things up."

I was furious. How any church could relieve a man like John from his post was beyond me. He was the most compassionate man I had ever met, wiser than any professor who had ever taught me, knowledgeable in all things pertaining to the Bible, fluent in New Testament Greek, and could always be counted on in a time of need. He was everything a pastor should be.

"That's fucking ridiculous," I spat. "How the fuck-"

John held up his hand with a smile. "Cool it, kid. No need to get upset. In fact, I'm a bit relieved this is happening. While it saddens me to leave so many dear friends, it has become apparent that it is time to move on."

"Wait. You're not leaving Eugene are you?"

He nodded sadly. "Afraid so. I need a fresh start. I'm sure you can understand."

A knot was forming in my stomach. I felt like I was on the verge of a panic attack. "What are you going to do?"

"I don't know. I've always thought living in the Appalachian Mountains would be nice. Find some small town untouched by the modern world. I assume there are still areas like that."

"Would you still be a pastor?"

He shook his head. "No. I hope to find a bar I could work at or something like that."

"What!"

Laughing at my disbelief, he replied, "Many things have changed since you have been away. I had thought you would come back to me when you needed me; however, you have come to me right when I needed you. I'm sorry to lay this on you, but I simply have no one else I can talk to face-to-face about this. While I do occasionally write to a Catholic priest whose acquaintance I've made about this, it is refreshing to say this out loud, face-to-face with an old friend."

"No problem, John. I'm sad to hear you are going, but if that's what you want…"

"It is," he said hastily. "It is. I did not feel that way at first, but that was attachment speaking as well as fear. Fear of losing my financial security. But I am selling my house and plan on living a simple life. Honestly, this has almost come as a relief."

"Really?"

He leaned back and sighed heavily. I could tell he was choosing his next words carefully. "Yes. That priest I just mentioned has opened my eyes to certain unpleasant truths about myself. Unpleasant depending on how you look at it. He, like many other priests, has lost his faith. Not his faith in God but faith in the Church. Considering how bureaucratic it has become, I can't blame him. That has always been one of my qualms with Catholicism."

"But they are still priests?"

He chuckled. "Well… yes. What else are they going to do? They've been priests for over twenty years, what other career options are available to them? So they continue the rituals they don't believe in while trying to find fulfillment in the small areas they do enjoy. For example, the priest I talk to has begun taking more of an interest in reaching out to drug addicts and the poor. In fact, he is sacrificing his chances of becoming a bishop to pursue more humanitarian work."

"That's admirable of him. Where did you meet him?"

"At a conference about reaching out to the youth I went to last year. We ended up grabbing some dinner. I always know when someone has something troubling them. After a few questions, he poured all this out to me. He said that he is one of numerous priests who have anonymously published articles about their lack of faith. It is sad to think what kind of inner turmoil he must experience everyday simply going through the motions with no one to talk to besides some eccentric Protestant who is losing his church. However, he said that sometimes, when in a group of priests, he can almost pick out the ones suffering as him. He said you can see it in their eyes, the resigned way they carry themselves; though, he also said they are the ones who serve their parish the best."

"Kind of ironic."

He shook his head. "I thought so at first, but then I reflected a bit about what I was doing. I serve the people best when I am not on the pulpit. In fact, I realized that I too was simply going through many of the motions like Communion."

"Do you still believe in a god?" I asked hastily. For some strange reason, I thoroughly relished seeing others suffer in the same ways I did.

A wide incredulous smile spread across his face. "Why of course I do. Your problem is you have a very narrow view of what God could be. An interesting article I read a while back about quantum physics discussed a theory on unified consciousness. While most of the article went over my head as I have no clue what string theory is, the part that stuck to me was this idea that there is a universal consciousness present in all things. Quantum physics has shown that consciousness can affect matter as well as that all living things, even plants and water, have some sort of consciousness. So the theory goes something like this. There is this original consciousness which permeates everything in the universe. In fact, it is the source of all consciousness. Humans, plants, and animals are nothing more than a filter for this universal consciousness. This theory validates the Buddhist concept of Nirvana. In fact, the river of Nirvana is a beautiful metaphor for this universal consciousness. While I have not done the research nor possess the knowledge to investigate this theory on my own, it coincides with many of my spiritual experiences and beliefs."

I nodded trying to take it all in. "So you are a hippie," I said very seriously.

He roared with laughter. "I used to be. Still am I guess."

"Michelle told me you used to follow the Grateful Dead."

"That I did. Dropped out of college to follow them. I actually saw Furthur a couple of months back when they came to town."

"That explains a lot," I said snidely.

He smiled and nodded. "So what about you? I can see something is troubling you."

"I'm fine," I said hastily.

"You're lying which is fine. If you aren't ready to tell me, I'm okay with that. But you got my number if you change your mind."

Shrugging my shoulders indifferently, I replied, "Will do, but I assure, everything is going smoothly in my life."

"Then why are your pupils the size of pin-holes?"

I jolted and immediately averted my gaze. He continued speaking in a compassionate tone. "No need to get embarrassed. I'm merely stating a fact. I can tell you are using some opiate or another. Obviously, you are not getting high since you seem fairly lucid. My guess is you are using simply to stay well."

I looked back up at him and nodded slowly. "You're right, as usual. You sure know a lot about drug addicts for a pastor."

"Takes one to know one," he said quietly. "I've actually been attending Narcotics Anonymous for over twenty years."

I groaned. "Please don't try to convince me to check myself into treatment."

Hastily, he rose his hands up. "I'm not. Never would either. Honestly, I don't think NA is the place for you. Quite frankly, I don't go for myself anymore. At this point, it's a way to give back."

I smiled knowingly at him. "I actually knew you attended those groups."

He raised his eyebrows in surprise. "How?"

"A client of mine was trying to get well. He recognized you from what I had said about you."

Laughing quietly, he replied, "Well, that was a breach of the twelve traditions. Oh well. I should have guessed you knew, considering your connections. I just hope you are not using heroin."

"I'm not," I said hastily. "Just a little methadone and morphine is all."

"Oh that's all," he scoffed. "That's reassuring. And just a little? I don't think so, Isaiah. I know you too well."

"Whatever," I sighed.

He stared at me compassionately. "If you ever want help kicking, let me know."

"Like you know anything about kicking."

He winced and pensively replied, "I know more about kicking than you would think."

I nodded slightly, a bit embarrassed by what I had just said. "I'm sure you do.

At that point, the conversation began to feel awkward. We each stared at a group of teenagers playing ultimate Frisbee for a few minutes until John cleared his throat.

"How's Tyrone doing these days? Michelle said you two split up."

"Yeah. He started fucking around with crystal, and shit went sour real fast."

Staring curiously at me, he said slowly, "That's too

bad. You two were really close." I could not tell if he believed me.

"Yeah, it sucks. But that's life."

"It shouldn't be. I hope you two work things out someday."

"Me too," I said with a hollow voice.

The conversation died off again for a few minutes. When it resumed, John and I reminisced about old times. We stayed at the park for nearly an hour. Then John had to go meet up with a married couple having relationship problems. We embraced warmly as we parted.

For some strange reason, I was extremely put off by John's critique of my drug use. Especially the part about the heroin as if I was not strong enough to use that. So to prove a point to myself, I did a little bump when I got back to my hotel room before I grabbed my cash and headed to my car.

My connection already knew the deal. We had a code when we sent text messages. He never talked on the phone. I met him a few years ago when he lived in Eugene. Not much of a talker. He called himself Lucas though I doubted that was his real name. He moved down to San Francisco because he had a supplier that wanted Lucas to push for him. Honestly, I always wondered if he was not the one manufacturing it and he only claimed he was dealing it to protect himself. San Francisco is a much better place to hide than Eugene plus San Francisco is more centrally located along I-5.

Lucas was all business, been like that since I knew him. Sure, he would attend raves, but he never danced, never used. He would watch people, study the crowd to see how the drugs were working. I think most people who had seen him at a rave would never recognize him on the street unless they happened to have bought a large quantity of drugs from him. Honestly, the first time he approached me, I thought he was a narc. It took a little time for me to trust him, a few good words about him from people I trusted before I decided to buy from him. The kid just looked too ordinary. Brown hair always buzzed on the sides with an inch or so on top. Clean shaven, never even a five o'clock shadow on him. His lower jaw had a bit of an under bite which only added to his look of docility. Cheeks neither sucked in nor puffed out. He had a large nose, not that it stuck out, but it seemed unnaturally wide. As to his build, he seemed like he was a runner. I had never seen him in any pants or shorts that were not khaki, and his torso always sported something with a collar. The biggest difference of his dress would be his feet, sandals, loafers, or boots, depending on the weather. He looked perpetually eighteen.

Of all the traits of his that I am fond of, the good drugs, the professionalism, the lack of drama, the inconspicuousness, perhaps my favorite was his unfriendliness. Never did he invite me over to his place to smoke a joint or ask me to join him for a beer. Or dealings had been as simple as exchanging matching backpacks. He texted me that he found a cool backpack at a certain chain store, I went out and bought that exact same backpack. Inside that back pack was twelve thousand dollars.

As I cranked up the air-conditioning, I watched in delight as the top of the convertible folded itself away in the back of the truck. Then I lit up a blunt, eased my way out of the hotel parking lot. I was eagerly anticipating the come-up from the heroin. I snorted it because I am not a junkie. That is the thing about hard drugs, as long as you are not shoving a needle in your arm every hour then it is safe to say you do not have a problem.

After I had made it a few miles down the freeway, I began feeling it. I was totally relaxed, a pleasant warm sensation washed over my body as the cool breeze caressed my face. I was completely and utterly at peace with the world. Life was perfect, simply perfect.

And yet, despite my elevated state, I was struck by the

absurdity of this situation. How does a society come to this, how does it create such people? For society does create individuals just as a conglomeration of individuals create a society. It is such a mind-boggling concept to think about. It is this cycle which has been going on for millennia. A society is started where pulling out hearts of captives and offering them to the sun god is the norm. No one thinks twice about it. But this same society, must have, at some point produced an individual who thought, "What the fuck is this all about? Is this not utterly absurd?" And then perhaps he had his heart sacrificed to the sun god, but he planted a seed in the collective mind of that society, a seed which blossomed into a whole new way of doing things. From a seed such as that spawned monotheism, the thought, or conviction perhaps, that there is only one god. Radical concept. One god who abolishes the existence of all other gods by the point of a sword. A vengeful, wrathful, war-mongering god crying out, "An eye for an eye, tooth for a tooth!" A society molded by this notion, by this monotheistic creed rises from slavery and marches out into the desert performing great acts of genocide that are lauded for thousands of years to come. What Sunday school child has not been completely enamored by the fall of Jericho? Imagine the great mighty walls struck down the horns of the Israelites, neigh, by the hand of Jehovah himself allowing the warriors to march in and put everyone, men and women and children, to death by the sword.

And after thousands of years of war and bloodshed, of captivity and exile, there comes another society, one that has absorbed countless other societies, the Romans. And again, captivity, destruction. Hedonism spreads throughout the lands. Read the old prophets. Four hundred years of silence from God, or so they say. And then comes one man, supposedly born of a virgin, telling everyone to get along. To have mercy on your fellow man, to bless those that persecute you. He too, was a product of society, an ideological seed that had been planted from some unknown source which blossomed into a philosophy that has shaken the world to its core. The salvation of mankind from itself is what he preached. A philosophy which conquered even the mighty Roman Empire which spread to all corners of the earth, an ideology that has in some way, shape, or form, molded each and every society on this planet today. Even Muslims have to pay tribute to what the call a great prophet.

Thousands of years pass, a religion is established, sects diverge, mighty persecutions burn heretics at the stake, and slowly the gears of society keep turning. The world is discovered to be round, the earth revolves the sun, slavery is abolished, monarchies overthrown, all these gradual shifts in human consciousness come about. Society keeps producing more individuals with even more progressive thoughts. The Age of Enlightenment then shakes Christianity to its core. Kant forms a metaphysical grounding for morality. Hegel preaches his World Spirit. Kierkegaard tries to find salvation from the absurdity of existence. Nietzsche heralds the death of God. All these ideas forming the world and how it functions. Then come wars which span the face of the glove, catastrophes unlike humanity had ever experience before. Genocides on nearly incomprehensible scales happen for the entire world to see. And then to rescue ourselves from the nauseating void of non-existence, here comes unbridled consumerism which is producing a new form of hedonism reminiscent of the good ol' days of Rome.

And in the grand, cosmic scale of this planet, this tiny revolving rock located on one of the arms of a spiral galaxy which is just one of the billions upon billions of galaxies we have located with our most high-powered telescopes in a universe whose workings and massiveness we are still attempting to comprehend, in all this, there is little Isaiah Edward Dummas, high on heroin in a convertible driving around with a backpack full of pieces of paper, which, inherently, are without any intrinsic value. These pieces of paper with the portrait of a dead man's face who did something important over a hundred years ago though not many students today could say what. And for these small pieces of paper, I am receiving a chemical whose peculiar molecular structure affects a human in strange ways, forcing the brain to release serotonin, a naturally occurring chemical at an unnatural rate. That is all. Nothing more, nothing less.

I grew up in a Christian home with conservative values though it was never really my home. I had a decent education, suffered little abuse, and yet here I am committing these so-called crimes. How does this happen? Was it because my English teacher in tenth grade made an off-hand remark about Nietzsche, and I, being infinitely curious, decided to inquire further into the matter. Was it because my best friend Tyrone came over one day with a bag of weed when I was fifteen and sparked it up while I was shaking in absolute terror thinking my friend was about to go insane on drugs? How and Why. Those are questions I want answers to.

How is it that I got here, and why aren't I somewhere else? Why is it that the police officer who would pull me over could come from very similar circumstances as I did, yet we are on very opposite sides of the law? How were these laws established, what sort of environment created these absolutely asinine restrictions? Was it not a moment of inspiration when a man wrote, in a move of unprecedented rebellion, that all men have "an unalienable right to Life, Liberty, and the Pursuit of Happiness." And all I do is help people pursue happiness in the way they see fit while making a shit load of money. Maybe it is the drug dealers who should be considered true patriots.

And I realize then that I am high and content and can passively ask these questions because the sun is shining brightly on the world, the breeze rushing against my face is cool and refreshing, and the combination of chemicals being carried by my blood cells to various places in my brain are giving me a feeling that a someone well versed in the art of linguistics would call "euphoric." And they could describe to me in detail how this word came about, its Latin or Greek origins, the connotations of that word. They could break down the various literary functions of the word, but they could in no way understand what I am feeling right now. High on heroin and weed and an assortment of pharmaceutical chemicals that are handed out like candy to the general population of neurotics. And how could one not be neurotic living in this world. A world where there is a shooting at a school on a weekly basis, a world where people live through their internet identities, a world where religious fundamentalists are beheading and burning infidels, a world where government agencies are feared, a world where everyone is scared of the person sitting next to them on the bus, a world where wars a waged for a variety of reasons which all turn out to be false, a world where advertising executives bathe in luxury by selling the world insecurity. How can one be sane in such a world? In fact, I believe it to be complete audacity that our society would even attempt to label insanity, for to truly do so it would have to condemn itself.

How and Why. The quintessential questions of our time. And philosophy has fallen into disrepute because no one cares any more so these questions will go unanswered. Instead of turning to the great intellectuals of our time to listen to their dissertations on the nature of our reality, we turn to People magazine to see what will be fashionable next fall. Utter insanity.

Though I pride myself for being well-read, I do know one thing and that is that I do not know very much. I do know that tomorrow I will be hungry and tonight I will need to sleep and to do these things I need to have money. To get money, I know I need to offer a service or my time. I know that I hate being told what to do; I know that whoever I work for is making more money than me. In fact, the only reason they make money is from my hard work. The trick to capitalism is to get as much work from a laborer while paying them as little as possible. To keep the laborer pacified, you dangle carrots in front of him much like a farmer would do to a donkey. These carrots are nice cars, nice homes, and nice lives all while indoctrinating their children with the same dogma at an underfunded school. For me, I am just too damn smart to be fooled by that nonsense and will forge my living by working for myself. A true entrepreneur. A true American.

Drug dealer. Such a crass term. What image comes to mind? Some big black thug wearing a flat-brimmed cap with sagging jeans, adorned with gold chains. I think that is what comes to mind for most. But really, we come from all walks of life. I have bought drugs from the children of lawyers; I have bought them from toothless women with scab-covered faces. We are college students and dope-fiends, rich and poor, black and white. Some do it for the money, some do it for the thrill, most do it for both of those reasons. Dealing drugs really is a high in and of itself. Come right down to it, dealing drugs is kind of fun. Sure there is the drama, the paranoia, but sometimes, in the filth and grime of the societal rejects one deals with on a daily basis, something beautiful will happen. For a few moments, one's pathetic, meaningless existence transcends to something bordering on the divine. No longer is one wasting away in front of a television in a dank, molding hotel room waiting for the phone to ring or the police to kick down the door. One is elevated to a higher state of consciousness, rolling down the freeway, top down, smoking blunts on your way to business deal that will put you one step higher on the corporate ladder of the drug world.

And then, as you look for a rest stop in order to roll another blunt and stretch your legs, you are hit by another revelations, whether it is due to the natural course of internal dialogue or simply because the heroin is wearing off as well as the pills, the revelation hits you nonetheless that you are completely and utterly alone. That these revelations, these high times, these moments of transcendence, despite all of that, all the lofty thoughts that you only have a slight idea as to what it is you are actually thinking about, all that, and you are still alone. Even if you were in a crowd of people, a crowd of people all anxious to give you a hug and tell you how much they appreciate your existence, you are still alone. Even if you were to marry, have kids that constantly hounded you every waking second of the day, you are still alone. And that is one constant to existence, something you can depend on, a sure bet, you are ever so much alone.

And that is the great curse of our species. Individualism, such a terrifying word, one with so much power that it can nearly drive a person who truly understands that word to suicide. It is humanity's greatest freedom, it's greatest achievement, and yet, as with most tragedies, our greatest weakness. A weakness that is driving this planet to extinction. While we strive so hard to present ourselves as individuals, to try to create some little quirk about us that is unique, we are afraid to do anything truly original. We spurn conformity while clutching it to our chest. In an attempt to lose oneself, organizations are created to fool people into thinking they actually belong to something, whether it is religion or a Facebook group, they are all pathetic attempts to help people forget that they are alone in this universe. While it is a common cry of teenagers that no one understands them, there is truth to it, yet they have yet to learn an even greater curse of the individual, that it is impossible to understand one's own self. We can only see ourselves through mirrors, mirrors clouded by preconceived notions and ignorance. So it seems the only thing to do is create an identity that is pleasing to others as well as gratifying to one's own self, an identity that assures a pleasurable existence. Only those with a strong will can accomplish that, who *attempt* to dissect their own Being, and I emphasize "attempt" because to truly do so is beyond our limited human consciousness.

Have I been successful at that? I am not sure, but what I do know is I have within me a strong desire to urinate so I pull off at the next rest stop, one which happens to be one of my favorites along I-5. It is tucked in the woods, not even the road can be seen through the thick wall of trees. I park my car and head for the bathrooms. There are children throwing a Frisbee back and forth between the trees. It is a nice rest stop, right as one enters California. High elevation, thick, burly trees, clean air. I stopped here every time I passed by. Real peaceful. And these children, under the watchful yet happy eyes of their parents who looked like they were enjoying a nice vacation, would squeal with delight whenever the Frisbee would hit a tree, would squeal with delight whenever someone caught the Frisbee, would squeal with delight whenever the Frisbee went overhead, would squeal with delight whenever they went chasing after it. And the parents, a nice, inviting looking couple, looked over at me as walked past them and stared. A look of concern if not disgust crept over their faces when I got closer. I could not comprehend why. They just did, and it enraged me to the point that I nearly went for my gun.

While staring at the urinal, I was nearly in a panic wondering why the disgusted looks. Was I merely imagining that? Did I not present myself to the world in a way where no one was the wiser about my true nature? Was there something about the way I looked which alerted them? Baffling. Perhaps they were merely overprotective. That had to be it.

I crushed up some pills in a bathroom stall, rolled them into a blunt, and went outside again. At the south side of the rest stop there was an open expanse of forest where one could wander around. After about five minutes, one could get so far from the freeway that only the aggressive honking of a semi-truck could be heard. After finding a suitable trunk upon to rest my world weary body, I sparked up.

In my Being, I find much confliction. I try not to think about it too much. Sometimes this conflict makes me revel in ecstasy; sometimes it nearly makes me stick the barrel of a pistol in my mouth. I had succeeded in creating several identities to pass through life as painlessly as possible, yet I still felt much pain. There was Isaiah the Cold and Calculating, Isaiah the Passive and Indifferent, Isaiah the Drug-Addled and Intellectual, Isaiah the Haughty and Scornful. I could pass through these identities and more in one conversation; I realize this and accept it. Yet as proud as I am of creating these personas, these masks, it only increases my sense of isolation. This gut-wrenching isolation. And perhaps there is a sense of fear, almost subconscious, that if one were to cast away these identities, these masks, one would find themselves in a more excruciatingly acute isolation. I say acute because I feel like it would be enough to dash my own cup of life on the ground. So for now, I play my various roles to various people and see the world through various lenses.

My thoughts wander to an old friend of mine, someone I lost touch with years ago. He had moved to Oregon from some Midwestern state. We first met when he starting hanging out in the same circle of friends as I did, apparently he was a co-worker of a friend of mine. While he never seemed uncomfortable, he also rarely spoke a word. There was something of that "good ol' boy" in him that many people took a liking too as did I. There was a certain meekness about him, for when he was in a large group, he kept to himself and smiled at his surroundings. He never shoved himself onto anyone, never tried to barge his way into the conversation, but would simply look around and absorb the experience. He was never well-groomed, his hygiene habits were obviously lacking, acne covered his face, but he never seemed ashamed of it, in fact, he would often pop pimples without regard as to who he was with. Like myself, he grew up religious yet took it to a much farther extreme than I which is how we first started talking. I walked off to smoke a cigarette and he anxiously followed me. Before exchanging names, he immediately started asking me how I fell out of the faith. While a bit weirded out by the forcefulness of his questioning, I consented to grabbing some coffee with him to discuss religion. And that is how I first started doing business with him.

Our business dealing primarily revolved around mushrooms and weed. He was always in awe by the weed. Apparently, the Midwest does not have the same quality as West Coast. Every once in a while, when I was not pressed for time, we would smoke out in his filthy apartment and discuss books. He was a reader as was I though he hid that fact from most. It was only by chance that I happened to discover this when he took me into his room to show me his record player. I was immediately struck by his book shelf, not merely by the quantity of books, but by the names of the authors. He was a man who enjoyed the classics, that was readily apparent. His apartment was a veritable definition of filth, dishes everywhere, clothes scattered about, and floors he proudly boasted had not been vacuumed in over a year due to the fact that he did not own one, yet despite the grime and chaos which cluttered his apartment, his book shelf was alphabetized and categorized. The top shelf was his philosophy section, then came religion, and last few shelves were crammed with fiction.

When I mentioned his collection, a look of utter self-satisfaction came over his face, one that I had never seen before. A haughty smile crossed his face and he began a prideful discourse about his collection. After that day, I always made sure we had time to talk.

I began to see an utter transformation in him. Not that he behaved any differently when in a crowd of people, but our interactions one-on-one were different. And this man, a quiet happy-go-lucky sort of kid as most people described him, turned into a talkative manic depressive before my very eyes.

One conversation, or more accurately monologue, that I remembered fondly was one when I randomly stopped by his apartment while he was tripping. Loud electronic music thumped from his apartment, and when I knocked, the music abruptly stopped, and he cracked his door open slightly. As soon as he saw me, he swung the door open, grabbed my arm, and pulled me inside. After ushering me to his couch, he simply stared at me with a smile, not even replying when I said hello. I was about to leave when he started talking.

As he puffed on a hand-rolled cigarette with an ironic smile, pacing back and forth, he said, "I love the Bible. The most influential book in my life, no doubts about that. And I have never read anything which contained such terrifying truth than in Ecclesiastes. Have you read Ecclesiastes?" He did not even pause for me to respond as he began pacing across his floor. "You should. Phenomenal, a work of true originality. 'Meaningless, meaningless!' cries the teacher. 'Everything is meaningless!' How true. And that was original. A true progression in human consciousness like Cain lying to God that he did not know where Abel was. Apart from being the first murderer, Cain was the first liar, lied to God for which I eternally praise him for because lying is one of my favorite things to do. Lie about myself by the way I conduct myself in front of others, present a false image, but you know this. We talked about chameleons before."

Relighting the cigarette that he had been waving around, he went back to Ecclesiastes. "You know The Birds and Kansas both use lines from that book in some of their songs. 'Turn, Turn, Turn' and 'Dust in the Wind' both pull from that book. That terrible book. So true except for the conclusion, you know, the part about finding meaning in serving god, but we, my friend, but we who have forsaken god, what do we have left?"

I can remember how is upper twitched and his eyes became widened with particular intensity. "Those who have never walked down our path will never understand what it feels like to lose the faith. For we were taught, indoctrinated, and molded by this idea that nothing in this life has value besides faith. Remember the man who wanted to follow Jesus but requested first to bury his mother."

I nodded my head and quoted, "Let the dead bury the dead."

He jumped up and shrieked with laughter. "What an asshole! Not your family, not wealth, not nothing has value compared to faith. And you grow up for years thinking and believing that, and then one day, you wake up and realize that it is all bullshit. Every last bit of it. Except for the meaningless part. No, that part sticks. Wisdom is meaningless, pleasure meaningless, folly meaningless, everything is meaningless. That is what the teacher cries. Or in some translations, they say 'vanity' instead of 'meaningless' but in our ignorant society, our Facebook-posting, blog-reading society, no one understands that word. The true connotation of the word 'vanity.' Oh, we live in an age of deluded pretension, my friend. Delusion is what makes the world go round. Some say money, I say delusion. But after all, what is money besides delusion."

Pausing for a moment to load a bong, his face contorted into something more somber. After passing the bong to me, he said quietly, "There is one thing I have in common with those religious fanatics. One thing only. And I say this to you, and only you. Because we are alike. We show the world lies for our own gain or perhaps to simply ease our own suffering and make life less troublesome. People think rather highly of us, but we know, beyond a shadow of a doubt, what rotten pieces of shit we are. If the authorities could read our mind, I am sure we would be locked up in a mental hospital."

I almost wanted to retort that could be said for him not for me, but I did not want to interrupt the flow of his monologue. "The truth is, along with those apocalyptic savages who pray for the Second Coming of Christ, I too want the world to end. I want to be there when the nuclear warheads fill the sky as many Christians predict that is the way God will destroy the world. I want to be there, standing next to those Christians or Muslims or whatever other superstitious idiots I find myself next to. And I want to laugh. I want to laugh as we bear witness to the extinction of our loathsome species and there is no god to save us. That is what I would do. I would laugh." He said that blatantly with an utter lack of emotion in his voice.

His manic fervor began to take hold of him again. "Is there any species more disgusting then homo sapiens!" he cried as he leapt to his feet and began pacing again. "Any creature crueler and more self-deceiving and more cursed than humans. You know, there is another quote I like, not from the Bible, but I suspect if there was ever a line divinely inspired it was this one. 'The only problem with suicide is that it is always too late.'" He burst out laughing. "Comedy, sheer genius comedy! God! How do we live ourselves, our sham of an existence? Delusion, utter delusion, is what we feed on, and I am the worst of all.

"But I can't bring myself to do the deed. I have thought about, contemplated it for countless hours, made plans, debated the pros and cons of each way to off myself, but I can't do it. I can't. You know why? Because I will be defiant to the end. Defiant. Yes, that's the word, one of my favorite words. Defiant and spit in the face of absurdity because I can. Either that or I am a coward. I don't know, and can never know because I can never look at myself from the outside."

It was right then I realized why I was thinking about this

particular friend. That moment in my life was the first time I had ever given thought about being able to see yourself for who you truly are. I had always thought it was given that I understood who I was, but then that little line about not being able to see yourself from the outside shattered that pre-conceived notion. I do not know what happened to him. Last I heard he got busted, and, unfortunately, in this line of business, friendships can be a liability. So I deserted him, as did everyone else I knew. Weird that I thought of him at such a time in my life as this. I had nearly forgotten about him.

Then again, these were strange times. Tyrone was dead, and I was desperately trying to judge myself. I did not go to his funeral. What sort of man was I? Defiant or a coward? I did not know and could never know.

My phone vibrated at that moment. It was my connection. He wanted an estimated time of arrival. Still had a few more hours to go. I texted back letting him know of where I was. Then he told me he would be at a small college campus in the library. I smiled. If you are going to do it, might as well do it big and for the entire world to see.

I headed back to the car feeling negligently narcissistic. The family I saw playing Frisbee was still there. Again, the parents shot me concerned looks, except this time, I did not lower my gaze and hurry past them. This time, I slowed down, stared directly at them, and smiled wickedly. Then I turned my gaze to their children, then back to them. I abruptly stopped in front of them causing the parents to jump a little in their seats. Still holding eye contact, I pulled out a cigarette, lit it up, inhaled deeply, turned towards their kids, exhaled, and then waltzed to my car.

When I caught a glimpse of my reflection in the rearview mirror, I noticed white and brown powder caked under my nose, very visible and very obvious what it was. Amateur mistake on my part. So that was why they stared so strangely at me. I howled with laughter, loud enough for them to here as

I started my car. Then I peeled out of the parking lot with one arm held high in the air with one finger raised on that hand.

The deal went down that evening. It went as smooth as it always did. I saw him sitting at a table in front of his laptop. I saw the backpack lying on the ground next to him. Taking a seat closest to the backpack, I struck up a conversation about the weather in San Francisco, a dreadfully dull topic. I set my backpack next to his. He related to me his first experience with an earthquake. I told him about my new car. Then I grabbed his backpack and walked away. We never had to test product or count money. There was a certain amount of trust between us. I attributed that mainly to the fact that he was too professional to want any drama in his business, and he knew that I knew that he knew people who could make my life very unpleasant if I crossed him.

Back in my car, I began the long journey home. Unable to contain myself, I dipped into my newly purchased molly. It was as good as the last batch. Pure as pure gets. And then I started to come up as I made it back onto the freeway. The setting sun was casting long shadows on the freeway, traffic was sparse, and the breeze was still warm. Nice end to my day. A long day, but the molly would help me power through another ten or so hours of driving.

In a peculiar state of intoxication, nearly trance like, I maneuvered my way through winding mountain roads as if I was on autopilot, absorbed as I was in happy contemplation. Things were happening, life was moving. I meditated on those six words for quite some time. There seemed to be something profound in that. Something extraordinary was about to happen, I could feel it. After the sorrow and the terror of the last few months, I felt at ease with how things were progressing. There would be a moment soon when all would be revealed. I was quite certain of that.

As I looked back on my kidnapping, a feeling a pride

swelled up in me. I had been punked and handled it like a professional. I did not allow my anger to make me act the fool. It showed me that I had promise in this sort of field. People would respect how I played my game. While there had been some serious setbacks along the way, I was overcoming those hurdles with leaps and bounds. I could run this town. With my experience in the big city, I could bring that sort of environment to Eugene and Springfield. While there was no shortage of wanna-be gangbangers, there were very few legitimate drug dealers unless it was crystal which was a whole other beast. After what I had was gone, I had no intention in trying to get back into that game unless I could score a good enough connection that would buy some serious weight off me. Then I might make a run back to San Diego. Hopefully, that connect would be Devante. If I could drop a few pounds on him every couple months, I could pay for a house in a couple years.

The oldies radio station I was listening to started playing Frank Sinatra's "My Way." Perfect song for a perfect moment. My anthem. The song I wanted to be played at my funeral. The rallying cry of existentialists. There is unshakable defiance in that song. The sort of defiance this world so desperately needs. Something to wake us from our complacency.

The longer I drove, the more molly I ingested. It had been a long time since I had rolled that hard. Normally, I would do a bump here and there to give me a boost, but that night, I snorted nearly a half gram. I was feeling it, and it felt great. The world was fluid, the road wobbly, the trees bright, the wind joyful, and I could hold the world in the palm of my hand.

When I arrived back at the motel, I nearly skipped my way to the door. Relaxing onto my bed, I did a few bumps of heroin, smoked a fat blunt, and slowly let a long and deep sleep overtake it me. It had been quite a rollercoaster of a day. With my life being so chaotic, it had been a long time since

I had time to ponder life, and I felt I had done some good thinking, and that felt good. Real good. I slept easy with a grand feeling of accomplishment.

The next few days were uneventful save for a chance meeting of an old acquaintance. Michelle and I were downtown having lunch outside of a small bistro when someone called out, "Oh my God! Is that Isaiah!" His voice was very feminine, and he talked with a heavy, exaggerated lisp. It was Evan.

I turned in my chair and waved at him. He was 6'6" and over three hundred pounds. Curly dark brown hair that ran to his shoulders framed a pudgy face and a plump button nose. With a pop in his step, he lugged his way over to where we were dining.

"My god! It really is you! Get up and give me a hug!" Evan demanded impudently.

I stood up, and he wrapped his thick arms around me. As I was lifted off the ground, I heard my spine crack.

"It is super good to see you again," he growled. "I thought you were getting butt pounded in prison."

I laughed. "You would like that, wouldn't you, Evan?"

In a low sensual voice, he replied, "It's what I think about every night before I go to bed, honey."

Michelle let out a surprised laugh which turned Evan's attention onto her. "And who's this cutie-patootie?"

"This is Michelle. Michelle this is Evan."

Michelle smiled up at him and held out her hand. "Nice to meet you, Evan."

"Pleasure is all mine, sweetheart." He wrinkled his nose. "Do I know you from somewhere?"

"I think so," Michelle said slowly. "Do you go to the University?"

"Yes. Hmmm… have you ever gone to any of the Occupy rallies?"

Her eyes lit up. "Yes! I have!"

"Oh my god, you were the Christian girl who went to Africa, right? You gave a presentation about the oppression of homosexuals over there!"

"That's me!" she piped up happily.

"Get up here, you, and give me a hug." They embraced. "Oh my God, sweetie, it's so nice to meet you. Loved, loved your talk. One of the best I heard at the camp. Seriously, oh my god, this is so exciting!" He waved his fat hands in the air.

They continued jabbering on about Occupy which caused me to grown inwardly. While I agreed with much of what the movement stood for, I simply could not see anything they accomplished. Sure, more people were now aware that corporations are fucking this country as a whole, but then came the question as to what to do about that. The answer was that there was nothing, absolutely nothing, one could do to stop that besides refusing to support those corporations. However, Americans are much too in love with convenience and money to bother with the idea of being an ethical consumer. The only other possible solution to this country's little problem would be for the millions of people associated with Occupy to take up arms and ransack some corporate offices. Maybe even lynch a few CEOs. However, that mentality did not receive many favorable responses, so I kept my mouth shut as Michelle and Evan bantered on about Occupy's greatness.

When the opportunity presented itself, I offered Evan a seat and forced him to order some food. He gratefully accepted. "Small world," I said with a chuckle. "You two knowing each other is something else."

Michelle looked at Evan skeptically. "So how do you know Isaiah?"

He paused and looked hesitantly at me. "Is it okay to talk around innocent little Christian girl?"

"Hey!" protested Michelle. "I'm not that innocent,

okay. If that's the case, I know Isaiah well enough to take an educated guess as to how you know him."

I replied, "And you'd be right. She's cool, Evan."

Evan smiled shyly and looked at the ground. "Well, that's good to hear. As you may have guessed, Isaiah and I used to be lovers."

Michelle burst out laughing as I scowled at Evan. He raised his hands in the air defensively. "I'm only joking! My god, lighten up, Isaiah. You look like you're going to pull a gun on me. Sorry, didn't mean to embarrass you in front of this lovely lady. No, sweetie, Isaiah and I used to slang ecstasy together. I used to get my shit from him."

"Speaking of which, you know where to get any good thiz around here?" I asked abruptly.

He shook his head. "Honey, I don't fuck around with the white drugs any more. I'm all natural these days."

"Why?"

"Why!" he cried incredulously. "Honey, do you have any idea what that shit does to your poor little brain? Besides, I got busted a little over a year ago for that shit. Almost did three years, but I got off with drug treatment and a suspended sentence. Did it once when I graduated treatment and nearly killed myself. So this guy right here only ingests things good Mother Earth provides."

"Same with me," piped up Michelle happily.

Our food was brought out, and we all began to eat. Evan was chatting up Michelle which gave me a little breathing room. It was nice they hit it off so well. A long stretch of time had passed since the last time I had seen Evan. He had never been skinny, but he must have put on another fifty since I had last seen him. Some hippies he ran with called him Papa Bear due to his enormous size and considerable hairiness. The two of us never hung out all that much, though we did take some mushrooms together. We travelled to the coast and ran along the dunes all night. By far, that time was my favorite trip. While we were not tight before and did not continue hanging out afterwards, the mushrooms broke down some psychological barriers that night, and we talked about some heavy shit. There were things he knew about me that not even Tiz or Michelle knew. Afterwards, we had always warmly greeted one another, but I always thought there was some sort of apprehension due to the fact we knew so much personal information about one another. He was a good guy who had some terrible shit happen to him as a kid.

With his mouth full of vegetables, Evan looked at me and said, "Isaiah, I'm absolutely in love with this Michelle. Sweetheart, I could eat you up like chocolate, and, if you couldn't tell by my thunder thighs, I love chocolate. Now I'm dying to know, how did you two meet?"

Michelle looked at me, and I shrugged off the question so she answered. "I've known Isaiah for a long time. We used to go to church together."

"Was he always such a little shit?" he asked snidely.

She chuckled. "No. He used to be a very sweet shy little guy. Always had his nose in a book."

"Really? Because the Isaiah I know always has his nose in a pile of drugs."

"He's changed alright." There was a sad tone in her voice which I did not like one bit. Perhaps I was irritated that my past was being talked about right in front of me.

"Well, it's real good to see him with a nice girl. So how long have you two been dating?" he asked innocently.

Both of us jolted in our seats and replied with hastily jumbled words. She was blushing. I probably was too.

"Slow down, sweethearts," he said holding his hands out. "It's just a simple question."

"Well, we aren't dating," stated Michelle flatly.

"Why not?" he whined. "You two look so cute together."

"He's too much trouble for me," she said dismissively. She shot me a strange smile.

If I had gone down a different path in life, I may have seriously considered trying to date her. However, in the criminal world, there is a saying, "Love makes you fat." I had no intention of becoming soft, my success and survival depended upon me keeping a clear head. Any attachments I would make would only serve as targets for my enemies, and I had no intention of stepping lightly in this town. What I had gone through only boosted my confidence. I was not one to live a quiet life. The mere thought of it was revolting. The whole idea of having some cookie-cutter house with a manicured lawn bordered by a white picket fence disgusted me. Having children and going to soccer games pretending you cared seemed straight out of Dante's *Inferno*. Plus, there is the cost of raising children, hundreds of thousands of dollars down the drain from some snot-nosed little shit. And while you devote yourself to helping them pursue their dreams, your ambitions go right to the shitter. Then you attempt to live vicariously through these little creations you have made, and in the end, they hate you for it. And as she said, I was too much trouble for her, and I was not about to change who I was for a woman.

Evan's shrill voice brought me back to the conversation. "Isaiah! Do you hear this girl? Too much trouble! If he ever gives you trouble, sweetheart, you call me, okay, and I'll come over and spank the shit of him. Spank that little ass."

"You'd like that too much," I retorted.

"Damn right I would," he said with a roll of his shoulders. "But seriously, you should two should really think about dating. You'd make a cute couple."

"Fuck, Evan. Since when did you become a matchmaker?" I asked with annoyance in my voice.

"Honey, I've always gravitated to strong couples. That's why I'm going into marriage counselling."

Michelle raised her eyebrows. "Really?"

"Bit ironic," I added.

"Not really," answered Evan a bit offended. "I think straight people find it easier to confide in a gay man, especially when it comes to sex. I think straight men find it easier to tell a gay man what their kinks are."

I shrugged. "Maybe you got a point."

We had finished eating, and all of us lit up a cigarette. Evan looked at his watch. "Oh my God, I am supposed to meet my cutie in ten minutes. Gotta run. Isaiah, it was great seeing you again, and, sweetheart, keep Isaiah in line for me."

She laughed. "Will do."

Evan made it about ten steps before he turned around with a gasp. "Oh my God, Isaiah!" he yelled as he hurried back. "I'm so sorry. I feel like a dick for forgetting." He wrapped his arms around me from behind. "I'm so sorry to hear about T. He was such a good guy. Are you holding up alright, honey?"

I patted his arm. "I'm fine. It sucks, but that's the game for you."

"Poor dear, going out like that. Well, you take care. Real sorry, but I gotta run, honey."

As he left, I could tell Michelle was staring at me.

"What happened to Tyrone?" she asked warily.

I cleared my throat. "He's dead."

"What!"

I nodded sorrowfully. "He got killed in LA a bit after he disappeared."

"Oh my gosh, Isaiah. I'm so sorry." Her sympathy helped her swallow the little distortion of the truth I told. "Do you know what happened?"

"Apparently, the people he was fucking around with shot him."

"That's terrible. I don't know what to say."

I shrugged indifferently. "Not much to say. It is what it is."

With that, the conversation broke off. I suggested we

walk around for a bit which she agreed too. For a half hour, we ambled around the city not saying a word. I could tell she was struggling with the news of Tyrone's death. Every once in a while she would clear her throat but said nothing.

Tyrone's death was something that I did not want to deal with. It was a kink in my path, one which I wished to hurdle over. Of course, I loved the man, loved him more than anything else, but he was gone. Not much more to say than that. Perhaps I avoided thinking about it because it was a failure on my part. I should have seen it coming; I should have been able to put the pieces together before it happened. Then there was the fact that he was one of the only people I could "be real" with. I needed no mask to wear when I was around him. With John, Michelle, and even Tiz, I had expectations to live up to, and image to uphold. With Tyrone, it was different. Not only did we mutually benefit from one another, a prime ingredient to any healthy relationship, but our personalities coalesced in a way where there was very little friction. I thought he was chill; he felt the same about me. We were familiar with one another to an extreme degree. Hell, I could hardly remember my life before I met him. And now he was gone. It was almost like I was learning to ride a bike without training wheels. But that was emotions speaking, or, in other words, that was weakness speaking. This was no time for weakness.

Michelle huffed, I sighed. I was uncomfortable and earnestly searched for a distraction. Coincidentally, we ran into Evan again who was walking around with some mustached man wearing flip-flops, khaki shorts, a button-up white shirt, and a rainbow colored scarf. Evan stopped us and introduced his friend, Logan.

"So what are you two doing not next Saturday but the Saturday after that?" Evan asked.

I shrugged. "As far as I know, nothing."

"Me neither," piped up Michelle.

"Marvelous," he said as he clapped his hands. "So Logan here is having a party at his uncle's cabin out by Blue River. You two should totally come."

"I don't know," I said hesitantly.

"Oh come on!" Evan huffed. "Please. It's going to be so much fun! We are all going to eat mushrooms and dance around. There'll be a bonfire and a drum circle and a whole bunch of fun lights! Please, please, please! You have to come."

Michelle laughed. "I'm down. I've never tried mushrooms."

"Oh my God, sweetheart, they are the best. How about it, Isaiah? You're coming. That's all there is too it."

I shook my head and inhaled through my teeth. "I don't know, man. Been awhile since I've shroomed."

"Come on. We had so much fun last time!" he pleaded.

Michelle nudged me. "Don't be a party pooper. This sounds fun."

"And he could use the fun," insisted Evan.

"That he could," replied Michelle with a chuckle.

I felt like I was cornered, so I agreed, having every intention of bailing at the last second. However, deep down inside, I knew if Michelle really wanted to go, I would be there. When we parted, I could tell Michelle was more at ease. Evan served as a distraction from the news of Tyrone's death.

"I absolutely adore him," said Michelle cheerfully.

"He's a good guy."

"We are going to that party. I hope you know that. No backing out like you usually do."

I shook my head. "You really want to try mushrooms?"

"Well....yeah. They're natural. Besides, I've heard so much about them that I am curious to try it at least once. Plus, drum circle and a bonfire. What fun!"

With a smile on my face, I agreed that it did sound like fun. However, internally, I was plagued by anxiety. Mushroom trips are intense. One has to be in the right state of mind for it to go smoothly. While I wanted to say that I was simply not in a good place to do them, I also wanted to be there when Michelle did them her first time. Besides, I had done them enough times that I believed I could control myself.

When we parted, she gave me a long hug, expressing her condolences for Tyrone again. She told me to call anytime if I wanted to talk. Assuring her I was just fine, I headed back to the motel. It was strange that now people knew Tyrone was dead, it suddenly felt more real. The more I told people he disappeared, the more I felt like he actually had. In fact, I felt a bit spurned by him. Yet the more the truth came out, the more I missed him. As I laid on the bed cutting out a line of heroin, I nearly broke down and cried, but as soon as the heroin hit, I felt just fine. Tyrone went back to just disappearing, not dying.

The next day, Devante called for some more crystal. Another half-pound of meth was gone, and I added another seven thousand to my stash. I also snagged a half gram of heroin. He told me when and where his contact for the molly wanted to meet me. There was a rave going happening that Friday. Short notice as that was only two days away, but I told him I could make it. Devante gave me a rough description of what he looked like and where he would be.

I hit up Tiz and asked her to accompany me to the rave. She seemed surprised that I actually was going to go. She was even more surprised when I asked her to bring a piece and be level headed.

"We gonna put a hit on some muthafucka or something?" she asked hesitantly.

"Nah. We'll talk when I pick you up. Just don't be too fucked up. I got business and want someone to watch my back."

I knew this was a bit heavy for her. She was not a

gangbanger even though she portrayed herself as such. Guns were not her thing. Fist fights, sure, but murder was something I did not think she had the stomach for. Despite the façade she maintained, she was not an evil-minded person. Just a fun loving gal, no more, no less. Admittedly, unconventional fun, but she was just in the game to have a good time. The only reason I asked her to accompany me with Jude was because that was her problem. This was different. This was my problem. However, without Tyrone I was vulnerable. I needed someone there in case anything went down.

We took a taxi to the show. I never liked bringing my car to these types of shows. Always the threat of someone busting in your car or the cops showing up. I trusted my feet more than any mechanical, four-wheeled creature. Tiz was nervous. I told her that I only needed someone to keep an eye on me from a distance. Also, I knew that whoever I was meeting with had eyes on the entrance. They would see me entering with someone. It was important for them to know I was not alone. Most likely, they would recognize Tiz which was a good thing. She had a reputation and knew a lot of people. Make them think twice about burning me.

I was feeling warm and relaxed. I attributed this more to the heroin than my own resilience. There was a part of me that was screaming out warnings. I had done this type of deal before, and I had lost my best friend because of that. But this was different. I had to keep telling myself that. This was different. This was Eugene, not Los Angeles. I knew people here. Gun shots do not ring out in this town without someone calling the cops.

The rave was taking place in a large warehouse that was surrounded by other similar looking warehouses. Obviously, whoever was putting this on was trying to hide the location, but due to the amount of traffic heading in, it would be obvious to any police officer what was taking place. That made me a bit nervous. However, I was smarter and faster and less intoxicated than most people in attendance, so I figured that even if the cops showed, I would have no problem running.

An absurd amount of cars surrounded the building. The usual crowd loitered outside. Teenage junkies, tweaks, ravers, and a few hipsters. All with dilated pupils. Soon, those pupils would be dilated thanks to me. This could be a hook that would help climb a bit higher. Three contacts to sell too, all that wanted serious weight. Push crystal to Devante, sling ecstasy to this unknown fool, and push the trimmings to Tiz. Though that might change. After establishing myself, I would not need to deal with her anymore. Maybe just pay her to watch my back. That might not be so bad. Hell, we could even get a pad together just like old times.

Loud bass vibrated through the concrete floor of the warehouse. People were jumping and convulsing to the beat. I pushed past them with my eyes scanning the crowd for my contact. There was a second level that was sparsely populated. There was a metal-grated platform which ran along the walls. It was about fifteen feet above the floor. There were a few catwalks that crisscrossed the warehouse where a few people stood on, looking at the crowd below while chain smoking cigarettes. Tucked in one of the corners of this second story was a makeshift bar where very few people were at. Not too many people were in the mood for drinking.

As I tried to make way up the staircase to that dark corner, a young kid with gauged ears and "541" tattooed on his neck stopped me. His intent was to sell me some molly. Curiosity got the best of me so I bought a point. Inspecting it brought a grin to my face. It was cut heavily with cocaine. Funny that cocaine has had such a falling out with the general population that it is now used to cut molly. Sign of the times. Me, I am old school, I prefer cocaine to molly, but molly is what sells so that it what I buy. Knowing myself, to be cocaine dealer would certainly mean a fatal heart attack before thirty.

I chuckled which caused the kid to glare at me. I showed Tiz the point, she chuckled too. Then she pulled out a point of our molly. The dude's jaw nearly dropped. He was even more taken aback that we told him to keep it.

"On the house tonight, mufucka," said Tiz as we brushed past him. "But if you gonna sell us coke, sell us coke, not some cut to shit fuckin' baby laxative."

When we made it to the catwalk, I had to stop and take it all in. The stage was little more than plywood set on some wooden beams. It was not even a foot off the ground. The kid making music with his laptop was probably sixteen. Not bad music, not so much my cup of tea anymore, but the drops were heavy, the melody listenable, and he added some humorous sound bites in his tracks. All in all, I would have loved it five years ago. Must be getting old.

But the crowd, that glorious mob of idiots stuffed with their bourgeoisie parents' money, that was a sight to see. It was fascinating to watch them react to the music as if they had no personal volition but simply slaves to the music and the drugs. That was my target audience. I could see them pop tabs, snort molly, smoke weed, and it filled me with glee. This was soon to be my domain. I could feel it. Soon it would be my drugs making them convulse to the music. Making my riches off their parents' paycheck. Beautiful.

For a few moments, I simply reveled in my hatred for these spawns of the status quo. Utter fools holding up their Iphones trying to record the moment instead of living it. One never saw that in my day. We did drugs, we danced, and we lived it. Never tried to immortalize it via the digital gods. These utter, self-deluded fools, who only do things so they can post it on Facebook. Their parents' generation had placed the noose around our society's neck, this generation would be the one to jump off the stool. Because when these kids grow up, when they realize that their childhood imaginary friends were more real and reliable then their Facebook friends, when their profile persona strikes them as a stranger, we will see a massive increase of suicides and addiction among the middle-aged. Already, it is happening. Clinical depression in this country continues to rise as the pharmaceutical companies continue to laugh their way to the bank as they continue to push their cures for the symptoms. And that is what those anti-depressants and anti-anxiety medications are, cures for the symptom but not the disease. In fact, they only assure the fact that the disease will never be cured, never managed. Because if the disease ever was conquered, they would lose a customer. So that is why anti-depressants have "thoughts of suicide" as a side-effect and anti-anxiety medications have withdrawals so intense that it can kill you. A detox center will not even admit someone withdrawing from barbiturates, the active drug in most anti-anxiety medication; they will send them straight to the hospital. And this is the shit that you feed to your kids on a daily basis. "Customa' fo' life, mufucka," as Tiz would put it. Mental illness has never been so financially seductive.

I turned my thoughts back to business. Already, I had seen a small room on the second floor that look like it had been used as a control center for the warehouse. The windows had been covered up. I figured this is where the deal would take place. But first, I had to find my contact. I told Tiz to watch from the walkway. If I did not turn up in twenty minutes, come creeping.

The bar was simply a flat metal sheet propped up on top of barrels. The bartender was a topless female covered with tattoos who stood in front of a shelf full of liquor bottles, all of it well material. There was a cooler filled with mixers and a keg on top of ice. Not much of a selection. My contact was easy enough to find. He was standing at the bar with shiny silver pants with an oiled mustache, just like Devante said.

I ordered a shot of bourbon, and then I ordered a gin and tonic for the man next to me. He turned and smiled as she poured our drinks.

His face was rodent-like, his hair fading which he tried to cover up with an ungodly amount of gel. It was plastered to his head. He turned to a group of men, all decked out in raver attire, day-glo, LED necklaces and bracelets, tie-dye bandanas, and grungy pants. A few of them had dreads. He whistled, and they came over to us. My contact and I downed our drinks, and, as expected, he ushered me to the room I had seen previously.

As I presumed, the room had been a control room for the warehouse at one time. There was a control panel which looked like it had operated a crane at some point. In the middle of the room was a desk with a chair on each side. He sat down at the side which faced the door. I was forced to keep my back to the door, something I did not like. His boys crowded behind him. Obviously, they were muscle and testers.

"So you are Devante's friend," my contact said slowly. He paused, I said nothing. He continued, "So, do you have a name."

"You can call me Josh."

"Alright, *Josh.* So tell me, why should I do business with you?"

I smiled wickedly. Homeboy was trying to flex. "Besides the obvious fact that you need a supplier. Devante told me you need what I got."

"And Devante should have told you to come alone."

"Well, there ain't nobody in this room besides me, you, and your homies. So I would say I came alone."

"You brought someone with you," he said menacingly.

I leaned in. "Would you really want to do business with an idiot? Of course I have someone to watch my back. I don't know you; you don't know me. I would like to keep it like that. This is strictly business. And I am not about to get burned. Not with this much product."

He nodded his head slowly. "So where is it?"

I had strapped a few thin fanny packs, the type tourists carry their credit cards in, around my stomach as I did not want to bring a backpack in the rave. That would have been too conspicuous. So I lifted up my shirt, blatantly displaying the pistol tucked in my waistband, and undid the straps. Before I even placed the molly on the table, I could tell he was impressed.

His cronies each did a bump from the bags. They whispered to my contact. He smiled and nodded. He pulled out a wad of bills. "Do you want to count it?"

I shook my head. "If it is short, I will let you know."

"It isn't," he said emphatically.

"For your sake, I hope it isn't." I began stuffing the cash in various fanny packs. Luckily, the man had enough sense to pay me in hundred dollar bills so it all fit nicely.

I cleared my throat, "So, do we exchange numbers, or we just go through Devante."

He leaned back in his chair. "Well-"

His response was cut short by loud frantic knocking causing my contact and his boys to go for their guns. But they tucked them away as quickly as they pulled them out.

"Raid!" screamed a panic-stricken female voice. I sat motionless, not wanting to get shot. One of my contact's men opened the door to the sight of the topless bartender. The music had stopped.

"The pigs are outside, full geared too!" she screamed. "We are going to get raided!"

My contact looked at me. "Get out of here!" he barked. Obviously, he had an escape route he was not going to share. I ran out of the room, the door was shut and locked behind me.

Sheer chaos erupted on the dance floor. Someone had opened the warehouse delivery doors, and people made a break for it only to be met with riot shields and zip ties. One girl slammed into a riot shield into the open arms of a police officer. Seemingly without effort, he slammed her to the ground and zip-tied her hands behind her back. Another girl broke through the line, only to get tazed in the back. The police were wearing gas masks meaning that the tear gas canisters were loaded. I had seen raids before, but never like this. The police were coming in full force, riot squad and all. I remembered what Devante had told me about the city councilor's kid OD'ing, and then it all made sense. They were going to make an example.

Engrossed by this spectacle of wailing partiers being forcefully thrown to the ground with their hands zip-tied behind their backs as a phalanx of baton wielding police marched into the warehouse, I had not even given a second thought as to how I was going to get out. Then Tiz grabbed my shoulder. There was terror on her face.

Without even giving her a warning, I grabbed the pistol from her waistband as well as one of her bandanas. I ran behind the bar, dumped some vodka on the gun and began polishing it. After I finished, I tossed it into the trash. I repeated that process with my own pistol. By the time I finished, we were the only ones on the second floor. Everyone else had tried their luck going down to the dance floor. It looked like a few had made it out.

I looked at Tiz and yelled to be heard over the din of raid, "You clean!"

She turned her pockets inside out, dumping an assortment of baggies filled with powder and tabs. I looked around. There was no way I was going down. I saw some officers look our way. Carefully, I scanned the room. In the corner opposite of us there was a ladder headed to the roof. I pointed it out to Tiz. The frantic screams of the arrested reverberated off the metal walls of the warehouse as we sprinted across the catwalk.

Without hesitation, I threw myself up the ladder. Heights are one of my greatest fears though this fear was conquered by my other greatest fear, the fear of prison. While I did not have anything illegal on me, it would be hard to explain the ten thousand dollars I had tucked into fanny packs. As I bounded my way up, I prayed that the trapdoor up top was not locked which it was not. It was rusted and hard to turn, but it was not locked. I threw all my weight into it and nearly fell off the ladder when circular handle finally budged. By the time I shoved it open, Tiz was screaming that the police were coming after us.

After we made it onto the roof, I slammed the trapdoor shut. I barked at Tiz to find something to put on top. All we could find was some scrap lumber and a few metal poles, nothing to hold the door shut. So I turned my attention to finding a way down. After running along the edges, I found one ladder which led down, but that was near the entrance which was swarming with cops. That left one option. On the south end of the building, there was another warehouse, slightly shorter than the one I was one. There was a six foot gap between the two, barely large enough to fit a car through. Apparently, only forklifts ever passed through this alley. Tiz frantically asked what we were going to do. I started sprinting because I heard the trapdoor open followed by orders to freeze.

I lunged off the edge of the warehouse while praying that I did not sprain my ankle. I curled my legs underneath me, trying to become as ball-like as possible. Instinctively, I leaned towards my left side. Poor choice. While I landed somewhat on my feet, those gave way quickly because my knees were tucked into my chest. My left arm and shoulder skidded across the metal roof. Immediately, I felt my wound reopen. Tears rushed to my eyes. I was paralyzed by pain for a moment. Then there was a loud thud next to me, and someone grabbed by arm and hoisted me up.

"Let's go!" screamed Tiz. Angry shouts were behind us. That woke me up. We ran to the edge. There was a ladder which led down the side, but it was one of those retractable ladders, and unfortunately, it had been retracted about eight feet off the ground to prevent anyone from climbing up. Tiz scooted her way down with me nearly stepping on her fingers. She did not hesitate when she reached the end and jumped down. I did the same, yet I twisted my ankle. I cursed loudly. Tiz hoisted me up again, slinging my arm around her shoulder.

"Come on, walk it off, bro. Fuckin' walk it off. We got to get the fuck out of here."

After about ten yards, I began to realize the gravity of the situation. Adrenaline started to push away the heroin induced complacency. I hobbled faster until I let Tiz go and started running by myself.

A shout came from behind us, "Stop or we will taze you!"

And then everything began to click. That is the only way I can describe it. Without even having to communicate, Tiz and I began sprinting and swerving. Whenever we passed a trash can, we threw it to the ground. In unison, we covered the small alleyway in trash and obstacles. We verged right down another alley which led to a tall, chain-link fence. We each jumped onto it and hurtled our way over it. My ankle cried out when I landed, but I paid it no mind. We kept running.

At the next intersection, we nearly ran into another group of police. They were huddled around a car, discussing something or another. When they saw us, they barked at us to freeze. We veered left towards the freeway.

A concrete wall about twelve feet high and a half a foot thick closed in the entire warehouse district. There were only two ways in and out by vehicle. I knew those ways were blocked off. So that left going over the wall. We ran along it, hoping to find an opening. What we found was a dumpster.

Again, no communication, we just worked in unison. We leaped onto it, Tiz put her back against the wall with her hands cupped together to give me a foot hold. My right foot landed in her hands, my left shoved off her shoulder, my arms made it over the wall, I heaved my body up, laid on my stomach with my right arm dangling down, Tiz grabbed my arm, I pulled as hard as I could, my body twisted off the wall, and we both went tumbling down into the bushes below.

"We good?" I asked as I jumped to my feet.

Her arms were covered in scrapes, some bleeding, and her nose was gushing blood.

"We good."

A steep embankment stood between us and the freeway. On all fours, we scrambled up, grabbing brushes and scraggly trees for hand holds. Then came the concrete barrier, thankfully this time only three feet tall. We bounded over that as headlights began blaring their horns at us. Without regard to anyone's wellbeing, we dashed across the freeway. There were screeching tires.

In a matter of seconds, we had leapt over the freeway and were in some serious brush. Thorns tore at my jeans and exposed arms. Yet we kept tearing through in silence. Over hills, under on-ramps, through streams and blackberry bushes. The only thought, "Go, go, go!"

We made it to a wooden fence, a happily residential fence. We peeked over it. There was a wooden play set, slide, swings, and even a small merry go-round attached to it. In the middle of the backyard was an above ground pool. Nowhere were there any signs of a dog. Good. Very good. The house, a larger two-story complex, was completley unlighted. Silently, we climbed over the fence, waltzed through the yard, unlatched the gate that led to the front yard, closed the gate, crept past the house, and finally, with a wave of joy crashing over us, made it to the silent, vacant streets of bourgeoisie suburbia.

Quickly and quietly, we walked past manicured lawns

and meticulously groomed flower beds. It was not until we made our way through the maze of suburban streets and onto Main Street that I felt completely safe. Tiz and I still walked in silence. A Taco Bell sign illuminated the night sky in the distance. Still on the same wave length, we veered into the parking lot and walked into the lobby.

After grabbing our order, we made our way, slowly and painfully, to a booth, sat down, and opened our bags. Tiz started chuckling. I followed suit. Within seconds, we were both convulsing with laughter. Whether the Taco Bell employees shot us strange looks, I will never know. I was too busy holding my sides, just howling.

The laughter died as quickly as it erupted. We nibbled on our food for a few minutes, still not saying anything. Yet neither of us seemed to be hungry, and most of the food we ordered went into the trash. I think we only needed a spot to sit down. I looked at my phone. It was almost two o'clock in the morning. We must have been running for almost an hour.

We headed outside and kept walking down Main Street. After spotting a bench tucked near the entrance of a convenience store, we sat down again. We lit up some cigarettes.

"That... that, muthafucka, was something else," said Tiz.

I chuckled. "Damn straight."

"Fuckin' tired as a fuckin' muthafucka," said Tiz with a yawn.

I nodded. "Me too. Probably should call a cab."

Our cab arrived in a half-hour. He dropped Tiz off and then me. I laid my head on the pillow, and fell fast asleep.

I awoke the next evening sore and famished. Grumbling, I hoisted myself out of bed. While driving to a restaurant to grab some grub, I called Tiz to see how she was doing. She was sore, but mostly, ecstatic about our escape. She told me what word on the street was about the raid. A few small-timers had gotten popped, but almost everyone had been processed then released. For the most part, there were mainly pissed off parents who were awoken at two o'clock in the morning to come pick their kid up from the police station. No word on my contact, but considering she had not seen his mug in the newspaper, he was probably safe. For the time being, at least. Most likely those who had been detained were being interrogated as to who their supplier was.

"If I was you, I'd stay clear of that fool," she said quietly. "There gonna be drama, you know what I'm saying. I ain't showing my mug at a rave for a grip. But you should grab a paper and read it yourself. They probably ain't gonna be doin' them now. People raising a fuss about that shit."

"Alright. Keep your ear to the street. Let me know if anything important comes up."

"Will do, bro. What a fuckin' night. Got me enough exercise to last a life time."

"I hear you there. Shit, my legs are killing me."

"Me too, bro. But shit, I got one my bitches comin' over to give me a nice massage, so I will talk to you later, aight."

"Enjoy," I said coolly.

"You want me to send one over to your pad?"

The offer was tempting. "Nah... I'm good."

I pulled into the restaurant parking lot, finished my cigarette, and then headed inside. I ordered steak and potatoes, seemed like a good choice. When I asked for a newspaper, I was given the tattered remains of the morning paper. A few sections were missing, but the front page was still intact. Headline news, "Illegal Rave Sacked By Police." Skimming through the article, I picked up a few pieces of information. Over fifty people had been arrested by the police. Most had been released, the others were being held for interrogation. A detective was quoted saying, "These illegal raves are breeding grounds for drug traffickers." There were some outraged parents calling for more aggressive policing of these unlicensed raves. Towards the end of the article were some statistics about drug use and overdoses. All in all, a load of journalistic rubbish. Fear-mongering and ignorant.

I had a thought, not a very pleasant one, but one that needed consideration. Was this my sign to get out of the business? I certainly could not go back to my contact to drop off more molly. That was my niche, my market. Now, narcs would be out in full force. All it takes is for one person to squeal, and then there is a domino effect. Personally, I felt safe, but it seemed to be only a matter of time before Tiz got popped. A little research would point them in my direction.

I shook those thoughts away. What was I thinking? It was not time to back down, it was time to step my game up. The more weight I pushed, the higher up I would be, and the higher up I was, the less likely I would be popped. As I munch on my steak, I decided I would call Devante to inquire about our mutual acquaintance. Worst case scenario, I would be stuck dealing with him and Tiz. Still, that was quite a bit of money headed my way.

Unfortunately, it was worst case scenario. Devante told me that his guy had left town in a hurry. Probably would not be back. Someone close to him had gone down. I sighed. So that was that. However, Devante was looking for some more crystal, but told me not to rush. He was getting out of town for a couple weeks as well. So it was time to head to San Diego. By myself. I had half of a mind to bring Devante and introduce him to my contact, but as Devante pointed out, how would I get my finder's fee. There was no way I could bring Tiz. They would see right through her. I was alone in this game, a dangerous place to be. So I would be dealing with men who, most likely, had connections to Mexican cartels, and I would be doing it alone. Perhaps Tyrone was right. Perhaps the meth game was too heavy.

But that was the weakness talking. I kept reminding myself of that. However, I could not shake the feeling that

I could be doing so much more with my life. Something a bit more meaningful. Yet that was weakness talking again. Nothing had meaning. Remember what the teacher said. So I headed back to the hotel completely conflicted as to what I was going to do.

A week passed without much happening. I spent some quality time snorting heroin and staring at the wall. Indecision was paralyzing me. I still had a pound of meth, enough for one or two more transactions. A couple times, I actually got into my car with the intent to drive down to San Diego. Even turned on the engine. But after a few moments, I would shut my car off, head back inside, and do some more heroin.

And then Michelle called sending me into a complete state of frantic uncertainty. She was calling to see if I was still going to Evan's party. I had forgotten about that. The last thing I wanted to do was trip on psychedelics. Inwardly, I screamed in protest as my drug-addled complacent voice said, "Oh yeah. I will pick you up. Saturday at four... Cool... Yeah... Yeah, I'm excited too... Sure, let's get lunch tomorrow and talk about it... Okay... See you then."

I savagely cursed myself when I hung up the phone.

Saturday came too quickly for my liking. I was high enough to not really care about what I was about to do so I tried to match her excitement. I discretely pocketed a small bag of heroin and some pills just in case I felt an itch.

The ride to the cabin was filled with nervous questions about mushrooms from Michelle. I answered to the best of my ability. She told me about all the stories she had heard and asked if she would really see leprechauns. I laughed and told her many people exaggerate. Tripping is not like how it is depicted in television shows and movies. It is much more subtle. Primarily, one sees a distortion of color as well as some geometric patterns that reside wherever your vision is focused. The patterns shift in shape and color, but they are also very vague. They do not block your line of sight but are always present in the background. At least that had been my experience.

The sun was beginning to set as we reached our destination. As we navigated our way through a mile long two-track which led to the cabin, anxiety set in. While there was not a large group of people, it was large enough for me to feel uncomfortable. There were twelve people altogether, including Michelle and me. Everyone except Evan, who was brewing the mushroom tea in the kitchen, was sitting around a large camp fire and greeted us warmly. Joints were passed around. Everyone there knew either Evan or Logan. Most of them were hippies which I mean in the best way possible. The conversation was easy going. For the most part, I sat back and listened. Michelle fit right in and soon was laughing and joking with everyone in the group. I left her to go find Evan.

He was happily stirring the tea which smelt like rotten death. The first few times ingesting mushrooms are easy. For some reason afterwards, most people gag simply smelling them. I was happy we would be drinking tea instead of eating them raw. That would help with the nausea.

"How are you, Isaiah?" he asked as he gave me a hug.

"Good." I stared suspiciously at the boiling water filled with chunks of diced mushrooms. "Smells fucking horrible."

"I know! I'm so excited for this. Michelle's here, right?"

"Yep."

He was grinning from ear to ear. "This is going to be great. I can just feel it. A truly bonding experience with a bunch of good people. Honey, we are going to have fun tonight! And my lordy, do you look like you could use it."

I was a bit taken aback by that comment. I thought I looked fine, but that viewpoint would radically change within the hour.

I helped Evan pour the tea into cups and assisted in

distributing them to the others. Each one politely thanked me for it. After everyone had received their cup, we all sat in a circle as Evan gave a toast.

"Tonight is a night for new beginnings. It is a full moon tonight, and we have many new friends joining us. For those unfamiliar with this area, the river is not far from here. Go enjoy if you want but be careful as it gets deep in the middle and the current is quick. Also, for those of you trying this for your first time, don't wander off alone. We all have our tripping buddies, so stick close to them. There are comfy beds in the cabin, so if you need to lie down, go for it. Otherwise, let us enjoy one another's company, and let the Universe take its course." He raised his cup. "To new friends, new experiences, and new beginnings."

With that, we all drank our tea. Michelle made a horrified face of disgust and coughed a few times. I was able to gag it down with a few gulps.

She chuckled quietly. "Wow. This is gross."

"It only gets worse," I assured her.

After we had all finished our tea, Evan and some of the others fetched bongo drums, and the drum circle commenced. I struggled to keep a steady beat as I had no musical inclinations. However, Michelle happily pounded away on her drum. The air reverberated with the pulsing beat. After twenty minutes passed, I started to feel the come-up. My stomach churned a bit, my vision became a bit shaky, and a peculiar sensation plagued my limbs which was neither pleasant nor uncomfortable. The best way to describe it was pent up energy.

Looking around me, I saw only smiling faces which seemed to be morphing slightly. Everyone was beginning to feel it. Michelle broke her rhythm to gently stroke my arm for a moment. I looked at her and forced a smile. However, I was far from comfortable. Anxiety began to overwhelm me, but I told myself it was simply the come-up. With every trip into psychedelia land, there is a nervous anticipation. Yet I could not shake a feeling of dread which was clouding my mind. And then came the itch. All I could think about was how badly I needed a fix. With a reassuring smile, I told Michelle I needed to use the bathroom.

Bathrooms are always a sand trap for one under the influences of psychedelics especially if the floor is tiled in small squares as this one was. As I sat on the toilet, I stared at the floor which seemed to be breathing with intricately patterned mono-colored squares. After spending quite some time quietly contemplating the floor, I reached into my pockets and pulled out the heroin.

The heroin mellowed me out a bit, but not as much as I thought it would. The mushrooms were taking hold. As I stood over the sink splashing cold water in my face, I caught a glimpse of my reflection in the mirror. How long I was transfixed by my own appearance will forever be a mystery.

What I saw in the mirror brought tears to my eyes. Perhaps I had subconsciously avoided the mirror in my hotel room because I had no idea just how bad I looked. Large swollen purple bags lingered under my eyes, my cheeks were sucked up, my hair was much grayer than I had remembered, and there was something very disconcerting about my eyes. They spoke to me of vacancy, of despair, of fear. I tore my gaze away from the mirror but was only able to restrain myself for a few moments before I looked at the mirror again. There was something unrecognizable about my face. I could not put my finger on it, but something had changed. This shadow of a man staring back at me was a complete stranger. He looked like a man on his last rope. He was a man shell-shocked and insecure who had no idea how transparent his façade was. Despite a hardened jaw and wrinkled brow, he still looked like a scared, lost child in a crowded mall. Geysers of watery desolation lay behind those shit-brown eyes. This was a face of someone who would die alone and miserable with no one to call friend. This could hardly be called a face. It was more of a cracking white-washed mask which saw only prison or death wherever it turned. And whatever those sunken eyes stared at, walls were built and bridges were burned. How could anyone live with a face like this? How had this poor, emaciated soul managed to not end its own loathsome existence? What narcissistic pomposity allowed this face to be seen by innocent children? This face which revealed the depths of human depravity. I did not recognize this face.

A loud knock on the door jolted me out of my melancholy thoughts.

"You okay, Isaiah?" called out a beatific voice which immediately made everything less rigid.

"Yeah... I'm fine," I replied as I opened the door. "I just got distracted."

Michelle looked at me with a reckless smile. "This is... it's... well... Wow, I'm tripping balls."

I wrenched my facial muscles into something which resembled a smile. "Yeah... me too."

A look of concern shot over her face. She raised her right hand and gently touched my cheek. "I'm really happy we're here."

"Me too."

"I mean it," she insisted. "I... I think we are supposed to be here. It's like my whole life has been simply leading to this moment, right here, right now. I don't know. It just... just feels so right."

I shrugged not sure what to say. "Maybe."

She grabbed my arm, and we headed back to the drum circle. For some reason, the beating drums only increased my anxiety. I tried to smile and play along, but my movements were completely off tempo. I played lightly, so no one could hear me. Every once in a while, I would catch someone giving me a concerned glance. Whenever that happened, I would smile harder and try to seem more relaxed. However, I knew, beyond a shadow of a doubt, that everyone saw right through me, especially Michelle. She would smile reassuringly at me, and I attempted to do the same.

The visuals were kicking in pretty hard. The flickering flames seemed to be moving in slow-motion. Everywhere around me was colorful geometry as T.S. Eliot tormented me from the grave. "Shapes without form, shade without color/ Paralyzed force, gesture without motion." Suddenly, those lines made perfect sense, and it took every ounce of self-control I had not to bitterly howl at the absurdity of it all. I felt like I was nothing but a hollow shell filled with straw and fishing twine.

Michelle must have sensed my uneasiness as she quietly suggested we go take a walk. Mushrooms have this uncanny quality that it seems one can read another's mind. I knew she could read me like a large-print book, for she seemed quite content playing the drums. So we stole away from the rest of the group and headed into the dark, inviting woods.

I began to feel more at ease when we were away from the rest of the group. The geometric patterns became more fluid. The world morphed into something with enough lucidity that I could handle. Neither of us talked for a long while, yet we seemed to be headed in a similar direction.

A river suddenly appeared before us. Without either of us saying a word, we sat down on a moss-covered log. I pulled out two cigarettes from my pocket. We puffed silently watching the smoke drift into the moonlit sky. However, Michelle made a startled huff as she grabbed something right next to me. It was a small plastic bag filled with powder. It was my heroin. It must have slid out when I was pulling out my pack of cigarettes. She picked it up and held it before her eyes in disbelief. Then she looked at me with pitiful eyes which filled me with rage.

"Isaiah," she whispered.

I could not take it. Forcefully, I snatched the bag from

her hands and shot to my feet. I planned on making a mad dash to my car; however, a hidden hole had other ideas for me. My right foot sank into the earth, my ankle twisted, and my left shoulder crashed against a tree. Normally, this would not be too devastating of a fall, but I immediately felt blood start gushing from my reopened wound.

"Isaiah!" squealed Michelle as I cursed angrily. "Are you okay?"

I was not okay. Not by any definition of the word or any level of my being. Emotionally, physically, psychologically, and spiritually, I was far from okay. And I lost control. Repressed tears came gushing out as I broke down weeping.

She hopped over to me and put her arm around my shoulder. "Isaiah. Shhh... it's okay. I'm right here."

Her hand recoiled as it touched warm blood. "Oh my gosh, you're hurt! Do we need to call an ambulance!" she asked frantically.

"No... no I'm fine," I managed to say between sobs. "It's just a re-opened wound."

"That's a lot of blood," she said still concerned. "Let me take a look at it."

Still sobbing, I had no power to refuse her. She rolled up my sleeve tenderly and took out her cell phone to use as a light.

"Oh my gosh, Isaiah, that's bad. Did you go to the hospital?"

"No."

"What happened? It looks like..." Her voice trailed off.

I managed a bitter laugh between tears. "Like a gunshot wound."

She went silent. For a few moments she poked around, and then tore a bit of her skirt off to reinforce the torn gauze around my arm. After she had managed to slow down the bleeding, she asked quietly, "Do you want to tell me what happened?"

I calmed myself down. She gently wiped some of the tears

off my face, and said kindly, "You don't have to tell me if you don't want to."

"No," I replied as I attempted to snort away the tears. "No. I need... I need to tell someone. I'm so sorry, Michelle. This is your first time tripping, and here I am sniveling like a little bitch."

She smiled sympathetically at me. "Don't worry about it. Just tell me what happened."

Struggling for words, all I managed to get out was, "It's my fault. I got him killed." Then I broke down again.

She pulled me to her. I rested my head in the crook of her arm and let myself go. Then nausea overwhelmed me so I jerked away and dashed off to vomit which made me feel slightly better. I walked back to her and let myself be cradled. She did not say anything.

"I got Tyrone killed," I said after a long swallow. "I was the one who wanted to push crystal not him. He was the one who said it was too heavy for us." I successfully fought back another break down. "We got jumped. Those motherfuckers... Those motherfuckers!" I unsuccessfully fought back another break down.

Wiping my eyes, I continued, "We met up with these guys, the Sanderros. We had been slinging ecstasy to them. Well, long story short, we got a hook for crystal in San Diego, so we started pushing it to the Sanderros in LA. Tyrone wasn't down. He even threatened to leave, but he was loyal. Loyal as fuck. He thought I'd get myself killed without him." I laughed miserably.

As I told her the story, the whole scene played out in my mind.

South Central Los Angeles. Not prime real estate location. Prostitutes and pushers roamed the dark streets. Next to me was Tyrone who was nervously puffing on a cigarette. Neither of us spoke.

Our destination was a massive rectangular apartment complex, seventeen stories tall with twenty rooms on each of the long sides. I had mapped out the building on my numerous stops to this particular complex. However, this time was different. This time I was pushing three pounds of crystal. Usually, I was dropping off some tabs or molly, but I had worked my way up the ladder of small-time gangbangers to some serious gangsters.

We headed to the elevator and rode to the top floor. I was excited as this was the first time going all the way up to the top. Seemed symbolic. During the ride up, we checked our pistols. Normally, I would only carry one, but I brought three to be safe. Two tucked in my waistband and another strapped to my ankle. My gut was doing somersaults. As always, I should have listened to my gut. I could tell Tyrone was uneasy by the way he shifted his weight from foot to foot.

Down the hallway were two men with poorly concealed pistols standing outside a doorway. I nodded at them. They knocked on the door which was immediately opened.

The room was scarcely furnished. There were two couches facing one another with a long coffee table between them. A fat, heavily tattooed Hispanic man was sitting on the couch. There were two other lean men behind him holding pistols.

Tyrone and I sat down on the couch facing the fat man. No one said a word, so I opened my backpack and pulled out a small bag of crystal. I laid it on the table softly.

The fat man picked it up, snorted a little, and then smiled wickedly at me.

"Impressive," he said quietly. "But I'm afraid we've run into a complication." He spoke eloquently for a gangster.

My mouth went dry. "What kind of complication?" I asked slowly as my hand crept towards one of my pistols.

"I'm afraid we do not have the cash available. So you are

going to have to leave this with us. You will get your money as soon as we push the crystal," he said in a matter-of-fact tone.

"That's not how I do business," I growled.

"Well, that's how I do business," replied the fat man.

As he spoke those last words, the other men raised their guns, but I was quicker on the draw. I jumped to my feet and lowered the barrel of my pistol right at the fat man's chest. Tyrone sat on the couch as if he was paralyzed.

A few silent seconds passed though it felt like hours. The fat man chuckled. "Listen, *ese*, do yourself a favor and put the gun away before you get hurt. Just walk out the door and forget this ever happened."

I picked up my backpack with my left hand. "That's exactly what I plan on doing."

"Leave the backpack," ordered the fat man.

"Fuck you," I snarled.

I liked to tell myself they fired the first shot. I liked to rationalize it, justify my actions. They had it coming. I had no choice. They forced my hand. It was self-defense. But those were lies, and unfortunately, I was one of the only people who could tell when I was lying. The truth was, I fired first. I pumped four rounds into his fat gut. Perhaps it would not have mattered. They were certainly not going to let us out of there without a fight. As the fat man rolled off the couch, his other two men began firing.

Instinct kicked in along with the adrenaline. With a leap, I made it behind the couch. Bullets slashed through the flimsy material. Tyrone's screams were muffled by the roar of gunfire. A strange calmness came over me as I sat with my back to the couch. A stinging sensation slashed my left arm, but I hardly noticed it. Entranced by the chaos, I breathed deeply, waiting for my next move to present itself.

The door burst open and the two doormen were greeted by three bullets a piece from my pistol. I tossed that one and grabbed another. Bullets tore by me, but the roar of adrenaline in my ears deafened everything but my own thoughts. These gangsters were untrained. They were firing frantically into the couch. I laid low and bided my time. Then I heard clicking. They were empty. Amateurs.

Boldly, I rose to my feet. I could see the fat man slumped on the floor not moving. Tyrone was laid out on the couch coughing up blood. Hatred, utter unfathomable hatred, quelled the shaking in my hand. I pulled the trigger. It seemed as if every motion I made was mechanical. It was all too surreal as if I was watching a movie or playing a video game. Yet the two men screamed very real screams, and the blood which splattered the walls and floor was real too. Only one man was still crying out as he hit the ground. I replaced the clip, slowly walked over to him and placed one last bullet in his throat.

Then the world stood still. The only sound I could hear was distant wailing sirens. A strange exhilaration came over me. I felt intoxicated. Then I heard someone coughing. My pistol led my eyes. It found the groaning body of Tyrone.

Suddenly, I became intensely conscious of reality. I dashed over to him and kneeled over him.

"Oh fuck! T! Stay with me, T." It was bad. From a quick survey of him, I counted six bullet wounds, three in the chest.

Tears were welling in his eyes. As he sputtered up blood, he wheezed. "Isaiah. I don't want to die. Not like this. Not like this."

"You ain't going to die," I said, trying to force a smile. "I'm right here, bro. Everything's going to be fine."

His dark brown eyes began to glaze over. Blood started gushing from his mouth. His last words were weak and full of despair. "Don't let me die, Isaiah. Don't let me go, bro. I ain't ready to die."

I sat down and placed his head in my lap as I gently stroked his frizzy hair with one hand. The other clutched my pistol. "Hang in there, T. We gonna get you to a fuckin' hospital, bro. Just hang in there." Indecision paralyzed me. And then I heard loud footsteps running down the hall.

There was no time to mourn, no time to digest what happened, no time to think, no time. Jumping to my feet, I grabbed the backpack and ran to the bedroom where I knew the fire escape was, leaving Tyrone wailing in despair as I deserted him. When I reached the bedroom window, I did not even bother trying to open it; I simply shot out the window and ducked out. Then I heard an angry Hispanic voice, and Tyrone screamed. There was one last gunshot, then silence.

I more jumped than climbed down to each landing. My vision blurred as well as my sense of time. Somehow I made it to the ground and was firing haphazardly at a group of people rushing me. They scattered leaving me enough time to make it to my car. Before I knew it, I was on the freeway heading north on I-5.

Michelle stroked my head. "I'm so sorry," she said choked up with emotion.

I was past the point of tears. "No need to be sorry. It was my fault."

"No, it wasn't. If they had been honest with you-"

"An honest meth dealer! That's a contradiction in and of itself," I snorted. Sighing heavily, I continued, "I should have known better."

Neither of us spoke for a few minutes. She continued stroking my head which soothed me. My mind was still reeling from the mushrooms, but I could feel myself acclimating to the trip. Michelle and I smoked a cigarette before she spoke again.

"Was that heroin?" she asked hesitantly.

I nearly cried again. With a hard sniff, I quietly replied, "Yeah... yeah. It's heroin." I added hastily, "I've only been using for a few weeks."

She grabbed my hand and squeezed it. "I hope you stop."

I looked her in the eyes. With firmness in my voice, I said, "I will. And not just that. I'm getting off the pills too. I'm sick of this. I'm fucking sick of everything. I'm through. I'm throwing in the fucking cards."

Smiling, she squeezed my hand again. "Good. If there is anything I can do to help just let me know."

I stood up and helped her to her feet. Then I wrapped my arms around her and held her tight. "You've done more than I could have ever asked for. Just knowing you got my back is help enough." It took an effort to release her.

I took out the bag of heroin, probably hundred dollars' worth of powder, and dumped it on the ground. A part of me cried out in disbelief, yet most of me felt very good about that decision. There were other decisions I was rapidly making. I had a plan, and it was a good one. I was out. To mark this decision, I pulled out my pistol. Michelle jumped back. I assured her everything was okay. Then I walked to the river, popped out the magazine, and tossed the two pieces into the water.

Michelle walked next to me and took my hand. She gave it a reassuring squeeze. Hand-in-hand, we walked back to the drum circle. Evan smiled at us as we rejoined the group. Michelle sat down and started playing the drums as I went to procure my first aid kit from my car. Then I went to the bathroom to clean up. The blood spurting out was blackish and full of puss. It hurt, but the pain was somehow refreshing. As I bandaged the wound, my mind raced with revelations.

My past came rushing back. Long repressed childhood memories appeared in my mind's eye. The memories were like pieces to the puzzle of my identity. Each small nuance of my upbringing took on a new significance. Each person's influence seemed more consequential. As the totality of my experiences was projected onto my consciousness, it appeared as if the superficial layers which I clothed my identity in began to fall away, leaving only the bare naked image of me. Again,

I stared at my reflection. However, unlike last time, I was not completely horrified. Instead of a hollow monstrosity, a blank canvas. There was a spark of life in those emaciated eyes.

I rapidly plotted my next few moves. First thing first, I had to get clean. Opiates have a way of robbing one of any sort of moral compass, of their ambition, of their ability to feel. It was a critical moment for me as I felt that I finally caught a glimpse of who I was. Or more accurately, who I was not and who I had potential of becoming.

The steady beating of drums reached my ears as I left the bathroom. The musical vibrations were soothing. I headed outside and sat next to Michelle. Joints were being passed around, so I decided to roll a few before I started playing. For the next couple hours, I pounded away my anxiety as I contemplated life. I felt at ease with the world, but there was a lingering dread as I knew how horrible the next couple weeks were going to be.

The group seemed to come down together. Hugs were distributed and numbers exchanged. Some people decided to crash at the cabin, but Michelle and I decided to head back to Eugene. We smoked a joint as the sun began to rise.

"That was fun," she said quietly. "I don't know. It was eye-opening. Definitely makes you look at things in a different perspective."

I chuckled softly. "That it does." I cleared my throat. "Look, I'm sorry for freaking out. I just-"

"Don't apologize," she said hastily. "I'm happy I could be there for you. I feel like I got my old Isaiah back."

I looked at her and smiled. "I do too."

"So... are you really going to get off everything?" she asked hesitantly.

"Yeah. Well, not weed, but everything else. I meant what I said. I'm going to drop off what I got to Tiz, and then I'm done."

"If there's anything I can do to help-"

I shook my head. "Afraid there isn't anything you can do besides everything you've already done. The next couple weeks are going to suck. I've tried kicking before, and I was using a lot less then."

"Can I at least check up on you?"

"Sure. Not sure if you are going to like what you see."

"That's okay. I can't believe I'm saying this, but you should use whatever pain pills you have one more time."

I shot her a surprised look. "What?"

She looked at me sternly. "I'm cleaning out that nasty cut you got. It's going to hurt."

"Look, I don't need-"

She huffed loudly. "Yes, you do, and I'm going to clean it out. Don't argue with me. In fact, let's do that right now. Let's go to your hotel room."

"You sure you are up for it?" I asked warily. Neither of us had slept all night.

"Just get me some black coffee with a couple shots of espresso, and I'll be fine."

We stopped by a small coffee shop. She ordered a small coffee with a quad shot of espresso. Sucking the hot liquid down, she shook her body.

"That's the stuff. Feeling more awake already."

When we arrived at the hotel, I took a deep breath. This was going to hurt. However, despite my own misgivings and Michelle's advice, I opted to not use the pain pills. Instead, I smoked a fat joint to myself.

We went to the bathroom and stepped into the shower. I took off my shirt and she inspected the wound. Clicking her tongue disapprovingly, she shuffled through my first aid kit. She pulled out some gauze, rubbing alcohol, the medical glue, and a needle. Then she asked me for a knife.

"What!"

She sighed. "I need to clean out the wound before I stitch it up. The blood clotting is dirty. There is a strong chance of infection which I can only do my best to prevent. I know I would be wasting my breathe telling you to go to the hospital, but you really could use some professional medical attention."

Without replying, I fetched a knife from my backpack and grabbed the belt I had bitten on previously. She looked at the belt as I folded it.

"Looks like you've used that belt before," she said, eyeing the deep teeth marks in the leather.

I sat down in the tub with my arm exposed to her. She kneeled on the floor with the knife in her hand and the first aid kit next to her. Closing my eyes I braced myself for the pain. However, no amount of preparation could prepare me for what I went through. I did manage to stay conscious the entire time, but the pain made everything hazy. I felt the blade dig into my arm scraping off the scabs. Then came the rubbing alcohol which seared the nerves. The stitches were not as bad as everything else by comparison, but it was by no means comfortable.

After she finished, I lay down in the tub. She handed me a cigarette to puff on while she rolled a joint. I am not sure how long I was lying in there, but it must have been close to an hour. Michelle asked me if I would like to lie down on the bed. She helped to my feet, and I wobbled to the bed.

For quite some time, we laid on the bed not saying a word. With long deep breaths, I managed to quell the pain. However, I started sweating and my body began itching. The withdrawals were kicking in. That woke me up. I offered to give Michelle a ride to which she kindly told me I should rest for a few hours.

"You don't understand, in a few hours I'm not going to be able to drive. I'm starting to fiend." My breathing was becoming short and sporadic.

"Are you sure you're okay?"

"Let me roll a joint, and I'll be fine."

The car ride back to her place was a bit odd. Though

my eyes were concentrated on the road, I could tell she was staring at me. I felt like doing something, not sure what, but something other than focusing on the road. Whether the pang in my stomach was from the withdrawal or something else, I will never know. However, when she got out of the car, I felt like I had left something undone. So I rolled down my window and called out to her.

"Hey, Michelle!"

She turned around. "What is it?"

"Just wanted to say thanks for everything, and if it's not too much to ask, do you think you could help me find a job when I get done kicking?"

She smiled. "I'd love too."

She walked over to the car and placed her hand on my shoulder. "I'm really proud of you, Isaiah."

"Couldn't do it without you," I replied, baffled by the tears welling up in my eyes. Then again, I was starting to kick.

"I'll see you soon," she said quietly.

"Yeah."

As I drove away, I called Tiz up. She was still awake from the party the night prior. Apparently, she was enjoying my product along with her clients. I told her I would be stopping by in an hour. At the storage unit I had rented, I grabbed the tabs and the rest of the molly leaving only the last pound of meth in there. Hastily, I drove towards Tiz's apartment combatting a wave of self-doubt.

Tiz was wide-eyed with severely dilated pupils when we met at her apartment. Even though it was morning, the party was still raging. Thirty people must have been crammed into that tiny space. I asked her to step outside with me so we could have a chat.

However, before she could leave, the sound of breaking glass reached our ears as well as some angry cries. We charged in. Two groups of people were mugging each other and for a very apparent reason. Some were wearing yellow; the other group was wearing red. The yellows were the Vessana family, the closest thing to a genuine gang in the Eugene area. Many of them came from south of the border. The ones in red liked to call themselves the Barger Bloods and were some of Tiz's first friends in the drug game. Knives were flashing as well as some jagged broken bottles.

Tiz charged in between them. I could not tell what she was saying, but she did not look angry. In fact, she was laughing most of the time. She pulled out a bag of tabs and started passing them out. Then as the music kept thumping, she started to breakdance in between the two groups. Soon enough, a circle was formed around her, and others began joining in. The onlookers cheered them on. It was a spectacular sight to witness. In a matter of minutes, a situation which could have turned bloody was diffused into a dance party. Some of the Bloods would take a turn in the middle of the circle then give way to Vessanas. Blunts were passed around the circle. A Vessana even walked with a tray full of shots distributing them to the Bloods. As things seemed to have cooled off, and everyone was having a good time again, Tiz stole away with me.

"Fuckin' drama," she muttered.

I smirked. "Well, you got to expect that when you got two rival gangs in the same room."

"Gangs?" she said with a chortle. "Those muthafuckas wish they was G enough to be in a gang. They ain't nothing more than some punk-ass high school clique."

"Nevertheless, that's quite the party going on," I said with a smile.

"Shit, bro you should have fuckin' been here!" she piped up happily. "What were you fuckin' doin' last night anyways?"

"I did some mushrooms with Michelle."

"That bitch from church?"

I sighed. "She's not a bitch, but yes."

Laughing, she punched me in the arm. "Fuck, I ain't judging, bro. Them church girls get hot in the sack, you know what I'm saying?"

Shaking my head, I replied, "No, I don't know what you are saying, but I'm not here to babble about bitches."

"What's going on? You look like shit."

"I'm getting clean," I stated flatly.

Her eyes widened. "Shit, little churchie girl got you hooked like a mu-fucka."

Controlling my irritation, I smiled painfully. "Whatever. I want you to take what I got left. There's twenty of the methadone left, maybe ten morphine. Not sure how much klonopin I got, but you can take that too."

"Shit, I'll just buy that back for what you paid for it."

"No. Just take it. I also brought the rest of the tabs and molly. Just push it and give me my cut."

"You just handing it all over to me?" She looked awed by the very idea. I nodded solemnly. "Well, alright, bro. I'll push it for you. Speaking of which, that bitch hasn't paid in over a week. What we gonna do about it?"

Shrugging my shoulders, I said, "I don't really care. You know the saying, 'fool me once, shame on you; fool me twice, shame on me.' Well, I guess shame on me."

"He can't just get away with that shit! I got my money in this too."

All I wanted to do was go back to the hotel room. I was feeling sick. So I told her to keep what he had given her. My only request was two ounces of weed to get me through the week which she freely gave without a second thought. Before she left with the drugs, we smoked a joint in my car.

"Shit, bro, I didn't even tell you why we partying," she said, noticeably controlling the tone of her voice.

"Why are you?" I expected a very dumb answer and was pleasantly surprised.

She rubbed her hands excitedly together. "I finished my album, and I got signed to a label, bro!" Then she squealed happily like a shy adolescent girl who was asked to prom by the captain of the football team.

I reached over and gave her a hug. "That's awesome, Tiz! That's fucking awesome!"

"I know. You got to get fuckin' well soon, bro. The album release party is in a couple weeks."

I smiled weakly at her. "I'll be there one way or another."

"Good. And this shit you dropped on me will make sure everybody's thizzin' for Thizzin Tiz."

She opened the door and popped out of the car. Before she dashed up the stairs, she turned to me and called out. "Take it easy, bro. Need anything just fuckin' call, aight?"

"I will."

"Proud of you, Isaiah. I knew you weren't no punk-ass junkie. Stay up, homie!"

My first task when I returned to the hotel was to roll up as many joints as I could. Having to constantly light a pipe can be exhausting when trying to kick. After grinding up nearly an ounce, I commenced to rolling as fat of joints as I could. Rolled them tight so they would not go out easily. It had been nearly twelve hours since my last fix, and my body was protesting a bit more loudly about its deprivation.

I had to keep wiping my hands off because the sweat was soaking the papers to the point that they were tearing. While marijuana does help quell some of the nausea, it does little for the pain. It is not pain in a conventional sense, not like stubbing a toe or getting shot. Those are very exterior pains. Kicking is a pain which seems to attack one at the cellular and spiritual level. By the time Michelle checked-up on me in the evening, I was in the fetal position in the corner of the room.

She had brought over a DVD player and some box set television shows. We lay on the bed and watched some Beverly

Hillbillies while smoking a joint. It had been a long time since I had laughed so hard. Granted, it was quaint, outdated humor, yet it was comedic ingenuity at its finest. Watching a screen helped distract from the withdrawals.

When she left, I nearly asked her to spend the night. It was gut-wrenching to watch her leave. Perhaps the withdrawals only aggravated my sense of loneliness. After she was gone, things became much worse. It was harder to distract myself from the ever-lingering cry for a fix, and one can only get so high from marijuana.

I was able to sleep that night for a couple hours at a time. Throughout the night, I would awake completely covered in sweat. My whole body itched. I would smoke a joint and turn on the television. Most of the next day was filled with fitful bursts of sleep. I figured if I was going to be miserable, might as well as try to sleep as much as possible. A good plan but one which was extremely difficult to actualize. Michelle stopped by again, and we watched more television. I fell asleep, and she was gone when I woke up.

The third day was horrible. My hands shook so bad that I was having trouble rolling joints. I could not keep down any food and simply swallowing water was an excruciating chore. When I thought it could not get any worse, someone knocked on the door. I cursed myself for chucking my last pistol. Shutting off the television, I tried to remain as quiet as possible. However, I was immediately relieved when the unknown visitor called out my name.

"Isaiah? Are you in there? It's John."

Stumbling my way to the door, I let John in and was nearly blinded by the sunlight.

"Hey, John," I groaned, not even considering how he knew where I was.

He looked me over. "You look horrible."

"Feel worse. I fucking promise you that."

"Michelle told me you were kicking."

"She also tell you where I was at?"

He shook his head. "No, she would not tell me so I have been scouring the town for places I knew you liked to hide at. I've been trying to call you, but you never pick up."

"Sorry. Been kind of ignoring it lately."

Waving his hand, he marched in and sat down on the bed. Right then, I noticed he had a large paper bag in his arms. "So I got you some things. There's some ginger ale because you probably are having a hard time keeping down food right now. It will help with the nausea. Then I got some niacin tablets. That'll help you sweat it out. Don't take too much or it will be unbearable. And here's some Epsom salt and baking soda. I assume you have a tub, so I suggest taking a hot bath with this. It'll help, trust me. Pulls the toxins right out of your body and will help with your aching muscles. If you get hungry, I brought some high-calorie protein bars. That way, even if you only can hold down a couple bites, you still can get a bit of nourishment. That leads me to some vitamin supplements. Make sure to take these once a day. Also, there are some melatonin tablets which should help you sleep. Don't overdo them. Let's see. What else do I got here. Oh yes, Michelle told me she brought over a DVD player so I burned all three seasons of the original Star Trek. Should keep you entertained. And that looks like everything."

I raised my eyebrows and whispered, "I don't know what to say, John."

"A thank you might be in order," he said cheekily.

A weak chuckle escaped me. "Yeah... thanks."

"Your very welcome, Isaiah. I was extremely pleased to hear you were kicking."

Worried, I asked, "Did she say anything else."

"No, but she wanted too. I could tell. Now, why don't you tell me all about what you are afraid that she might have told me?"

With a sigh, I told him about Tyrone. He listened intently

to the same story I told Michelle. When I finished, a dark scowl ran across his face. As I sobbed a bit, he nodded slowly as if he was contemplating what he was about to say.

"Let me ask you. Do these Sanderros have vulture tattoos?"

Startled, I nodded my head. I was trying to roll a joint, but my hands were shaking too fiercely. John took the weed and papers from me and rolled one up for me. When I expressed my shock at his ability, he laughed it off saying it was like riding a bike. Then his face resumed to darkly scowling.

"So, I am sponsoring this young guy in NA. Real nice kid, about your age. He's from Los Angeles. Got a wife and kid. Used to be some sort of gangster, but now he has a good job at a factory and is trying to live a clean life for his family's sake."

"Alright. What's that have to do with anything?" I asked confused.

"Well, he's got a bit of dilemma. Some of his old associates are in Eugene. He is struggling because he wants to help them, but he doesn't want to delve back into that lifestyle."

"What did you tell him?"

"I told him that it was not his problem. He has started a new life and to jeopardize that would be utter foolishness. But that is not the point. The point is that this kid has a vulture tattooed on his neck."

Then it clicked. "And what are his associates doing in Eugene?" I asked slowly.

"Apparently, someone stole a bunch of money from them and killed a few of their people."

I sighed and ran my hands over my head. "Fuck."

"Pretty much," he replied emphatically.

"But they didn't have the money," I whined. "Not like that fucking matters. Fuck, John! What the hell am I going to do?"

John sighed heavily. "The way I see it, you got a few

options. You could run, you could pay them off, or you could try to fight them."

"I probably don't have as much money as they are looking for."

"Then you two options. I would opt for running."

Shaking my head slowly, I whispered, "No. They'd only come after people I know. They'll repay blood for blood."

He scowled sternly at me. "You think that fighting them will make it any safer for those around you."

"No... no, I don't think so. But there is another option."

He looked me in the eyes. With a sad tone in his voice, he replied softly, "You're right. There is one other option."

We lapsed into silence. I burned the joint trying to focus on the problems at hand but was too sick to think clearly. With a sigh, I said, "I guess there's not much of a point in kicking then."

"That's not true," barked John harshly. "While it might seem pointless, you are taking a step in the right direction."

"Like that matters," I scoffed.

"It does. Trust me, keep making the right moves, and things will work out in the end."

Chuckling bitterly, I retorted, "Oh, I have no doubt it will all work out in the end. It'll work out with me six feet under."

John leaned in and stared directly into my eyes. "Isaiah. If I have one vice, it's my love of being right. I've been right about you so far whether you believe me or not. Trust me when I say that if you continue to make the right steps, you'll make out alright. Maybe not where you want to be, but you will be alive and well."

Shaking my head, I said, "I don't see a way out of this. Besides, it's not like I don't have it coming."

Exasperated, he threw up his hands. "That may be, but I believe people can change. That they can atone for past sins, and you, my young confused friend, have so much potential that I just don't see you being killed if- if you do the right thing."

"And what's that? Tell me, my old omniscient friend, what is the right thing to do?"

He smiled curiously at me. "I don't have to tell you because you already know."

That was the end of that conversation. So I began questioning his plans for the future. His last sermon would be next Sunday. He was going to take a few days to say his good-byes then planned on leaving Eugene. When I asked him where he planned on going, he shrugged and said he was confident he would find where he was supposed to go. As he had said before, the Appalachian Mountains appealed to him so he thought he would wander around there first. The desert was his second option, yet he was willing to go anywhere he felt led to.

After he rolled me several joints, he asked if there was anything else he could do for me. I told him I was fine and thanked him for everything, especially the information. After he left, I called Michelle. I told her not to come by anymore. It was not safe for her to be seen with me. When she pried me for details, I told her the Sanderros were in town. She demanded to come by at least one more time. I sternly told her no, but she hung up on me after saying she would stop by later.

She was frantic when she arrived that evening. No amount of assurance would calm her. She asked me what I was going to do, so I told her my plan. She did not like it. Not one bit. She urged me to run. For some reason, I could not bring myself to say that the only reason I was not running was because of her. If the Sanderros were in town, they would waste no time in locating me and those I associated with. She would be a prime target as would Tiz, but Tiz could handle herself.

It was a teary good-bye. I promised that I would talk to

her before I made my move. Then I laid down on the bed and watched some Star Trek. It was a good distraction.

A week passed before I began to feel a bit normal. Deciding it would do me some good to breathe a little fresh air, I went out for a walk. The midnight air was oppressively humid. A storm was brewing, I could smell it. Everything was still and silent. Not even a breeze rustled the trees. For some reason, a passing white cargo van caused my stomach to churn.

I walked with no particular direction in mind. Being a weekday, very few people were out so I had free range of the streets. I passed downtown and headed towards the residential area. Then I realized where I was going. There was a little park I was fond of not far away. I spent my hours as an adolescent smoking weed there. It was large enough with plenty of space to do your business in peace. No one ever bothered you.

Besides a few sleeping bums, the park was vacant. I sat down on a swing, rolled a joint, and quietly rocked myself back and forth. A similar if not the same white cargo van I had seen earlier rolled by. A knot formed in my stomach. Though it was extremely dark, I could make out the driver. He was Hispanic. Perhaps subconsciously, I wanted them to find me. I was exhausted, physically and emotionally drained, and I wanted this all to end one way or another. The vacancy that the absence of pills and heroin left in me was filled by complete apathy towards my own self-preservation.

About twenty minutes later, the same van passed by. Then my suspicions were confirmed. With a sigh, I rose to my feet and started walking towards it. However, it drove away. While somewhat relieved, I was also severely shaken. For what seemed like hours, I stood on the side of the street waiting for them to return. Perhaps I had scared them off.

Yet they returned, this time driving more slowly. The

sliding side door opened, and I was greeted by three men pointing guns at me. With a cigarette hanging in my mouth, I slowly raised my hands. My heart was racing. This was it.

However, I was pleasantly surprised when one of them holstered his pistol and walked out of the car. He was well-dressed, wearing khaki dress slacks and an orange striped polo short-sleeved shirt which displayed his many tattoos. His mustache was well-groomed. Slowly, he looked over me, and then told me to turn around with my hands still in the air.

As he patted me down, I said with the happiest tone I could muster, "I've been expecting you."

"Have you now?" he said slowly. "Then where is your gun?" He had a heavy accent but was fluent in English.

"I'm not looking for a fight," I said quietly.

He ordered one of his men to accompany him as he escorted me to a picnic table where we sat facing each other. I rolled a joint as they stared me down. When I offered them a hit, they politely declined.

"We must talk business," the man said.

Nodding my head, I replied slowly, "Apparently so." I did not bother asking for names.

"You have our money. We want it back, plus interest."

I shook my head and chuckled. "Look, I don't know what the fuck you think happened, but your people jumped me. They didn't have the money. They pulled guns on us."

Shrugging indifferently, he replied, "I do not care what happened. What I care about is the money."

"How much?"

"Fifty thousand," he said flatly.

I whistled. "They sure as hell weren't paying us no fifty g's for three pounds of meth."

"Consider it a fee for cleaning your mess."

Waving my joint angrily in the air, I spat, "My mess! Your people are the ones who acted the fool. They didn't have the money, so whoever I was selling to must have done something else with it."

He stared at me not saying a word, so I continued, "You know who I am, and likewise, you must know my reputation. The only reason your people did business with a nobody like me was because I had a reputation for being on the level. Now, I don't know much about whoever I killed, but my guess is that they did not have a reputation for being on the level."

He nodded. "Correct, which is why you are not dead. We thought that is what may have happened."

"So where do we go from here?"

He sighed. "If you do not have the money, then I must ask you for a favor."

"What kind of favor?" I asked suspiciously.

"You come work for us."

I could not control my laughter. "Seriously?"

He scowled. "Seriously. You obviously have talent for this type of work. You killed five men who came at you. Good shots too. Your spread was most impressive. You can work off your debt."

"I don't like the idea of being your bitch."

Shaking his head, he replied, "It's not like that. You have contacts here. We want you to push our product here and only our product as well as sell whatever we may require to us at a discounted price."

I chuckled in disbelief. "I've already sold for you and to you, and I got shot."

"You will not be working for fools."

I scrunched my brow trying to concentrate. "Do I have time to think about it?"

"Yes, but not long. Two weeks."

I smiled hard. "Fair enough."

"And I don't think I need to tell you what will happen if you run," he said slowly.

"No… you don't," I replied with a grimace.

We decided against exchanging phone numbers. Instead, we would meet up at a secluded wooded area outside of town. My gut protested as I could think of many advantages for them having our rendezvous in such an isolated spot and none for me. However, I consented to their plan. I was not looking for an argument.

They left as abruptly as they appeared. Left alone, I smoked a cigarette and thought about this new development. I was quite pleased. More than pleased, in fact, I was flattered that they were offering me work. I thought about how this was the break I had always dreamed of. All my dreams, the money, the cars, the women, all that was in spitting distance. The fact I was still alive was testament enough to my potential. He was right to about my shooting ability. Anyone can be a marksman, but only a few can be that accurate with bullets whizzing around them. This was another way out of my predicament. To think I had been so stressed seemed laughable. I was like an employee going to work expecting to be fired but instead is given a large promotion.

I wanted what the man who talked to me had. He was calm and collected, respected by his men, and, most likely, was decently wealthy. He probably took a different girl home every night. His car was probably a luxury vehicle, classy but without the flash. I did not take him to be the kind of Hispanic who put chrome on everything. This was the kind of guy I dreamed about doing business with.

Walking back to the hotel in high spirits, I breathed easy in the night air. The fresh air was doing wonders for my state of mind. While I would have stayed out longer, I was out of weed. However, my happy mood was shattered by the sight of my door wide open. Frantically, I ran in. The weed was gone as well as all my clothes. I opened the grate to the heat duct. I breathed a sigh of relief. My money was still there.

After scooping up my possessions, I found another hotel even though I still had another five days paid for.

Since I had a bit of money saved up, I upgraded my hotel room. It was nothing fancy, but it did have a continental breakfast. I plopped down on the bed which was much more comfortable and considerably less stained. Luckily, I had some weed stashed in my car, so I was able to roll a joint to congratulate myself on my recent stroke of luck. No, it was not luck. It was me finally receiving what was rightfully mine. I slept for five hours straight for the first time in a week.

The next afternoon, Tiz called completely frantic.

"That muthafucka jumped town!" she screamed into the phone.

"Who?"

"Who you think, bitch! Jude!"

I chuckled. "Figured. My hotel got robbed last night. Must have been him."

"What!"

"Didn't lose anything besides my clothes and some weed. Which reminds me, do you think I could stop by and pick some more up?"

"Yeah, no problem, but how the fuck did he know where you were at?" she asked.

"That bitch that was with him probably told him."

"And how the fuck did she know where you were at?" Her tone was very accusing.

With a laugh, I answered, "We may have gone back to my place after all was said and done."

"Fuckin' idiot," she snarled.

"I'll see you in a bit."

Since I had no clean clothes, I went out and bought some more. At the mall, I browsed stores looking for the right apparel for this next phase of my life. However, I could find nothing which looked appropriate. I even tried on a suit, but I nearly fell on the floor laughing when I looked at myself. I spent hours there trying on clothes. Yet nothing seemed to look right. I finally decided on some black slacks, a button-up shirt, and a coat to match.

When I saw at myself in fancy clothes, there was something disconcerting about it. Even when I was tripping, I seemed to look more like myself than I did right then. I saw a man trying to be something he obviously was not. However, I walked out of there dressed in business casual apparel. Every time I passed a window in which I could see my reflection, I winced. I looked so fake.

It seemed like the party was never stopping at Tiz's place. There were at least twenty people present, causing some sort of ruckus or another. Tiz proudly proclaimed that she had not slept in three days.

"You should take it easy, Tiz. Don't want to overdue it."

"Fuck that!" she snapped. "Got to be on my game for the album release party. You still coming?"

"Of course."

She looked me over. "Lookin' classy there fool. What? You get a job at a fuckin' bank?" she said snidely.

Smiling, I replied, "Whatever. Fuck you. It's about time someone in this town had a bit of class."

She shrugged her shoulders. I wanted to talk to her about my recent encounter with the Sanderros, but I held my tongue. There were still some things I needed to sort out in my head. Plus, the more she knew, the more danger she would be in. It was completely feasible that they would still kill me. Yet, if I decided to work for them and did not pay them, then there would be no profit in my death.

With a quick farewell, I headed back out, deciding to take a trek up the butte. There were dark clouds on the horizon which must have scared everyone away because it was deserted. My body was still coping with the withdrawals to some extent which made for a very grueling trek to the top. I was not even a quarter of the way there when I seriously contemplated just turning around. But something was driving me. For some reason, it seemed of the utmost importance that I make it to the top.

When I reached the top, I was panting for air and soaked in sweat. Yet the view revitalized me. The dark clouds had covered Eugene and were quickly approaching the butte. Sitting down on a large rock, I smoked a joint. My future seemed so bright at that moment. It seemed like I had reached a peak in my career. While I smiled thinking about my metaphorical golden ticket, I could not shake a nagging misgiving which was plaguing my conscience. At first, I thought it was simply that it was too good to be true, but then I realized that perhaps my partnership might be the start to another vicious cycle. I remembered what John had said about doing the right thing. I still knew what that was. However, this new deal seemed so enticing that I thought I would be a fool to turn it down. Yet it was definitely not the right thing to do. While I would be gaining powerful friends, I would be gaining many new enemies. Who knew what that might lead to. For one, I would have to distance myself from everyone I cared about. I could have no Achilles Heel. On top of that, I would be dealing with another level of law enforcement. No longer would my concerns be about street cops, I would be dodging them at a federal level. If one gets busted by the feds, ten years is least amount of time one will get off with. As the old saying goes, "More money, more problems."

However, to not work for them would certainly mean death for me or someone close to me. Which really left only one option. Undesirable for me, to say the least, but it was the only way to protect those around me. With a sigh, I made up my mind. I would enjoy these last couple weeks before it was time to face the music. I looked up at the sky for relief and was greeted by the sight of black clouds overhead.

I could hear the rain before I felt it. It crashed onto the

surrounding trees. Then large droplets splattered me. In a matter of seconds, I was drenched.

The walk down was a bit tricky as the rain made the rocks slick and the dirt trail quickly turned to mud. I took my time, still enjoying the walk. The rain was warm and the air still. I felt at ease. I tried to soak up every moment, engrain a mental image in my mind of each passing view. I made a vow that I would live life to the fullest while I had still breath in my lungs. It is strange how when one stands face to face with death that one learns to appreciate living more. Or perhaps it is not so strange. Living is something most people take for granted. When that certainty is stripped away, when one stares at the void of non-existence, it sparks a renewed gratitude for the small things.

At that moment, I was thankful for everything. For the rain, for the moss-covered trees, for my friends, the dead and the living, for the struggle, for every bitter tear, for every moment of joy. Looking back on my life, I was pleased to some extent as to how things had been handled. There had been plenty of mistakes made, but I planned on atoning for them as John said. With a firm resolution, I vowed to do the right thing, even if that cost me my life. At least people could say I died doing my duty to protect the ones I cared about after a lifetime of making every wrong turn possible.

I thought I would be a professor someday or a famous social activist. I thought I would be yelling into a microphone as tens of thousands applauded. I thought the history books would be plastered with my name. That was before I caught that felony which squashed every dream I had of becoming something. Perhaps it was poetic that I would most likely die in a shallow grave which probably would not be discovered for a long time- if it was ever discovered. The Sanderros would get away with it. There was no doubt in my mind about that. Actually, I hoped they would get away with it. I knew the game I was playing. It was not their fault things played out the way they did. You cannot let yourself be punked in this game. Whether or not their associates were in the right was not the point. As someone who values loyalty, I understood where the Sanderros were coming from. Even if their associates were in the wrong, it was not like they could simply walk away. Not after blood had been spilled.

A peace beyond understanding overwhelmed me. I knew I was making the right decision. With a sigh of relief, I felt a large burden roll off my back. I took a deep breath and relished the feeling of my lungs expanding. It had been a long time since I had taken such a breath, and I swore to myself that I would take more of them in the next couple weeks.

With a peculiar sense of well-being, I hopped into my car, not even thinking about how I was mudding up the interior. I headed to the hotel room, took a shower, and got into some dry clothes. While the television begged for some attention, I decided not to waste any more time vegetating in front of a screen. I headed out to a bar. This new appreciation for life made me thirst for some socialization.

The rain had left the sidewalks vacant. The bar was nearly empty and deathly quiet. I took a seat at the bar and ordered a whiskey and a beer. I sipped on these for a long time before I went out for a cigarette. When I went back in, I contemplated moving to another bar. There were very few people present, and no one looking to talk to a complete stranger. While I tried to talk up the bartender, he was too engrossed with ESPN to hold much of a conversation unless it was sports related.

As I finished my beer, two men walked in the door. Both were wearing plain jeans with windbreakers. Even though the entire bar was empty, they decided to sit down next to me, one on each side. The one on the left was the taller of the two. He had bleach blonde hair with green eyes. I knew this because he stared at me with no embarrassment. In fact, there was a sly smile across his face. He ordered a shot of whiskey for him and his friend. Then he ordered one for me, and I politely thank him for it.

For some reason, the hair on my neck was sticking up. My blood was pumping. Something was not right. The man on my right was black-haired and hefty. He looked like he could throw his weight around in a very destructive manner. He too stared at me unabashed with the same smile. We took our shots. I thanked them again and told them that I was on my way.

The blonde-haired one on the left grabbed my arm. "Hold on a minute. Don't I know you from somewhere?" His voice was too friendly for my liking.

I shook my head and pulled away. The black-haired one piped up, "He does look familiar doesn't he? Though I can't place the name."

The man on the left slammed his hand on the bar. "I got it! Josh right?"

My stomach dropped. I dumbly shook my head.

The black haired man shook his head. "No, that's not it. Chris, maybe?"

Then my heart dropped. I dumbly shook my head again. They rattled off three more names each one only adding to my despair. In my line of business, it is not always wise to give one's real name to clients. They were listing off half the aliases I had given over the past three years.

The blonde-haired one forced a laugh. "Wait. I got it. It's Isaiah. Isaiah Edward Dummas."

Clearing my throat, I mumbled. "Yeah. That's me."

"You know who we are?"

"I could guess." My mouth was completely dry. "We doing this here?" I whispered.

"Perhaps you misunderstand our intention," he said quietly. "Let's get a round of beers and find someplace quiet to talk."

Before we headed to a table in the back, they escorted

me into the bathroom where I was patted down. The blonde-haired one, who said his name was Tom, was surprised not to find a gun.

"Trying to clean up my act," I offered in an apologetic tone as if I was sorry for not having anything illicit on my person.

"Good. We can help you out with that too. Just play it cool."

We sat at a booth. Tom sat across from me while his partner, Bill, sat next to me. Made sense to stick the big guy right next to me in case I tried to run.

After we finished a beer in silence giving me enough time to quell a panic attack, Tom cleared his throat. "So I take it you know who we are."

"DEA," I stated flatly.

Tom laughed. "You are a smart one, but we already knew that. And I am sure you can guess why we are here."

"I could, but there's that whole annoying Fifth Amendment thing so why don't you tell me why you are here," I said with bitter softness.

Shrugging his shoulders, Tom replied, "You seem to have gotten us all wrong. We aren't here to bust you; we are here to help you deal with the visitors you recently had. This is a 'you scratch my back, I scratch your back' sort of situation."

I huffed. "I got it. Cut to the chase, and let's talk plainly."

Tom held his hands out disarmingly. "Whatever you say, boss." His wide smile showing off his pearly white teeth was seriously beginning to irk me. "Let's say you are a small fish, and your friends are big fishes. That makes us big bad fisherman. Now we could catch us some small fish, but we want the big ones. Catching big fishes gets the fisherman trophies and medals and promotions and hefty Christmas bonuses. You follow?"

"Yeah."

"Now, these big fish are going to devour you unless you can come up with something else for them to eat. Am I correct so far?"

There was no point in lying, so I numbly nodded my head. He continued, "Now the problem is that you don't have something sufficiently satisfying to quell their appetites. Now the big bad fisherman wants the big fishes, so he's going to give the small fish something to give the big fishes. Something to eat. However, that something is bait, so the big bad fisherman can track those big fishes."

I lowered my head and whispered, "Marked bills."

Tom continued smiling painfully at me. "Well, now we got ourselves a smart little fish. That's right. What is it you need again, little fish? Fifty worms?"

Nodding my head, I replied, "You sure know a lot about this whole situation."

"That's my job," said Tom happily. "You know, for a little fish, you sure get around some dangerous big fishes."

I was nearly past the point of control being called a little fish, so I changed the subject. "How do I know that you won't just lock me up after I help you?"

Tom shook his head slowly. "Why would we waste our time? Too much paperwork. Plus, you got rid of some undesirables during that little stint of yours in LA. Consider it a token of our gratitude."

"So if I help you this one time, that's it for me? I can go about my business without any fear of you two stopping by my door again."

"If you keep your nose clean, then you are absolutely right. You can find an honest job, bag yourself a wife, have some kids, and then die of lung cancer when you're fifty." He leaned in, his smile disappearing, and lowered his voice menacingly. "But if you try to run or cross us, the Sanderros will be the least of your problems. We'll find you and throw the book at you. You'll be getting ass-fucked for the rest of your miserable life in some federal prison. I'll personally make sure of that."

I sighed heavily. "Mind if I step out for a smoke?"

Tom leaned back and smiled. "Not at all, but I would advise you quit. It'll kill you someday."

Staring at him hatefully, I muttered, "Everybody dies someday."

Bill moved out of my way, and I walked outside. Tom called out after me, "Don't wander off too far."

Hiding underneath a small overhang, I lit up a cigarette. I took a long drag and held it for a few seconds. I wanted to freeze time for a few years, so I could think this all over. Things sure had become interesting within the last few days. Now I had multiple options to contemplate. This new one certainly was appealing. All I had to do is hand over the cash, and all my troubles would simply disappear. However, that went against everything I stood for. I was not a snitch. While it may seem laughable to most, even criminals have a code of ethics they follow. At least the good ones do. I had always prided myself on following my own code. To aid the police, the DEA no less, contradicted that. For years, I had been a vehement opponent of the War on Drugs even when I was not an enemy combatant in said war. To aid the government in their corrupt war was, to me, morally reprehensible. In fact, it is one of the few acts I believe warrant capital punishment.

By the time my cigarette was done, I had come to a hasty decision. I marched back in the bar, ordered three shots of top-shelf whiskey, and brought the liquor to the table. Tom and Bill were sitting next to each other whispering, leaving me to sit by myself which suited me just fine. After handing them the shots, I toasted, "Here's to ending this whole fucking mess."

We downed our shots. Tom smiled wickedly at me. "So is it a deal then?"

"It's a deal."

He nodded solemnly. "You are doing the right thing, Isaiah. Who knows, after you clean up your act and start acting like a respectable member of society, maybe you can eventually bag that fine little piece of ass you've been hanging out with."

I shot him a dirty look. "I think I am good on your life advice."

"Well, shit, if you aren't going to take a crack at her maybe I'll make my move. Them churchie girls love a badge," he said snidely.

Deciding that was my cue to leave, I stood up without responding. Tom tried to get me to join them for another drink, but I was shaking with rage. I have never enjoyed people prying into my personal affairs, especially the police. Tom handed me a card with his number on it. I told him I would need the money in a week's time.

Once in the safety of my motel room, I lit up a joint, watched some cartoons, and then stared at the ceiling until the sun rose.

Thankfully, nothing too eventful happened for a few days. I spent most of my time on the butte or wandering along Blue River. I had a lot to think of, but I was still resolved to carry out my original plan except now there would be an additional twist. A good one too. One that might just save my life, but also might send me to prison. If that was the case, I hoped the Sanderros would just kill me. I am not the kind of man to be kept in a cage.

I met up with John one last time before he left. He had sold his house and bought an old Volkswagen bus. I could not suppress a laugh when I saw him pull into the parking lot of the coffee shop we were meeting at.

"Like the ride," I called out as he exited the driver seat.

He smiled guiltily as he walked up to me. After a warm

embrace, he said, "I saw it yesterday and just had to buy it. Plus, their easy to fix. You can jimmy-rig them easy enough."

"It figures that you know all about these busses."

He smiled and rubbed his hands together. "I guess I am an old hippie. But enough about the car. How are you?"

I shook my head as we sat down at an outside table. "Life got real interesting. I have had some visitors."

His eyebrows rose with curiosity. "Do tell."

"About a week back, I ran into the Sanderros at a park."

"And you are still alive," he said a bit surprised.

"For now, at least," I replied with a hint of bitterness in my voice.

"And what came of that?"

"They want their money or they want me to work for them. Apparently, they were impressed at how I handled myself."

He snorted. "I would not take that as a compliment."

"Actually, I do. The fact that they respect the way I do business is the reason why I am sitting in front of you right now and not buried in some shallow grave."

"But you don't have their money," he pointed out.

"Interestingly enough, I actually have the money or will have it thanks to some other visitors I met at a bar."

He looked skeptically at me. For some reason, I was enjoying myself. With an old friend sitting across from me, the whole situation seemed a little less real. Life was progressing like a cheesy movie or a poorly written book. There was some sick pleasure I took in finally coming to John with a problem for which he would be stumped to come up with an appropriate solution. This was not some adolescent angst driven whining but a serious problem with dire consequences.

As John said nothing, I continued, "Some DEA agents met up with me at a bar. They want me to pay off the Sanderros with marked bills."

John breathed a sigh of relief. A wide smile spread across his face. "That's great, Isaiah. I told you if you did the right thing that things would work out. Wow, the Lord works in mysterious ways," he said though his last sentence had a bit of a facetious tone to it.

"I'm not a snitch," I said quietly.

His eyes nearly bulged out of his head. "You can't be serious," he gasped in disbelief.

"You should know me well enough. I've got my code, and I plan on sticking to it-"

"Even if it kills you!" he snapped.

Calmly, I replied, "If Socrates had walked away from Athens, he would be another obscure, forgotten Greek. Yet he stuck to his guns and is remembered as the father of philosophy. Or if Jesus had simply-"

He threw his hands in the air. "That's ridiculous!" he snapped. "This is an entirely different situation. These are bad men you are dealing with who deserve to be locked up. They murdered Tyrone."

Shaking my head, I said quietly, "I dealt with the ones responsible for his murder."

He looked at me pleadingly. "Isaiah, don't throw your life away. You got so much potential."

"I'm not!" I retorted indignantly. "Remember what you said John? You told me if I did the right thing that everything would work out fine. And even if I played along with the DEA, what happens when the Sanderros find out I was working with the feds? You think they'll just shrug it off? No. I will die very slowly along with anyone close to me. I'm doing the only thing I can do to make sure no one gets hurt- besides myself. But like I said, it's not like I don't have this coming. Reap what you sow, right?"

"You're not going to work for the Sanderros are you?" he asked morosely.

Laughing that question off, I retorted, "I told you that I

am going to do the right thing, not get mixed up with some cold-blooded killers."

"Then what is your plan?"

After I explained exactly what I was going to do, John seemed more at ease with the whole situation. He stood up, and walked over to me. As he placed a firm hand on my shoulder, he told me that he was proud of me. He told me I was a good kid. Tears were welling up in his eyes. If truth be told, my eyes became a bit watery. Our food was delivered, and as was our ritual, we ate in silence.

After the meal, I lit up a cigarette. John was staring thoughtfully at me. I knew our time was short together, but I could think of nothing to say. We decided to walk around which we also did in silence. I chain smoked cigarettes as he twiddled with his beard. When we made it back to his van which was packed with boxes and clothes, we hugged for nearly a minute. It was tough to part.

Looking at me with tears running down his face, John sniffed hard and wiped away the tears. "You know, I still believe what I said. You are doing the right thing. I might not agree with it, but it is right for you. And if you don't mind, let me make one more prediction."

"Go for it."

He stared into my eyes. "We will meet again, Isaiah. That I am sure of."

"You mean in the next life?" I asked a bit cheekily.

He shook his head and weakly chuckled. "No. We'll meet further on down the road. Life is a journey. We all go down our separate paths, yet those paths are always intersecting. We may go down our separate ways for now, but our journeys will intersect once again before our lives are done."

I nodded solemnly. "Thanks, John. For everything." Those were the only words I could choke out.

"Don't mention it. It's been my pleasure."

"Any idea on where you are going?"

He sighed. "Like I said before, the mountains sound appealing. Last night I opened the Bible and happened upon the part where Elijah is on the mountain listening for God."

"I know the story. The wind howled, the lightning crashed, earthquakes, the whole nine yards, but he didn't hear God in any of that."

Smiling, he nodded his head. "You're right. He did not hear God in all the commotion but in the silence which followed after the storm. Perhaps it was coincidence, but it only reinforced my idea of heading to the mountains."

"Sounds peaceful," I agreed.

It was time for him to leave. We both knew it but could think of nothing to say. So we hugged again. When we parted, we said nothing. John hopped in his van and slowly pulled away. I watched him disappear around a corner then smoked a cigarette as I stared blankly down the street.

The next day was Tiz's album release party. I had not seen much of her, so I was alarmed when I met up with her. She looked like she had not slept in a week. Her pupils were huge, her skin deathly pale, but she seemed in good spirits. It was impossible for her to sit still for a moment. While at her apartment, I saw her rail nearly a quarter of a gram of molly as well as pop a couple triple stacks. I could tell she was nervous and was obviously compensating by using an ungodly amount of ecstasy. When I told her that she should ease up, she laughed it off.

"I can handle my shit, bro. Don't you fuckin' worry about me. This shit helps me stay on top my game."

I shrugged and said nothing.

Her label had rented out a music hall on the east side of Springfield. It was fairly large, and I was shocked to see the place packed. So was Tiz. Her manager or producer, I was not sure which, took her back stage. He was a fat, pimply, greasy looking middle-aged man who looked like he might not have a septum. I did not like the looks of him. While Tiz demanded I be allowed backstage, he insisted that I was welcome after the show not before. I waved them off and wished her luck. Then I shoved my way into the crowd.

As I made my way through the throng of people, I noticed many people doing my drugs which brought a smile to my face. There was a good energy in the room. While there were plenty of wanna-be thugs, no one seemed to be looking to start trouble. I attributed this primarily to Tiz's connections. She was well liked by many and had beef with few.

When Tiz walked onto the stage, the crowd roared with excitement. I could tell she was nervous by the way she crept onto the stage. Yet when the bass started pumping and she started spitting, that all disappeared. This was her moment, and she killed it. By the end of the first track, the crowd was engrossed. People were dancing and waving their hands in the air. When she yelled out that she wanted to smell some herb, smoke immediately filled the room. While I myself typically do not enjoy rap shows, I found myself dancing along and chanting with the crowd.

At that moment, I could not have been more proud of her. To go through the shit she did as a child and come up swinging was admirable. It was hard to remember her as the quiet shy little girl she had been when we first met. That was a long time ago, and she had grown up so much since then.

As she continued to pump up the crowd with impeccable rhymes, I began to see her in a different light. I had never taken her very seriously. In my eyes, she was a lovable but laughable little girl who acted tough. I thought she was just another young kid with dreams of becoming a big time rapper. Yet seeing all her idle talk manifest itself in reality rattled me. She had gone from some shy little girl to a punk teenager and now she was transformed into a woman. A fiercely independent woman, one who made her way with blood and sweat. Not a conventional woman by any stretch of the imagination but that was fine by me. I loved her more for that.

While I always disdained Robert Frost's poem, "The Road Not Taken," it's most famous lines came to mind when I looked at Tiz. However, she did not take the road less travelled; she simply bushwhacked it through the forest. And I loved her for that. She made her way in this world with bloody knuckles and broken noses. I knew right then she was going to make a name for herself. Everything was flowing so naturally for her.

The song before the intermission stopped me dead in my tracks. It was one I had not heard. It was called "The Prophet." She dedicated it to someone in the audience. I wondered who it was, but as I listened to the words, I began to tear up.

> "I call him the prophet.
> He's been my guiding light,
> The one who showed how to chop it
> Taught me to fight.
> He's always had my back
> Helping make those stacks.
> While he aint' got a name
> He's the one who brought into this
> muthafuckin' game."

She was talking about me. I was deeply touched. She talked about the trouble we got into as kids, and even mentioned how I was kicked out of our foster parent's house because I stood up for her.

I was seventeen. She must have been fourteen or so. I was the only person at that point who she had come out of the closet to besides her girlfriend. However, her girlfriend's parents had found out about their relationship and immediately called my foster parents. I was in my room listening to my headphones when I heard a loud thud from Tiz's room which was right next to mine. When I took off the headphones, I heard the familiar snapping of my foster father's leather belt, and I heard her crying. Normally, the belt was reserved for me.

Rage poured into my veins as I stormed over to her room. I saw him standing over her, belting her viciously as she curled herself into a ball in the corner. Without thinking, I tackled him into the wall. We grappled with one another on the ground until I finally was able to pin him. As I managed to wrench the belt from his hands, I stood up, and when he tried to stand, I swung the belt hard. The buckle caught him right in the face. He looked up at me with hateful eyes which I rewarded with another brutal blow from the belt. Then I lost control. With all my strength, I snapped that belt striking him relentlessly. Soon it was him who was curled into a ball. Tiz was wiping the tears from her eyes as she watched me beat him.

Suddenly, my short, squatty foster mother, or "The Troll" as Tiz and I called her, burst into the room shrieking. She grabbed my arm holding the belt. However, a swift elbow to the nose made her crumple to the ground. My foster father managed to rise to his knees and lunged at me. Grabbing my legs, he brought me to the ground. I got him in the guard position which did little to stop his fists. After taking a few blows to the face and feeling quite disoriented, I managed to catch one of his arms. I pinned it next to my head and bit down on his fatty wrist. I could taste blood.

He howled and wrenched away which gave me the leverage I needed to shove him off with my feet. While I rose to my knees, something hard hit me in the back of the head. It was the small TV in Tiz's room that my foster mother smashed on top of my head. If I had not been driven by rage and adrenaline, it probably would have knocked me out cold.

However, it only succeeded in pissing me off even more. I jumped to my feet and knocked her out with a vicious right hook.

My foster father was struggling to his feet. I grabbed the belt again and began to mercilessly punish him. I do not know how long I struck him. It was probably close to five minutes. The entire time he squirmed and howled. If he tried to get up, I kicked him back down.

When the rage subsided, I was left with an icy hatred. I lowered myself on top of his quivering frame and pulled a knife out of my pocket. His eyes widened. He tried to say something, but I silenced him by shoving the knife against his neck.

I was surprised to find tears running down my face as I spoke. "I'm leaving, and if you ever fucking lay a hand on her again, I swear to Jesus fucking Christ I'll kill you."

He stared up at me with terrified eyes. I got off of him and looked at Tiz. She sniffled a bit then rose to her feet.

"Let's go," I said. I had nothing in that house I cared about. We left in a hurry; however, it was only be a matter of days until the police showed up at my new apartment and took her back. That began the long struggle of her running away and the police fetching her again. Eventually, Tiz said something to our foster father which made him relent in his pursuit of her. I am not sure what she said, but I could guess.

Before the intermission, Tiz told the crowd she was going to smoke a blunt and advised them to do the same. I decided to try my luck making it backstage. The security guards let me through after a brief discussion. Tiz was slumped on a couch with two girls who were nuzzling her neck. When she saw me, she squealed and ran over to me. I scooped her up in my arms and twirled her around as she laughed recklessly.

"Was that not the fuckin' shit, bro!" she cried happily.

I smiled. "You're fucking killing it, Tiz! Fucking killing it! The whole crowd is into it."

She sighed happily. "This is it, bro! This is fuckin' it!"

Her manager was rolling two enormous blunts which we passed around. Tiz pulled from a bottle of top-shelf vodka and railed a few lines of molly. I was slightly concerned with how much she was doing. While I had no doubt her tolerance was extremely high, she was going harder than usual which was to be expected. However, I estimated she snorted nearly half of a gram in a fifteen minute span as well as killed a good portion of the fifth she was pulling off of.

As she headed for the stage, I noticed her stagger a bit. Her eyes widened as she caught herself by grabbing onto a large amp.

"You alright there?" I called back to her.

It looked like she was trying to say something, but she only managed to smile dumbly and give two thumbs up. I shrugged it off and headed to the floor. Yet I could tell something was not right when her second set opened. Slowly walking onto the stage, she mumbled something into the mike as the beat began pumping through the speakers.

She managed to get through the first few songs alright. Most of the crowd was too fucked up to notice she was slurring her words. Her lyrics were becoming more and more incomprehensible. Yet the crowd loved it. People kept handing her shots which she took without hesitation. My gut sank when I saw someone dumping a large quantity of molly into a shot. I tried to stop them, but the crowd was in my way. I resolved to not let anyone else serve her drinks. One punk nearly took a swing at me when I told him to fuck off.

The crowd was chanting with her as her song "OD'in" was winding down. Tiz shouted, "Gonna die before I'm twenty-five." The crowd echoed her. And back and forth it went for a nearly a minute. A strange feeling of dread began to restrict my chest, and it only increased each time that line was repeated. Tiz's speech was becoming more and more unintelligible with each repeat. The music was fading which I assumed signaled the end of the song, but Tiz just kept stuttering the same line over and over.

My back had been towards the stage to fend off people from handing her more shots, and as I turned around to see if she was alright, I saw her stagger. Dropping the mike, she began plunging forward, yet there was nothing for her to grab onto. She face-planted on the ground and did not even attempt to catch herself. I jumped onto the stage and shoved my way past the security guard who tried to stop me. Her manager beat me to her. I kneeled down next to her in a complete panic. Her pulse was weak, very weak, and her forehead was on fire. She was barely breathing.

I pulled out my phone and her manager asked me what I was doing.

"Calling a fucking ambulance!" I screamed.

He snatched the phone from me. "She'll be fine. Just give her a minute."

I did not even ask for it back. Giving no warning, I laid him out with a jab to the face. I grabbed the phone and called 911. What happened between then and when I made it to the hospital is a complete frantic blur.

She was in a bad way. I did not need a doctor to tell me that. As I paced the waiting room floor, I did something I had not done in a long time. I prayed. I prayed to anyone or anything that might be watching over her.

Finally, the doctor walked in after nearly six hours of waiting. His face was grave. My heart sank, and I began weeping before he even spoke. I did not make out everything he said, but I understood the gist of it. Her brain had overheated from the molly. They would run more tests, but, at that point, things did not look good. While it was too early to make an accurate prognosis, it was probable she would be in a vegetative state for the rest of her life. Irreparable brain damage most likely had taken place. They had her on life support because she could not even breathe on her own.

I asked to see her. While visiting hours were over, he was kind enough to let me. I told him I would be sleeping there. He did not argue.

My heart broke when I saw her. There was an oxygen mask over her face. The steady beeping of the heart rate monitor echoed in the room. I pulled a chair next to her bed. I held her hand and stroked it tenderly. I wept, burying my face into the hospital bed. I awoke the next morning in that position.

The next few days I did not leave the hospital. The only time I left her side was to smoke a cigarette. They were continuing to run tests, but each test only made the prognosis graver. When they asked if there was any family that needed to be contacted, I told them I was the only family she had.

On the fourth day, I was passed out on the chair. It was mid-afternoon but I had not slept in thirty hours. There is only so much a body can take before it finally shuts down. I awoke to someone whispering. For a brief moment, I thought it was Tiz. My heart leapt with joy, but it was a false alarm. There was someone else in the room. They were praying.

I looked up wearily and said quietly, "It won't help. I've been doing that since I got here."

Michelle sadly looked up at me. "Well, I thought I would try."

I stood up, and she walked over to me to give me a hug.

"How bad is it?" she asked hesitantly.

I was choking up just thinking about my response, so I asked her if she wanted to go smoke a cigarette. We walked down the corridors of the hospital in silence. When we finally made it outside, I smoked half of a cigarette before answering her.

"It's not good," I said with tears in my eyes. "It's not fucking good at all. She's being kept alive on life support."

"Oh my gosh. I'm so sorry, Isaiah." She gave me another hug before she asked, "What are they are doing?"

"Running tests to assess the damage. However, it looks like she has irreparable brain damage."

She inhaled sharply. "What happened?"

I sobbed a little. She grabbed my hand and squeezed it. "She… she got too high on molly. That shit makes your body temperature rise, and… she just fried her brain."

"Is there anything they can do?"

I shook my head. "It doesn't look like it. I will know tomorrow just how bad it is."

"Then what's going to happen?"

It seemed if all the air left my lungs. I wheezed for a moment as I was blinded by hot tears. Flinging myself against a concrete wall, I slammed my head against it and sobbed. I punched the wall a few times before I said bitterly, "If there isn't anything they can do… then I'm… Fuck! Goddammit!" I cried out in anguish. She put her hand on my shoulder which comforted me enough to finish my thought. "Then I'm going to pull the plug."

She spun me around and brought me to her. I buried my head in her shoulder and burst out crying. My legs began to fail me, and I dropped to my knees. She kneeled down with one hand rubbing the back of my head. It sounded like she was going to say something but stopped. We stayed in that position until I managed to compose myself enough to rise to my feet.

As we walked back to Tiz's room, Michelle held my hand. There were a few times I had to lean on her for support. I was weak from the weeping, and I had not eaten in two days. While I protested the idea of her bringing me food, she insisted. I ate but was not hungry. Every motion of mine seemed automated as if I was nothing more than a machine carrying out my programmed function.

PORTRAIT OF A DRUG DEALER

Michelle stayed with me for nearly five hours. We hardly spoke. She left when visiting hours ended. She gave me a long hug before quietly walking out the door. I sat back down and held Tiz's hand. Then I fell asleep.

While I already knew what the doctor was going to say, it still cut me deeply to hear it. He used a lot of medical jargon I did not understand, but the long and short of it was that there was absolutely no hope. As he began to discuss options for her care, I cut him off.

"Pull the plug," I choked out.

He nodded and walked away. I insisted on being there for it. They took off her oxygen mask and undid the sensors strapped to her body. The IV was taken out, and they left me alone with her for a few moments. I stared at her face for a long time. It was strange seeing her without her normal apparel. The oxygen mask and other medical devices had hindered a good view of her. I was startled by how beautiful she was. Her nose was slender if a bit crooked from all the fights. Slender cheeks gave her a dignified look. Her plump red lips could have belonged to a lip stick model.

This could have been the face of an elegant ballerina gracefully performing for a room full of royalty. This could have been the face of a tender kindergarten teacher comforting a crying child. This could have been the face of a loving mother bandaging her son's skinned knee. This could have been the face of a scientist discovering the cure for cancer. However, this was the face of an innocent little girl who had passed from one abusive home to the next until she had the utter misfortune of meeting me.

I longed to hear her laugh one more time. I wanted to tell her how much I loved her, how lucky I was to have her for a sister. There were so many things left unsaid. As I held her hand feeling her pulse weaken, I whispered all the things I wished I would have said years ago. Her chest stopped rising.

The doctor came in to record the time of death. When he called out the time to the nurse, he looked at me with surprise when I let out a brief gust of bitter laughter. Thizzin Tiz died on July 10th, 2013 at 4:20 p.m.

The next couple days were a haze of paperwork dealing with death certificates and funeral arrangements. The mortician seemed a bit mortified that I did not want her to have any make-up on and insisted that she be wearing her favorite red bandana. I would not even listen to his suggestion that she be put in a dress. No. She would be wearing a pair of Air Jordans, some baggy red shorts, and a Chicago Bulls T-shirt. There would not be a funeral service as I knew she would have hated it. I was able to pull a fast one and have "Thizzin Tiz" engraved on her tombstone. Other than that, the tombstone was quite plain. They refused to let me put "The Alpha Bitch" on it though I hardly argued with them.

Before I could take it all in, I was standing in a cemetery with Michelle by my side. The sky was clouded over which seemed to trap in the suffocating humidity. I looked around me. There were around fifty people huddling around the grave in color-coordinated groups. The Vesanna family was present. Then there was the Barger Bloods, pasty white-skinned punks in all red. A few Crips loitered in the back. It was nothing short of a miracle that these people were not pulling knives on one another. Only Michelle and I were dressed in all black.

We all stood around the open grave in silence for a long time. Finally, I cleared my throat. My words came out in short bursts as I was fighting back tears. "We all knew Tiz. She was one hell of person. She made people laugh. She was honest and fair. She never caused problems unless you caused problems for her or anyone she cared about. She was a dear friend to us all. She was one in a billion. There wasn't anyone else like our Thizzin Tiz." There was a lot more I wanted to say, but a torrent of tears stopped me. I wish I had prepared something because that was a piss poor excuse for a eulogy.

No one else spoke. One of the Crips, a scrawny black kid, had brought a small boom box with him. He played the only appropriate song- Tupac's "Thugz Mansion." As the music played we all paid our respects to the dead. I pulled out a blunt from my pocket and tossed it on the grave. Others followed suit. Some threw nugs on the casket, other's sprinkled molly or tossed tabs. One of the Bloods poured a bottle of Grey Goose on the casket. When everyone finished paying their dues, there was probably close to a grand of drugs in the grave.

I was the first to dump a shovel full of dirt into the grave. There were only two shovels so the rest passed the other shovel around. When the grave was filled, people went their separate ways. I stood by the grave for hours with Michelle standing silently beside me. I was paralyzed by grief and guilt. If there was ever a time in my life I wanted to use opiates, it was then. All I wanted to do was make every feeling disappear. Yet I deserved to feel this. It was my fault. I tried to tell myself that she was a big girl who could make her own decisions, and that was true. But I gave her a hefty push down the road she had travelled. While I had tried to do what I could to help her, I had failed. That was the second person I had failed. All within the short span of a few months.

As I walked to my car, I seriously thought about killing myself. It seemed the only thing left to do. I had nothing to live for. Then I looked over at Michelle, and at that moment, I also remembered the Sanderros. I had completely forgotten about them. I was nearly a week late meeting up with them. I panicked thinking about what they might do. I had to reach them before they did anything to her.

I sighed with relief when I reached my car. There was a note underneath my windshield wiper. It was from the Sanderros informing me to meet them at the designated spot in three days. They were even thoughtful enough to offer their condolences. I was grateful that they had understood my tardiness.

Michelle stared curiously at me. "What is it?" she asked quietly.

I explained my situation. We had not talked much about anything since Tiz had been hospitalized. Michelle was surprised when I told her I had been approached by the DEA. At first, she took this as good news, but her face dropped when I told her my plan. She protested and pleaded with me, but I had made my decision.

When I dropped her off at her apartment, she began to cry. I would have too, but it seemed as if I had run out of tears. "So this is good-bye then," she choked out.

I nodded numbly. She exhaled heavily. "And you won't be coming back."

"No. One way or the other, I'm out for good."

"Where will you go?"

Shaking my head, I answered, "I don't know. Somewhere far from the West Coast. Try to find work in some little town in the middle of nowhere. Somewhere that neither the Sanderros nor the DEA will find me."

"Wait here," she ordered abruptly as she darted out of the car and into her apartment.

I got out of the car and smoked a cigarette as I waited for her. I said a quiet prayer that the Sanderros would just kill me. It would make everything so much simpler. After the Sanderros had been taken care of, there was absolutely nothing left to live for. If I lived, I would probably wind up on the streets somewhere, homeless and hopeless. Probably would get on heroin again. I would die in some trash-strewn back alley with a needle sticking in my arm. If the Sanderros killed me, at least I would go out like a gangster not some punk-ass junkie. I would happily dig my own grave for such a dignified death.

Michelle returned holding a small picture in her hand. It was a picture taken of us a few years back at the Youth Retreat. We looked so young. I was bashfully looking at the camera as she had her arm around my shoulder pulling me close to her, smiling that reckless smile that I loved so much. On the back was her phone number.

Choked up, she said, "I figure you would probably be ditching your phone, so I wanted you to have this. I want you to hold onto it, and if you ever find yourself in a good place, promise me you will call."

"I promise," I said hoarsely.

We hugged for a long time, pressing our bodies close to one another.

"I love you, Isaiah," she whispered.

My heart throbbed. "I love you too, Michelle."

Then we parted a little. Michelle looked expectantly into my eyes. I nearly leaned my head in, but I pulled away at the last second. There was no reason to make this any harder than it already was. I told her not to try to find me as it would not be safe. When I drove away, I could see her in my rearview mirror, watching me drive away with tears in her eyes.

When she was out of sight, I pounded my steering wheel with my fists. Life was too much for me. All I wanted to do was find a rock to die under, but I had business to accomplish. I called up Tom and told him I was ready for the money. We met at a bar that night. I was an hour early, so by the time he showed up with his partner, I was dead drunk. After a few smart aleck remarks from Tom about Tiz, I took a swing at him. Bill caught me before my fist connected. I was quickly escorted out of the bar by the bouncer.

On the street, Tom and Bill led me to their car where I was given a small backpack. They politely thanked me for doing business with them, and I politely told them that they could go fuck each other.

All I had left to do was wait for three days. I spent the first two days drinking copious amounts of alcohol. Yet the third day, I spent sober. I went to the butte and sat still as the hours trickled by.

Deciding to treat myself for my final meal, I hit up one of the classiest restaurants in Eugene. I ordered a steak and lobster tail with the most expensive glass of red wine. Though I thought this was to be my finest meal, it was an utter disappointment. The wine tasted like vinegar, the steak was chewy, and even the lobster tail was a letdown. It was way too salty. In pretty glum spirits, I paid my bill, and headed to my car. Luckily, my cigarette was as delicious as ever. After taking a few long drags, I turned on my car and headed to meet the Sanderros.

I had the fifty thousand in marked bills still in the backpack Tom had given me. In my own backpack was twelve thousand of my own money as well as the last pound of meth. And that was everything I had to my name. For all the bloodshed, the sweat, and the tears, twelve grand did not seem like much. However, even if I had ten million in the trunk, it still would not have seemed like much. Not after what I had lost. Nothing seemed very valuable to me, and what I had, I hated bitterly. I hated my car, my money, my drugs, my fancy clothes. I wanted to burn it all in a giant pile with my body smack dab in the middle.

The night sky was clear, the air motionless. I drove down the dirt road thinking about nothing in particular besides that it seemed like a good night to die. I caught sight of two parked cars with three men sitting on the hoods. There were guns in their hands. When they saw me, their guns lowered at me. I flashed my headlights letting them know it was me.

As I opened my car door, I immediately held both my hands out to them. Then I slowly exited the car. Without being told, I turned around and put my hands on the hood so they could frisk me. After a thorough search, I told them they could find two backpacks in the backseat. The mustached man told one of his men to fetch them.

Clearing my throat, I said, "In that backpack there is fifty thousand. In the other, there is another twelve thousand along with a pound of crystal."

The mustached man looked surprised. "That's more than is necessary."

I looked the mustached man in the eye and said slowly, "I know. I was hoping you and I could have a private conversation."

"About what?" he asked.

I tried to smile. "If I told you, there would not be much of a point in having a private conversation. You can stick a gun to my head the entire time. I'm not trying to pull a fast one on you. Just tell your men not to open the backpacks. There is a reason the money is separated."

One of his men protested, but he silenced him with a curt rebuttal in Spanish. Then the two of us walked down the road. He made me walk ahead of him and had a pistol in his hand.

When we far enough down the road, he told me to turn around and face him. Then he said, "I am sorry to hear about your sister."

"Yeah, me too." I liked him more and more.

"So have you thought about my offer?"

"About working for you?" He nodded. I shook my head.

"Now why the extra money?" he asked slowly.

I sighed heavily. "Because that fifty grand is marked."

He raised his eyebrows but said nothing, so I continued, "A couple days after we met, I was approached by the DEA. They knew everything. They knew you were here, they knew I needed fifty grand." I paused. "You have an informant."

He nodded thoughtfully. "That confirms many suspicions of mine."

I huffed sadly. "I didn't know what to do. I thought maybe you could find some use for marked bills."

"That does not explain the extra money and crystal."

I lit up a cigarette to quell the shaking in my voice. "Because I am hoping that will be sufficient payment enough not to retaliate against anyone close to me."

"Like the girl," he said flatly. I knew he was talking about Michelle.

"Precisely."

"And you are sure you do not want to work for us? You could be a rich man."

I could not suppress a chuckle. "You still want me working for you even though I am being watched by the feds."

He shrugged. "Good point." Pausing for a moment to light a cigarette, he looked thoughtfully at me. Then he asked, "So what happens now?"

"That's up to you," I said quietly. "I understand you probably have your orders. I don't really give a fuck what happens now."

He did not say anything for a long time. I could tell he was thinking long and hard about his next words. "You are right. I do have my orders. If you did not decide to come work for us, I was supposed to kill you. If you ran, I was supposed to kill someone close to you. The girl."

My heart was racing. I braced myself for the bullet.

He cleared his throat. "You can rest easy about the girl. Nothing will happen to her. You have been frank with me, so I will be frank with you. I do not wish to kill you, but I have my orders. However, I do not think killing you will be of any use, and though I have known only for a short time, I know you are a good man. I respect how on the level you have been. However, there are friends and family of those you killed who wish you dead. If I do not kill you and you are seen, it will be bad for me and even worse for you."

I smiled weakly. "So I guess there is only one option."

He shook his head. "There are two."

He paused which I assumed meant that I should finish his thought. I smiled wistfully and spoke slowly. "I get out of town and never come back."

Nodding solemnly, he replied, "That is what you must do. I believe that is the best option for everyone."

"So that's it then?" I asked as a mixture of relief and disappointment poured through my veins.

"Yes. But I have one question. Why did you not just give us the marked bills? Why did you tell me it was marked?"

I lit up another cigarette and took a few drags before answering. "Because it was the right thing to do. I may not be a conventionally ethical person, but I have my code which I live by," I explained. "I'm not a snitch. Besides, if you had found out those bills were marked, you would have come back for me and anyone close to me. And if I worked with the feds once, they would have me on the hook. All they'd do is wave more time at me to make me work for them again. I'll be dead before I'm some fed's bitch. Really, I did not have a choice in the matter. I was going to come to you with what I had, but when the feds gave me the money, I thought at least I could pay you what you wanted even if it was marked."

"And yet you were willing to die to follow your code."

I chuckled bitterly. "It's not like I have much to live for."

He shook his head. "That is not true. A man like you will be successful in whatever you put your mind to. I know this for a fact." He held out his hand. "I'm sorry things turned out this way. We could have had a very mutually beneficial business relationship."

I shook his hand. "Such is life," I said quietly.

"Words of the wise," he said softly.

As we walked back to the cars, he said, "I wish you luck on your journey."

"Same to you. Watch your back."

We had returned to the other two men. He looked at me and smiled wide. "That is what I am doing."

He walked up next to one of his men, shoved the pistol in his face, and without a moment of hesitation, pulled the trigger. The dead body crumpled to the ground. The mustached man explained something in Spanish to the other man. I could not understand what was being said, but judging by the grave yet understanding look on the other man's face, I knew he must have had his own suspicions. I offered to help with the body, but the mustached man politely declined my offer saying I had done enough. Then he reached into one of the back packs and pulled out the twelve grand I had given him. He handed it back to me, thanking me for the information.

I hopped in my car and slowly drove away. I chain smoked cigarettes as I made my way onto the freeway. All I knew was that I was heading east.

Morning Motel Raid Leads To Arrest Of Oregon Man

At approximately 4:00 am, police swarmed Peaceful Meadows Motel and apprehended Isaiah Edward Dummas, an Oregon man, wanted for multiple counts of murder and drug distribution. License plate recognition software on an Iowa State Police squad car alerted authorities that the man was wanted by the Drug Enforcement Administration. After being ordered to "monitor but not engage," state and local police placed surveillance on the motel where Dummas was residing. After two days of surveillance, federal agents with the help of state and local law enforcement raided the motel room where Dummas was arrested without incident. Details of the arrest will not be released until a full report has been made.

Dummas, 25, is being held at Delmont Community Corrections without bail where he awaits transfer to Oregon where he faces a first-degree murder charge as well as multiple drug charges. Officials believe he was an accomplice to the vicious murder of a federal informant.

The murder of a federal informant to prevent testimony in court is considered a capital offense according to federal law. If convicted, Dummas could face the death penalty. Details as to the identity of the informant have been kept classified until a full investigation has been conducted.

Dummas also faces multiple murder charges in California for his suspected involvement in a shootout which left six men dead. Authorities believe it was a drug deal gone wrong.

Along with the murder charges, Dummas is facing allegations of interstate drug trafficking and distribution for a variety of drugs including marijuana, methamphetamine, cocaine, and ecstasy. All of these will be tried in a federal court. Each of these offences carries a minimum ten year sentence, although a federal prosecutor's aide, speaking on a condition of anonymity, stated that due to the severity of the crimes, a life-sentence could be pursued.

This is not Dummas's first run-in with the law. When he was 19, Dummas was convicted of the manufacture and distribution marijuana in Eugene, Oregon.

A Drug Enforcement Administration agent at the scene, using the code-name "Tom," gave this statement to the press. "This is a good day for everyone involved. I would like to thank both the Iowa State Police and the Delmont Police Department for their vigilance and bravery helping take down this violent criminal. This operation demonstrated the perfect coalescence of law enforcement agencies from every level."

ABOUT THE AUTHOR

Tom Cellar was born in Michigan where he spent the entirety of his childhood. After dropping out of college, he moved to Oregon and started his own business distributing plants and fungi. Unfortunately, an unexpected visit by undercover police halted his operation forcing him to become, yet again, a professional wage slave. He now bounces back and forth between the two states working odd jobs accompanied by his wife and two cats.

Printed in the United States
By Bookmasters